The Sands of Gower

THE FIRST PENNY WEAVER MYSTERY

Judy Hogan

Hoganvillaea Books 〜 Moncure, NC

Hoganvillaea Books,

Cover design: Anne Kachergis

Paperback ISBN-13: 978-1515191063

Published in 2015 in the United States of America

Hoganvillaea Books
PO Box 253
Moncure, NC 27559-0253

For Edith Merrett,
my good friend and landlady with whom I spent summer weeks on Gower between 1981 and 1996.

ACKNOWLEDGMENTS

I am deeply grateful to my two readers, Carol Hay and Suzanne Flandreau, who have faithfully read this book and many of those which came after this first one. They have given me excellent suggestions as well as believing in Penny Weaver and her stories. I owe a great debt also to Rhodri Williams, of the Swansea Police Department for his help in making the crime scene and other details of the investigation more correct than I could have done. Any remaining errors are mine alone. This book was written in 1991, revised many times, and is being published third, instead of first, because *Killer Frost* was a finalist in the Malice Domestic First Best Mystery Contest in 2011. I owe a lot to all my supportive friends, many of whom were made though Sisters in Crime and their subgroup The Guppies. John and Sharon Ewing have for years supported my writing projects and books. They keep me in Northern Virginia during the annual Malice Domestic convention, and are real morale-boosters. I'm also grateful to those indefatigable Malice women who give us such amazing conventions every spring, where I have learned, net-worked, and had opportunities to show off my books.

A special thanks to The Swansea Tourist Board for the use of the cover photo of Three Cliffs Bay. © Produced by permission of the City and County of Swansea.

The Sands of Gower

ONE

They had left Cork an hour late, and the three-hour crossing had already become four when the ferry's loud speakers announced that they had engine trouble and would need to dock in Tenby. Penny had thought she'd be in the Swansea bus terminal by six p.m. It was after seven, July 2, but in the British Isles, when it was cold and rainy, it felt like winter in North Carolina. She'd gone into the loo, dragged all her warm clothes out of her shoulder bag, and put them on. She'd stayed in the glassed-in cabin. She hugged herself for warmth and watched the rain slashing across the deck, then blowing back as if in some deliberate attempt to clean it by sloshing a river of water onto it.

She hadn't slept well on the plane, and then she'd had to get herself to Cork, where she had a reservation for the night. The breakfast at the B & B the next morning was plentiful so she only ate biscuits and fruit for lunch. The cup of tea and a scone around four in the ferry canteen had helped, but it was closed now, and she was so hungry she would have gladly eaten the thick, tasteless soda bread served at breakfast that she'd left on her plate. The ferry's main passenger room was barely lit, perhaps to save the engines, and she couldn't see well enough to read the book she had brought along.

The engines idled another twenty minutes, and then the ferry set off slowly, limping. Now she could see the Welsh coastline, its rocky cliffs and little bays remarkably like the Gower coastline, her destination. Would she ever get there?

This would be her fifth summer to stay at Evelyn Trueblood's Pobbles House in Pwll-du. She'd told Evelyn to expect her by eight. The other passengers were mostly Welsh and Irish, wearing subdued colors, dark greens, browns, greys. Pensioners by and large, and a few young families with children. They sat quietly, passive, the same way they waited in queues, with endless patience and forbearance. Two men in jeans and cable-knit sweaters were walking back and forth, smoking, restless. Undoubtedly Americans, judging by their confident strides, the flamboyant reds and blues of their sweaters.

She'd never been in Tenby, where they were going to be put on buses for Swansea. She hoped the bus out to the Gower peninsula was still running. Taxis were expensive. Sometimes she wished she weren't so determined to do things off the beaten path, take these risks that went with traveling alone.

Penny was dropped at the Swansea bus terminal at 10 p.m., but the last bus to Gower had already departed. Evelyn would be fit to be tied. Penny took the first taxi that pulled up.

Gwyr. Finally, in the pitch dark, rain still sheeting down, she saw the first signpost with the word in Welsh and English, *Gwyr* and *Gower*, from the back seat of the old-fashioned heavy black taxi as it lumbered in the direction of the sign. I'm almost home, she thought. The taxi had a heater, so she'd stopped shivering. Once at Evelyn's, all would be well. She could collapse.

They passed the turnoff to Murton, where Evelyn had done a window last summer in one of the two Methodist chapels on the peninsula. Evelyn had been in a real swivet over that window. The closest Penny had gotten to it was seeing the sign announcing that the chapel was having a flower festival August 20–23, "Women of the Bible," as her ambulance went through the village on the 23rd, to pick up a lady who had broken her leg. She herself had only a sprained ankle. It was embarrassing to go back to the hospital for her follow-up appointment in an ambulance, but Evelyn had no car. She had planned to see the flower show with Evelyn, but she had ended up spending most of her holiday in bed with her foot elevated.

Maybe this summer on Gower she would find a partner who wouldn't mind her poetry. She scared men off when she let them know she was interested, especially if she wrote them a poem. Fifteen years out of a miserable marriage, and she hadn't yet found a new love. She did have her own individual goals. She wasn't going to waste her postmenopausal zest years hung up in some man's idea of how she should serve his needs.

Her three children were launched now, theoretically, and her ex-husband, whom she was very sure that she did *not* want to remarry, could be held off more firmly. She could create more time for her poetry. She did want to remarry. She was sure it was possible for a woman to have both a marriage and her own quest plot.

As she looked out the window on the road down to Pwll-du, she knew the sea, her sea, was out there in the dark, and the three cliffs that gave the bay its name.

Ten years earlier, on that first visit, Evelyn had made Welsh cakes while she was out battling the Gower wind and a fine stinging rain in order to see the castle Evelyn had insisted she go in search of. She was chilled, hungry, and exhausted from six hours out in the wind with showers off and on that hadn't daunted the Welsh, so she stayed out, too.

But when Evelyn had offered her tea and Welsh cakes freshly made on a cast iron griddle—a baking stone, Evelyn called it—and had laughed with her and teased Penny about putting Evelyn into one of her poems, she had felt quite at home. Wales was more beautiful, wilder than England. As soon as she had seen its green rolling hills and glimpsed the sea from the train window, she had known she'd write poetry here.

So she kept coming back. Her youngest child, Sarah, was newly married, so Penny was rewarding herself with a two-month stay. Evelyn, who, each time they said goodbye, wondered gloomily if she'd ever see Penny again, as Evelyn herself was seventy-five now, had agreed to give her her regular single room. She could write a whole book of new poems and settle into the more human rhythms she always found here.

Only herself to see to. Only her teeth to worry about getting brushed; only her money to be sure not to lose. As they turned into the village of Pwll-du, she felt the familiar tug of that wonderful time alone. She would write. She knew it. The words were already taking on a presence in her mind. They'd passed the golf links, the post office, where Helen sold newspapers, little green apples, and the twelve-pence notebooks she bought to do her writing in. She told the driver to take the first right turn after the shops.

When he pulled up in front of Evelyn's house, she paid him, climbed out, grabbed her shoulder bag, which he'd already set on the sidewalk, slung it over her left shoulder, her purse over her right, gathered up her straw bag of odds and ends, and her walking stick, and walked through the little gate and up the drive. Evelyn had left a light on.

The Sands of Gower

Eleven p.m. Embarrassingly late. Then Evelyn opened the door. "Penny, my stars, what happened to you? Did you miss the ferry?"

Evelyn looked as sturdy and welcoming as always, her short white hair brushed back, a robe over her night dress. Evelyn was never effusive, but her relief and happiness on seeing Penny were in her eyes and her voice. "Go put your things down, and I'll make you a cuppa. I bet you're knocked up. Are you hungry?"

Penny followed Evelyn in and then down the hall to her familiar room. "The ferry from Cork had engine trouble, and I didn't have a chance to call you. I'm sorry. I'd love a cuppa, and maybe some biscuits. I haven't eaten since this afternoon. I'm tired, but I won't have any trouble sleeping here."

"I'll get you a milky drink and a sandwich then," said Evelyn and bustled off.

To enter her same room, to see the pale lavender passion flowers on the wall outside in the porch light, and the yellow rose bushes under them that matched the yellow duvet on her bed, was to feel, yes, she was free again, to be herself, a poet and a human being. Not anybody's mother or teacher or ex-wife. Nothing to do but write poetry.

Once she'd dropped her things and used the bathroom, she walked back into the lounge, settled in Evelyn's big chair, and let her limbs relax as they hadn't on the whole trip. Here was Evelyn with a cup of hot Ovaltine in a mug, two slices of bread, some cheese, and pickled cucumbers and onions, with Welsh cakes, her favorite. She'd read of crumpets and scones, but never, until Wales, had she heard about the rich scones with currants in them in which the Welsh took such pride.

"What a treat! I haven't had Welsh cakes for a year. Thanks. You know I love them."

"Maggie was visiting, and she wanted to make them. She's gotten so big, helps me in the kitchen now. Tell me what happened with the ferry. It's usually reliable."

Penny explained briefly. Then while Evelyn chattered away about her granddaughter, Penny let herself enjoy feeling completely indulged. She still ached with fatigue, but everything, being on Gower, the warm drink, listening to Evelyn, provided just the bone deep comfort that she so longed for and never found anywhere else. It was like drinking cool water cupped in her hands from a spring she once found in the mountains after she'd raked the leaves away. She took a deep breath and drank deeply.

She was almost asleep when she heard Evelyn talking about "the newlyweds who've been here a week tomorrow. They're staying on another week. He's real sweet. I wouldn't mind marrying him myself. But she's a typical Prussian. Very bossy. I don't know what he sees in her. Oh, she's lovey-dovey. They practically climb in each other's laps at breakfast—when she finally comes to breakfast. She insists she has to go swim every morning to keep her figure and that missing my big breakfast is probably as well. But they paid for it, didn't they? It drives me up the pole when she's late to breakfast and I want to get the washing up done before Harold comes in about ten with the paper. He likes to have a cuppa with me, you know."

Penny did know about Harold, the widower next door. The summer before she had wondered if he were flirting with her and had decided probably not. For all his love of talking, he was pretty timid, but he and Evelyn could and did natter up a storm. Harold always took over the conversation and steered it his way, but Evelyn put up with him, grateful for his taking her into Swansea on Fridays for her shopping. He always picked up her morning paper when he went out for his constitutional. He was a great one for walks, all weathers. "Out early, back early," he'd say, "and then you feel good the whole day."

"Then Friday," Evelyn went on. "Last Friday, I had to tear to get ready for Harold. I nearly held him up. He has his cronies down at the club, and he likes to go down for a pint in the late afternoon, and then he has his chores to do before that. So he likes to be back by three, but this Prussian woman—."

"What's her name?" Penny asked, amused at how already Evelyn was full steam into gossiping about her guests. She used to have Hal to talk to. But after he had died four years ago, Evelyn had had to find other people to laugh with about the more outlandish of her guests. The summer before she had gotten Penny to listen to her stories. There was the French couple who had hung their laundry all around the room and then went off during the night and never paid.

But this Prussian, as she called her, really had Evelyn going. "Christine is her name—I don't know what her German name was. She's Prussian to the bone. Her husband is James Hampton, III, probably rich—

you should see their car, a brand new big Rolls Royce. The clothes she's got! She must wear three outfits a day. Oh, he acts happy most of the time. She tells him off plenty, and he doesn't even peep. I wish he'd stand up to her—somebody should. She runs over him—it drives me up the pole. Friday, I just know she'll go for that swim and be late for breakfast. Then I won't be on time for Harold. I hate to make him wait. What do you think I should do?"

"Tell her she can only get her breakfast if she's in the dining room by nine. That's reasonable. Explain about your shopping. You can do that," she added in answer to the face Evelyn was making.

"I guess I could speak to *him* about it. It's not asking too much?"

"No, of course not. Who else is in?"

"That's all now. That's enough. But two of your fellow countrymen are due tomorrow night. They're in for two nights. From New York. Do you think I'll ever visit New York?" Evelyn asked wistfully.

"I don't see why not. Maybe they can give you some pointers. Look, Evelyn, I'd better get to bed before I fall asleep in this chair. Okay? Don't let that Prussian woman get to you now. Tell her. You can do it."

"Easier said than done," said Evelyn. "Last night they came in the lounge to watch the telly with me—couldn't even agree on the program they wanted to watch. Kept changing it from one program back to the other. Drove me up the pole."

"It's good to be back, Evelyn. No one else like you. I'm off to bed then." Penny handed her the tea cup and pushed herself to a standing position.

"Your ankle healed all right?"

"Oh, yes, it's fine, though they say after a bad sprain like that, it's always weaker. I believe Harold told me he'd had a lot of sprains. Always the same ankle. He advised wearing hiking boots, so I brought some this time. Wait'll you see me in my boots with my stick."

"Now don't go and fall again now. I thought I'd have a heart attack when that ambulance drove up."

"I know, I know. I should have called you first. I promise not to sprain any ankles this time. I'm going to walk—carefully, and write and write and write."

But events were already in motion that would change things for Penny and those around her, which she had no way of knowing about at the time.

TWO

Penny's first thought on waking was that she had to hurry and get up. Then she remembered: there was nothing to leap out of bed for except breakfast. Her alarm hadn't gone off yet. She hadn't opened her eyes when she heard the fast slap, slap, slap of footsteps approaching the house, and then the splat as the morning post went through the door and onto the floor in Evelyn's front hall.

Probably no letter yet. Still it was worth opening her eyes. Her first full day on Gower. Quarter of eight. She wrapped her robe around her, opened the door a crack. The bathroom door was ajar.

She was in and out quickly, but Evelyn had noticed and left her a cup of hot tea on the dresser, with a letter beside it. She smiled and climbed back in bed. Cathy had mailed it the day before she left. Now that was the kind of letter-writing friend to have, one who wrote to you before you left home.

A week in the life of Cathy hadn't changed much. Her husband, Rick, was out of town; the older boy, Neill, off to visit his grandparents; she'd splurged on a full-time babysitter for baby Joe and planned in this free week to do research four hours a day, write four hours a day on her thesis, clean the back porch, mow the lawn and weed the garden; have dinner every day with a different friend; see three movies she'd been wanting to see, and give the house a thorough cleaning.

Penny laughed aloud. Was it because Cathy was thirty-four instead of fifty-four? She'd have to ask her what she had actually accomplished. Reading about Cathy's plans for her week "off" was so tiring that she returned with relief to think about her goals for today: visit Three Cliffs Store, buy cards to mail home to let everyone know she'd arrived safely; also get some digestive biscuits, peanut butter, and green apples. Go to the P.O., get stamps and some little notebooks from Helen. Should she splurge on a whole pint of milk? She loved British milk. It was so fresh and creamy.

Evelyn knocked lightly and pushed the door open. "Your breakfast's ready any time."

"Okay, thanks. I'll be right in."

"Nice letter?"

"Yes, from my friend Cathy. You spoil me, bringing me letters and tea. It makes me lazier than I already am."

"No hurry. I got it ready early. Just wanted you to know. Ta." She went back to her breakfast makings.

Penny hunted for all her warm clothes—her room was chilly and the sky was cloudy—probably cold out, too. She had slept in her under-shirt and underpants. To save weight she hadn't brought a nightgown. She remembered aching arms from carrying even one light suitcase two miles to find the B and B the Tourist Board had sent her to. She had brought a warm, lightweight robe but no gown. Anyway, it made her feel young and sexy to sleep in her underwear. Skip the bra today. She'd not be taking her sweater off, even if the sun came out. It must be fifty degrees in this room. She looked with affection at her breasts under her undershirt. She still looked and felt young. Maybe this was the summer she would have a love affair on Gower. She put on a long-sleeved tur-tleneck, the heavier of her two sweaters, and her warmest pair of long pants.

As she took her place at the table, Evelyn carried in a pot of tea and one of hot water. "Look at you in your jumper. It's going to be seventy-five today."

"It isn't there yet, Evelyn, and I'm cold."

Evelyn collected Penny's juice glass the minute she emptied it and said, on her way back to the kitchen, "You'll see. You'll be burning up by lunch time. I'm burning up right now." Evelyn was wearing a short-sleeved cotton blouse and fanned herself with one of her potholders to demonstrate the heat that Penny was foolishly ignoring.

Penny was on her third cup of tea and her last piece of buttered toast generously spread with marmalade when the newlyweds appeared. Apparently the swim had been missed this morning.

"Oh, good morning. Good morning. You must be Mrs. Weav-er. Mrs. Trueblood has said so many nice things about you." This was

James Hampton, III, a man of about forty, bald, well-rounded, definitely well-fed, dressed in casual but elegant clothes, beaming at her in a way that seemed good-natured but made her uneasy. What had Evelyn told them?

"We understand you write poetry," said his wife, Christine. She was strikingly voluptuous, with long blonde hair swept up on top of her head, with very green eyes (contact lenses?). She was wearing a light blue dress that emphasized all her curves, and she exuded sexual power. Penny wondered how some women did that. She knew she didn't, but she recognized it.

"Call me Penny. Yes, I do write poetry," said Penny and thought, so this is the terrible Prussian. She doesn't seem so bad. Maybe she can't help being sexy. She does have an accent. That's probably it. The Brits have never forgiven the Germans. Penny smiled at them both as they settled themselves, and then he reached for her tea pot.

"Actually, that's my pot," she said, "though help yourself, as long as you don't mind sharing yours when it comes." She knew that Evelyn gave every guest or couple a teapot and a pot of hot water.

He pulled his hand back as if she'd bared her teeth. "Oh, sorry."

"We can wait," he added, manfully. But Christine couldn't.

"If you really don't mind? She brought us a cup before breakfast, but I could use another one now," and she helped herself, taking the last cup in the pot, which Penny had planned to add some hot water to and put in her thermos. Evelyn bustled in with an even larger stainless steel tea pot and another pot of hot water on a tray. Mr. Hampton immediately began fussing with it, opening the lid. Evelyn said, "Let it sit a minute. I just poured on the water. Now do you both want a full breakfast?"

"Oh, yes, thank you," said James.

"What do you think, Jim? Should I? I haven't had my swim."

"Just as you like, dear. We've paid for it. Take it, and then don't eat it all if it's too much."

Penny was surprised that an obviously well-brought up British gentleman, or one who appeared as such, would even suggest wasting food. Then it occurred to her where Christine's unfinished breakfast would probably end up. The same thought must have occurred to Christine.

"Now, James, I don't want you eating it. We're both on a diet, remember?"

"I remember, dear. But breakfast does come with the room. I hate to waste it. If you insist, I'll only eat mine. Don't worry. I plan to skip lunch."

"You promise?"

"Yes, dear. I promise."

Penny didn't believe him, and she didn't even know him. But she was still surprised when Christine turned back to Evelyn who had been standing waiting, trying not to look mad, and said, "Two breakfasts then."

"Full breakfasts?" asked Evelyn, like she had played this scene before and didn't enjoy it much.

"Yes, Mrs. Trueblood," said James Hampton meekly, like a small boy who is trying to get back into the good graces of a teacher who has caught him out of his seat for the fourth time. "We'll each have a full breakfast, and we won't waste a bit of it."

"Now, James, you promised!" Christine began in an uncannily unsettling tone of voice, a cross between a whine and a wheedle.

Suddenly Penny wanted to get out of there. They had each poured themselves a cup out of the fresh pot and hadn't offered her one. She could grab the pot and help herself, but there was something peculiarly irritating about these two that made her want to stay as far away from them as possible. She had been in a very pleasant "first day of my writing vacation, rum-tee-tum" mood, wondering happily what she should do today, and feeling like there was, for the first time in days and days, a clean piece of paper inside her. These two were scrawling all over it like a couple of spoiled kids having a heyday with black magic marker. Her peace of mind was gone.

"I'll be off," she said, as she stood up, trying not to sound as angry as she felt.

James grabbed his napkin and rose, too. "Maybe we'll see you later then. I notice you have no car. Can we give you a lift anywhere?"

"Thank you," she said, feeling like she'd have to sprain both ankles and break both arms (so she couldn't even crawl) and all the National Health service ambulance drivers would have to be on strike besides, and the Hamptons owned the only car left on Gower, before she'd accept a ride. But she said, "That's very kind of you." Why did she say that? "I like to walk."

18

"We heard that you sprained your ankle last summer," said Christine.

"Yes," she said, moving toward the lounge.

"Do be careful," said James. "I expect there are a lot of holes on these moors. Do you call this a moor here?"

Penny wanted suddenly to scream, but before she could say, "No, these are chalk cliffs," Christine was answering him. "Of course not, dear. That was the other place we were. This is Gower. Cliffs, you know, and sand. We came so I could swim. You remember?"

"You're right, my dear. Why was it you didn't swim this morning?" he asked meaningfully, staring steadily at Christine and looking coy.

"You know the answer to that, my dear. Why mention it?" At this point Evelyn came in with two platters of bacon, sausage, eggs, fried tomatoes, and mushrooms, and Penny fled.

She retreated to her room, got Cathy's letter off the dresser and climbed back under the covers. Cathy had teased her to be sure and fall in love and send the details. I'll answer Cathy's letter, she thought. It will help me think about something else. For Pete's sake. She had peeked out her curtains. The cloud cover still looked like it might turn to rain. I'll write Cathy a quick note, and out I go. I'm getting the hell out of here. These two are worse than having three children all fighting with each other and dinner not ready and the peas scorched and the dog peed on the floor, and someone I don't like wants to talk to me on the phone. I may have to stay out on the moors—chalk cliffs, she corrected herself angrily—to get any peace at all for the next week.

Then the cloud cover broke, and a ray of light came through the place where the two curtains didn't quite come together. An omen. I'm going out, tea or no tea. I'll write to Cathy up at the top. Maybe I'll buy myself another cup of tea up there. For cat's sake. She put on her hiking boots, found her raincoat, stuck pen, some paper and envelopes in her backpack, along with a five pound note, and opened her door. The coast was clear. She walked quietly out into the front hall, leaving her door ajar so Evelyn would know she was out, opened the front door, closed it behind her firmly, and walked quickly along the walk out to the street.

As she approached the cliffs, a forty mph wind cleared her mind of the breakfast scene. She felt bad about abandoning Evelyn on her first morning, but Evelyn would cope, and they'd laugh about it later. The newlyweds were pretty outlandish. At Three Cliffs Store few people were sitting outside. A young girl—Stanley's daughter?—was wiping off the tables and benches. The postcard racks were out, although it couldn't have been ten minutes since the sun had appeared.

A middle-aged man was writing at one of the tables. Writing? She had never seen anyone else on Gower writing. He looked rough, seedy even. A large man, his greying hair cut shaggily. Unshaven, in rumpled clothes, like he'd slept in them. She'd never heard of that in Wales. He had a serious air and acted proprietary about his table. A cup of coffee, a bottle of milk, and a backpack lay on the table near him, and he was scribbling away in a little notebook, exactly the kind she used on Gower.

She suddenly didn't want to do her postcards here. It was like watching a bad imitation of herself. She stopped at the racks to pick out half a dozen cards of Gower, stepped over the lintel and into the shop. She hunted up digestive biscuits, peanut butter, apples, and, yes, a bottle of milk.

Stanley Jones appeared to wait on her. Stanley was a pensioner, but he still worked long hours running his store. He wore his dark hair combed straight back, and dark-plastic-framed glasses. He had the typical stature of the Welsh, fairly short with a compact body. He generally didn't talk much, but today he seemed pleased to see her. "Oh, hello. So you're back for another summer, are you?"

"Yes. It's nice to be on Gower again. I get to stay two months this time."

"You're staying with Mrs. Trueblood again, aren't you?"

"Yes."

"That's nice for her, isn't it? I know she enjoys you. She's been lonely since Mr. Trueblood died, hasn't she?"

"Yes. She's doing well though. She doesn't slow down for much."

"No. Do tell her hello, won't you? That's two pounds, thirty-eight." Penny handed over her note.

"Newlyweds she's got staying there, too, now, I think, hasn't she?"

"Yes." Penny wondered what was coming. Stanley wasn't a gossip.

"The wife likes to swim. I see her when I'm having my morning walk. A very beautiful woman, isn't she?"

Penny nodded. Not the first thing I'd say about her, she thought. Badly behaved is more to the point.

"They were in here yesterday. He's very pleasant, isn't he?" Penny nodded. What was on Stanley's mind?

"I'm not sure they understand our tides," Stanley went on. "I tried to explain to them how we have one of the longest tidal changes in the world, and how it can be quite treacherously fast if you're swimming. You can get stranded because the incoming tide moves so fast, you know, and there's sometimes a bad undertow. I'm not sure they understood the danger . . . maybe you—." He broke off.

"She seems like a woman who can take care of herself," Penny said. "She probably heard you all right but didn't let on. Was the tide like that this morning?"

"Yes."

"There you are, Mr. Jones. She didn't swim this morning. She must have heard more than you thought."

"I hope so."

"Don't worry, Mr. Jones. That one can take care of herself. I'm sure of it."

"I hope so." He turned to another customer.

Penny had a thing about post offices. She had always made friends with the postman, the mail person, or the postmaster. In Pwll-du, the post office had many functions. She loved Helen Harcourt. The sign over the door said T. Harcourt, Ltd. But whoever T. was or had been, Helen was the one in charge now of all the postal operations, which included serving the pensioners who came to get their monthly stipends. They could also save money in their post office account. You could buy your newspaper or pick it up, if you were a subscriber. Helen also carried postcards, stationery, school notebooks, apples, potatoes, and candy bars. She had the best buy on little school notebooks. Today Penny was buying notebooks, airmail stamps, and a couple of air letters.

Suddenly she heard a familiar voice with a German accent. Christine was at the counter. The Hamptons looked to be her nemesis today. Ten a.m. must be rush hour, or pensioners' day? Six people stood between her and Christine, all elderly, all having that stoical look the British get when they're waiting in a queue, several with papers tucked under their arms.

"You haven't got any commemoratives?" Christine spoke loudly, in an offended tone, as if to be sure everyone noticed: she was not getting good service.

Penny couldn't hear what Helen said in her quiet voice. If the British were usually cautious, even timid, with strangers, Helen was especially timid, and always carefully polite.

"What about in 32p stamps? Or 30p? None, either? Don't they give you any? Isn't this a regular post office?"

Again Helen said something low. This must be hard on Helen, who was obsessively polite. Penny caught a glimpse of her slight frame. Helen always held herself ramrod straight, but she looked frail enough for the strong Gower winds to blow her right off her feet.

"All you have is queens?" Christine said. "I'm sick of Queen Elizabeth. No, frankly, the Queen Mother isn't what I had in mind either. Nothing but queens then?"

Another murmur from Helen.

"Where is the nearest full-service post office then?"

As Helen murmured her answer, someone shifted place in the line, and Penny caught Helen's eye. She looked exhausted and worried about her other customers whom she was glancing at. She barely smiled when Penny smiled her sympathy.

"Swansea? Swansea?" said Christine loudly. "I have to go all the way to Swansea to get a stamp that doesn't have a queen on it? Good lord, help us!" Helen hadn't broken the news to her that every British stamp had a queen on it somewhere.

Christine turned suddenly and walked out, oblivious to the visible signs of relief in the six British pensioners, whose tensed bodies all relaxed, as they now moved a step or two closer to the counter. If she saw Penny, Christine didn't acknowledge her. Penny never noticed clothes much, but it was unusual on Gower to see someone on holiday this gussied up. Christine had changed since breakfast. She now was wearing a startlingly white blouse with a beautiful, many-colored wool sweater, with browns and oranges and blues in it, all mixed up, and a pleated white skirt that swirled slightly as she walked. Every pleat was perfect. She must have sat down to ride to the P.O. But not a wrinkle. Penny heard the purring of a well-made, expensive engine. The Rolls Royce appeared as Christine left the post office. Penny saw James III hurry around, moving amazingly quickly and dexterously for a stout man, to open her door. She thought he bent his face down toward her before handing her in, but he stopped the motion a few inches from her face. Christine was not in the mood for kissing. James III saw her adjusted and arranged, closed the door carefully, and walked very slowly around to the driver's side.

The man is a blathering idiot, Penny thought, but I don't envy him the ride to Swansea.

"Are you in the queue?" an elderly woman asked, startling Penny.

"Oh, yes, thanks." In those few minutes Helen had taken care of five out of the six customers ahead of her, and Penny had been so fascinated by the drama happening at the door of the Rolls that she had not noticed the drama of the vanishing queue inside the post office.

"Oh, hi, Helen. It's good to be back. How are you?" she asked.

"Pretty busy, actually. This is the morning most people come for their pensions. Then that German woman—I felt bad I didn't have the stamps she wanted, but I don't sell that many airmail stamps—commemorative—like she wanted, so I didn't have any. It seemed to upset her a lot." Helen brushed her short white hair back with one hand while she hunted out the stamps.

"I wouldn't worry." Penny laughed. "They're staying at Evelyn's, too. Evelyn also has a hard time pleasing her. Don't take it personally. It's her, not you. But if you do get any commemoratives, I'll buy them. I'll be here two months, so I should be able to buy out your stock."

Helen smiled faintly but kept looking at the remaining people in the queue now behind Penny.

"Just queens today," Helen said quickly. Penny told her what stamps she wanted and handed over all her money but her last ten p piece and a couple of pence.

"Here you go," said Helen. She was already making eye contact with her next customer.

Penny stopped outside the shop to tuck her booklets, stamps, and air letters into her backpack. She'd go by the library next. A poem a day was her rhythm on Gower, and after she'd done her day's writing, she liked to tuck up with a good detective novel. She wondered if the library had any that she hadn't read yet.

She could write to Cathy there, do her cards, mail them across the street, and then head over to Three Cliffs Bay. The tide would be in, and she could watch the ocean from the cliffs and have her lunch. If she found a good book or two, that, after a good "write," would be the perfect omen to add to the sunshine which was still holding its own, though more and more clouds were blowing over, and Penny was still glad for all her layers. Lucy Straley, the librarian, was one of her best friends on Gower and its only resident feminist, and she wanted to say hello.

At supper that Wednesday night Penny learned that the Hamptons had been back for a long afternoon "nap" but were gone now for their dinner. It was Evelyn and Penny over their lamb chops, boiled potatoes, and cauliflower. Penny told Evelyn that she was planning to start the new detective book that Lucy had recommended.

Evelyn laughed at her for her addiction to detective fiction and tried to get her addicted to the telly instead. Evelyn had for years tried to get Penny to come into the lounge in the evening and behave like a regular B and B guest. When she was on holiday, Penny loved to spend a whole evening alone in her room reading. It rested her mind for poetry.

"There's a detective movie on," Evelyn told Penny. "You might like that."

"What is it?"

"Agatha Christie."

"I'm not wild about Christie."

"I like it. It's a series. Jan Fisher plays Miss Jane Marple. She's stunning. You'd better see it to see her. I've seen the others."

"Okay, okay. I'll try it. If I like it, I'll stay. If I don't, I'll go read my library book. But what about the Hamptons? I wouldn't like to get all involved and then they come in and start changing the channels."

"Oh, they've gone all the way to Cardiff for dinner. They won't be back before ten. It's on from eight to ten."

"To Cardiff. Good grief."

"Yes. They have the petrol to waste, I guess. They liked a place where they ate in Cardiff on their way down here and decided to go there tonight. I think they were celebrating their first week of marriage. I heard him on the phone ordering champagne. She showed me three different outfits—she must have two trunks full of clothes—before she decided what to wear. Come for a holiday and bring that many clothes? I can't see it."

"He must like it."

"Oh, yes. He likes it. But he likes them all—all her outfits. I've heard him tell her so. Still, even so, he lets her go buy more. They're going shopping tomorrow. Today they had to go to Swansea anyway, and she found the perfect swimsuit. Forty pounds for nothing. Not enough even to cover her where she needs it. I'd be embarrassed. A big beautiful blue swimming robe to go with it. She gets cold, she says. No wonder. She'll be practically naked in that thing."

"Oh, Evelyn, you've admitted it. Some of us do get cold on Gower."

"She goes down there at six a.m., and it's usually still cloudy. The water's warm."

"Warm? You couldn't get me in that water. I can't even wear shorts without freezing to death."

Evelyn was stopped in her tracks but not for long. "You, Penny? You're different. I can't get you to take off your jumper when it's eighty."

"Oh, yes, I do when it's eighty, Evelyn. I might even swim if it was eighty."

"I bet you didn't bring your suit."

"I did, and I promise, when it's eighty and the sun is out, and the wind dies to only twenty miles an hour, I'll go in."

"I'll believe it when I see it. Will you watch the Christie?"

"Yes, I'll watch the Christie, and if those two come in, let me hold the channel changer. Okay?"

"All right. You can fight with them, and I'll go to bed. Actually those Americans are due. I'll have to wait up for them."

"Americans I can handle."

Penny was to fail utterly with these Americans, however, and though she was thoroughly and easily hooked by Jan Fisher's performance as Miss Jane Marple, and although she'd read the book years before and forgotten it enough to enjoy the plot again—to be genuinely puzzled and to entertain herself trying to guess the murderer—she wasn't destined to see the whole program.

The Americans called from the village club about ten minutes after eight, when the Christie had just started. Evelyn had been fretting, as they'd said they'd come in before dinner, but finally the call had come. He said they were running late, had had their dinner. They were having a pint at the club. If it was okay, they'd be over in about half an hour. Evelyn said she heard a woman's voice in the background say, "Tell her an hour," and the man had then corrected himself, "in about an hour, if you're sure that's okay?" Evelyn said yes, relieved they had at least showed up. She got in a swivet when people reserved a room and were late, afraid they weren't coming at all, and sometimes she had had to turn other people away. She had, in fact, only that afternoon.

She and Penny had settled to their mystery and were fully caught up in it, when, an hour later, as promised, the doorbell rang. Evelyn jumped up without hesitation, but she considerately closed the opaque glass door behind her, welcomed the Americans in the hallway, and then took them back to see their room. Penny had no interest in meeting Americans. The Americans she had met in Great Britain had embarrassed her and made her feel ashamed of her country. They were generally so insensitive to cultures other than their own and so insular in their thinking. She liked it when people thought she was from Canada or Australia. Once on a long walk in an unfamiliar part of Gower, a shopkeeper had thought she was French. She had loved that.

She had almost forgotten these Americans when the glass door opened and Evelyn led them in, picked up the remote control, and turned the sound way down. What could Penny do? She smiled, as she was introduced. "Mr. and Mrs. Rosewood, your compatriots. This is Penny Weaver. She's been with me several summers."

"Where are you from?" asked Mr. Rosewood.

"North Carolina," she said. "A small town called Riverdell, near Chapel Hill."

"We're from Manhattan. I'm Eloise," said this dark-haired woman, who was probably in her fifties. She had a European accent—French? She reminded Penny of a lithe greyhound, ready to spring up and run out the door, given any opportunity. "And this is my husband, Ernest."

Ernest nodded, smiled, and gazed at her directly. They were both of middle height, about five feet six. He was also slender and looked fit. His greying hair and mustache added to his sophisticated, urbane look. He had a New York accent—urban Northeast anyway. He was in his fifties, maybe sixties. He always made eye contact when he spoke, Penny noticed. Eloise, with dark hair and eyes, who looked younger, was possibly tipsy and seemed very amused by something. He was not amused by whatever amused her.

"He dragged me away from the pub. I wanted to have one more pint, but he was worried we'd keep you up. But you're watching something. Don't let us keep you. Ernie, you see, you were ridiculous. We have time to go back to the pub."

Evelyn corrected her. "The club, you mean? They close early—at ten. It's already 9:30 now. I'll need to lock up at 10:30, though there are pubs..."

"No, no," said Ernest, more firmly. "We're here. We'll stay in. But don't let us keep you from your program. We—."

Evelyn stepped over near the television, pointed the remote control, and turned it off. Penny thought, there goes another unsolved mystery. I'll see if the library has the book. She was on the point of getting up and excusing herself, figuring she'd take a shower, while they chatted with Evelyn, and then climb into bed with her library book, but Ernest was speaking to her: "We understand you're a writer. How interesting. What books have you published?"

That nearly always kept her in the conversation. "I write poetry. I like to come here to write. I have three books out, and the last one is about Gower. I write my best poems here, and Evelyn looks after me. She's a great cook. The best British breakfast you've ever had."

He smiled. "Have you ever been up to Snowdonia? We've just been there. It's lovely."

"No," she said. "I fell in love with Gower. I keep coming back here. I don't have a car, and I can walk or ride the bus here and see a lot of different kinds of scenery. Not too many Americans come here, or even British, but the Welsh love it. Evelyn's been coming here since she was a little girl."

He turned to Evelyn. "Oh, are you Welsh then?" He ignored the fact that his wife was fidgeting and had already said, "Ernie," once. He was soon deeply engrossed in a conversation with Evelyn. She was telling him about her childhood. Penny heard him ask: "How long have you actually lived here?" Evelyn loved to tell the story of how she and Hal had decided to retire here and had bought this bungalow some twelve years before; how, years before that, they had honeymooned on Gower. Ernest was entranced, but Eloise was shifting in her chair.

"Ernie, dearest..."

Penny decided to tackle her. Her program was shot. But Evelyn was clearly happy, and that was something. For a man, Ernest was good at drawing people out, putting them at ease. He was probably a psychiatrist. She turned to Eloise. "You liked Snowdonia?"

"Oh, yes. But we got here about seven, and it is really lovely here, too. There's an old castle right on the cliffs—you know that, I guess. I want to go see it early tomorrow and then go down to the Worms' Head point—is that what it's called? How is that?"

"I like it a lot, though it's best on a clear, sunny day. It's right on the Atlantic and not very pleasant if it's raining and blowing. Interesting wrecks in the sand though. If you like to walk, there's a house, halfway between Worm's Head and the village Llangennith that's supposed to be haunted."

But though Eloise smiled and tried to look interested, she was clearly preoccupied.

"Dear Ernie—."

"Yes, Ellie?"

"I think we should let these people finish their program and go back to that pub. We've still got almost half an hour, and I'm not sleepy. I'm really not."

Ernie stared at her, looking like he wished he had a different wife or no wife or a wife who understood polite behavior better. Nevertheless, he did what Penny would never have predicted from his firm, polite, genuine way (almost a bedside manner—probably a therapist's chairside manner) with her and Evelyn, he yielded to his wife. He turned to Evelyn. "You lock up at 10:30 then? I guess we'll go back out until 10:30. We're not quite ready to turn in. I apologize for interrupting your program." He stood up.

Eloise had started for the door and now said, as nice as pie, "So good to meet you both. See you later then?"

Penny said, "I'll see you at breakfast, I expect." She stood up, too.

Evelyn went out with them to give them directions to the nearest pub. Penny looked at her watch. It was five to ten. The BBC news started at ten. The mystery would be solved, and besides, she didn't know how to operate the remote control. She went out the other lounge door, through the dining room and kitchen, and slipped through the hall to her room. She heard Evelyn saying "Bye" outside on the walk as she closed her door behind her. Safe back in her own room.

If today was typical, she was going to be stepping to get a poem every day and any reading done. Still, Evelyn was right. People were amusing in their own way, especially if one could laugh with someone else about their foibles.

28

☙

Evelyn knocked gently.

"Come in."

"What did you think of your compatriots?"

"They're okay. He's probably a psychiatrist."

"A psychiatrist?" Evelyn looked shattered, as she called it. "What makes you think that?" Penny knew the whole topic of psychology made her anxious.

"He draws people out well for an American man. They live in Manhattan. That takes a lot of money. Psychiatrists are rich in America."

"They do have a big rented car, much bigger than they need for the two of them."

"I wonder if she's his wife," speculated Penny. "Maybe he's having an affair with one of his patients."

"Oh, no, she's Mrs. Rosewood all right. She's French. She told me they'd been married so long they didn't even care any more where they had their fights. I don't like her much, but he's all right."

"You say that about all these couples, Evelyn."

"No, just these two. Didn't you think she was strange?"

"I thought she was spoiled. I bet they're late."

Evelyn looked worried. Then the outer door opened, and Evelyn dashed off, closing Penny's door. The newlyweds. If she hurried, she could beat them into the bathroom. She grabbed her toothbrush, paste, and robe. She made it.

THREE

Thursday morning it was the milk bottles in their metal holder being set down by the front door that woke Penny. She stretched and re-curled her body under the covers but didn't open her eyes. The milkman came about seven. She could sleep another half hour. Then she heard voices in the front hall. Evelyn? The key turned in the front door, and it opened, and someone stepped out and walked quickly away. Penny heard Evelyn muttering and getting in the milk. The door closed. Could the Prussian be going for her swim? This was too good to miss. Penny got out of bed, got her glasses off the dresser, and opened the edge of the curtain cautiously.

Yes, there went Christine in her royal blue bathing robe, and a big orange and blue beach towel over her arm. There was no shortcut to Pobbles, the nearest beach. You had to walk up to the top and along the cliffs, or go through the village, cut through the lane opposite the P.O., and take the footpath between some dunes and the cliffs. Christine was half way up Heatherslade Lane. Penny watched, curious which way she'd turn. She turned left. Through the village then and the public footpath. Evelyn must have told her about it.

Suddenly Penny saw the red Royal Mail truck zoom down the lane and stop a couple of houses away. She was in her underwear. She dove back under the covers. She pulled her robe around her shoulders and reached for her diary. She heard the sound of the shower in the bathroom. The Americans had the room with its own shower and toilet, so it must be James III. She hoped he was a four-minute shower man. Back in North Carolina everybody would be taking four-minute showers. They had a drought, plus a heat wave and a water shortage.

Whatever. She was in Wales. Today, the gods willing, she might write a poem. She'd have her breakfast as early as Evelyn had it ready, take digestive biscuits and peanut butter, a thermos of tea, and head out regardless of the weather. The library opened at ten Thursday, so if it started raining, she could go there. Lucy had been doing a story hour for pre-schoolers when Penny arrived the day before, and then an old gentleman had needed her help finding books on the history of Gower. Morning got busy in the library around eleven. Maybe she'd go when Lucy first opened and have a chat.

The sound of the post going through the door slot onto the hall floor startled her. Then Evelyn knocked quietly. "You awake, Penny?"

"Yes. Come in."

"You have a letter. Would you like some tea?"

"Sure."

Evelyn came in with the tea in one hand and a postcard in the other. "I thought we probably woke you up when the Prussian went out. I'm sorry."

"Don't worry about waking me. Actually, it was the milkman. So the bride is off to swim, huh? You've given her strict instructions when to be back if she wants to eat, right?" Penny grinned.

"Oh, Penny, I'm not like you. I'm not that tough. I did tell her husband that I'd like to serve them breakfast no later than nine. I can do you at eight, if you like, and I told the Americans 8:30. But Mr. Hampton said he'd like to eat earlier, so he may be in with you. He was sure his wife would be back by nine, but I doubt it. She does whatever she likes. She certainly never does what he says."

"True," said Penny. She looked at the card. "It's from Cathy. Another record for the British postal service. This was mailed Monday, the day I left."

Evelyn had disappeared again. Penny looked out the door. The coast was clear. She dashed for the bathroom, peed, splashed water on her face, and ran dripping back to her room. She always forgot her towel. Ah, the luxury of mail and tea before breakfast, and being able to go back to bed when you were already wide awake. She had smelled bacon as she came through the hall. Not even having to cook your own breakfast. Later she'd go onto her routine of having the smaller breakfast—cereal, toast, juice, tea, and a poached egg—but for now she was enjoying the works.

Cathy's card showed a cat with a huge fish. It looked to be half of a salmon. The cat was in the attack mode with its tail raised as if it were lashing it back and forth. Two smaller fish hung from a meat hook. Who would let a cat in with freshly caught fish? It was called "Still Life with Cat and Fish," but only the dead fish were "still." Cathy had written: "I forgot to tell you I've discovered a great feminist detective writer: Sara Paretsky. She's American but appropriate for your British holiday. Enjoy your sweater weather. It's 97 degrees here, with 99% humidity. Love, Cathy."

A new detective writer. This was worth getting out of bed for. Quickly she shed her robe and undershirt. Today might warm up. A bra day and a white cotton blouse, in case she got to take her sweater off. The sun was already out. Who could tell? It might hit eighty and only her second day. She put her sweater on for now. Evelyn's house was cold. She undid her braid, brushed and re-braided her still light brown hair—no gray yet—and went to breakfast, handing Evelyn her cup at the kitchen door.

She wondered, as she reached for the cornflakes, if Evelyn had read the card. Evelyn wasn't a feminist, though she had tried to dissuade Penny from getting remarried. What did she need a man for? Didn't she enjoy her life as it was? If she had a husband, she wouldn't be able to go traipsing off whenever and wherever she wanted to. "I did love Hal, and I miss him terribly, but men are a lot of trouble."

"I know," Penny had said. Yet she had always assumed there would be someone else. So far no Odysseus had washed in to take up a permanent place in her affections. There had been a series of interesting possibilities, but some had been married and had opted to stay with their wives; some had panicked when they had gotten to know her better. Others had been interesting to her, and sexy, but she apparently hadn't been interesting or sexy to them.

Her friend Lucy at the library thought it was the age. Lots of women right now were becoming who they wanted to be, but there weren't many men ready for that yet. She said she knew a whole lot of British and European women who couldn't find a man who was up to them. It wasn't the end of the world. Life was interesting on its own terms. There were advantages to being on your own. But she liked men, some men.

At this point James Hampton III startled her by appearing to her left. "Good morning," he said, "so you're an early bird, too."

He smiled at her in a peculiarly ingratiating way.

The man doesn't act married, she thought. Oh, help! Why doesn't Christine come back?

"Oh, hi," she said in her most matter-of-fact voice. That usually settled them down. "Yes, I decided to get an early start. Looks like a good day." She gestured toward the window where the early morning sunshine was glinting off the drops of moisture on Evelyn's prize yellow roses.

"A gorgeous day, indeed. Will you write a poem to this fair sun and those golden roses?"

Although Penny distrusted blatant flattery, hated buttery words, and didn't like the man, he was trying to be nice to her, in his way. Maybe he was feeling guilty about yesterday morning's intrusion on the part of his wife into the territory of her teapot.

"Ah, my tea." He beamed as Evelyn came through her swinging kitchen door. She had brought him a small pot today. As she collected their juice glasses, she handed Penny her platter of bacon, sausages, eggs, mushrooms, and fried tomatoes.

"Great, Evelyn," said Penny. "It looks beautiful."

"I hope it's all right," said Evelyn. "I'll have yours ready very shortly," she went on to James III. She set the cornflakes box near him and smiled.

"Do you think I dare eat cornflakes, too? Christine says they aren't necessary and have no nutritional value."

"No nutritional value," exclaimed Evelyn. She nearly lost her hold on the juice glasses. "Why, look at this side panel. Every vitamin you can think of, just about, is in these cornflakes, and probably some you never thought about, too. I've eaten them for forty years."

"Have you now?" asked James, looking reassured. "As a matter of fact, so have I. My mum says the same as you. Of course, I do need to lose weight. Christine—."

"Not on your honeymoon!" protested Evelyn. "Surely a few cornflakes won't make that much difference. Christine will never know."

"But then there's your big breakfast," he said, smirking, as he poured a bowl of cornflakes so full that Penny wondered what would happen when he added milk. He was gazing longingly at her sausages though, not yet concerned about whether the milk would fit into the bowl.

"So?" said Evelyn. "It will hold you all day. You'll be out and about. You need a good breakfast. But it's up to you. What will it be? I can leave out the sausages."

"Oh, no," said James III. "I love sausages."

"Well?"

"Just give me the full breakfast. Christine will kill me."

"She doesn't have to know," said Evelyn again.

Did this mean they were all supposed to lie when the man's wife returned from her swim? He can fend for himself, she thought. I refuse to help him out. If he's going to overeat, he'll have to deal with his own consequences.

"Oh, she'll know," he said sadly. "She reads me like a book. But I have a harder time dieting than she does. Oh, dear. I hope she won't be too mad." He continued to gaze affectionately at Penny's eggs and sausages. Penny looked out the window and stared at the roses, but they didn't help. Another breakfast that was not proving to be much fun. Finish and leave. That was the ticket.

"Hello, everybody. Good morning, good morning." It was her fellow Americans. Evelyn was back in the kitchen. Where was she when she was wanted?

"Oh, hi. How did you sleep?" Penny yielded regretfully to the role of hostess.

"Just great!" said Ernie.

"Have you met James Hampton? This is Ernest and Eloise Rosewood. They're from New York. James is from—"

"Coventry. The West Midlands. Very nice to meet you. Are you enjoying your holiday?"

Ernie answered, "Very much. We have been up to Snowdonia, but, alas, tomorrow we have to head back to London and get a plane home. Too bad. We'd love to stay longer. We like Gower, what we've seen. We got here last evening."

Evelyn reappeared with their tea, asked how they'd slept, and ducked back into the kitchen. Penny was opposite Ernie, with James catty-corner, and Eloise beside her, helping herself to tea and trying to ignore James, who was clearly eager to talk. Oh, Christine, she thought, no wonder you work so hard on your clothes and your figure. This man flirts with every woman he meets.

"Are you planning to write a poem today?" Ernie asked, friendly, interested, not flirtatious. What a relief.

"You never know about a poem, when it will come and when it won't, but, yes, I hope to."

"What do you find helps you get started?" he asked as though he cared to know. He wasn't a cornflakes man. Nor had he noticed his juice.

James was asking Eloise what she'd liked best about Wales, and she was answering with less reluctance than Penny had expected. The man was a solemn fool, but he did understand some things about women. Was it his obsequiousness that was attractive? Do we all like that in spite of ourselves? For someone to act like we're impressive to him? I fell for it, too, she admitted, more than I meant to.

Still, she'd rather talk to the psychiatrist. He wasn't quite leveling with them, but she had two friends at home who were shrinks, and people tended to shrivel up when they found out. She asked Ernie how he liked living in Manhattan.

"It has changed a lot," he said. "Most of the people living on Manhattan now are very poor. It's difficult for them. So few jobs, yet most immigrants still come there first."

That subject was boring. Try another tack. "Your wife said you might go back to see the castle near here."

"Oh, yes, she is quite taken with it."

"There's a legend about it."

"Eloise, she says there's a legend about that old castle we saw last night. You wanted to go back to it today."

"A legend? Excellent," said Eloise, abandoning her conversation with James, who looked at Penny with respectful interest. He had polished off his cornflakes and was on his second cup of tea. There were no cornflakes or milk around his bowl. I have underestimated this man, thought Penny.

"I read it in a book in the library," she said. "It goes back to the 1100s. As you know, the French conquered England." She smiled at Eloise. "They built castles in the last part of the eleventh century. The legend is from a hundred years later. The fairies in the story may be the native inhabitants who had kept secretly to their old ways.

"The lord of this Gower castle was a famous warrior, and another lord asked him to come help him out in a battle. After they won the battle, the other lord offered him whatever he'd like, and the Gower lord took his daughter, who was afraid of the Gower lord, but she went with him. Once back at the castle, they had celebrated with a big wedding feast until late at night in the big hall.

"A lookout was watching, and he heard some eerie music, and

it scared him. He told the lord in the big hall, who then, with all his knights, rushed out of the castle and down to the plain below where the fairies were dancing. They drew their swords and rushed into their midst. But the fairies vanished, and their swords met only the air. Then they heard a fairy voice say, 'Because you have ruined our singing and dancing, this night your castle will lie in ruins.' The voice disappeared, laughing as it faded away.

"That night a big sand storm came up and buried the castle, all the people, and all of the nearby village as well. There must be some basis in fact because the castle is still besanded, and when I walk along the cliffs, it's easy to imagine the stones there were once part of the village that got buried."

There was a hush, so that, when Evelyn swung open the door, carrying two more platters, she startled them all. She put one down for James, and one for Eloise, and said to Ernie, "I'll be right back with yours. Is everything all right?" She looked worried.

"Oh, yes, fine. Your poet has been entertaining us with a legend," said Ernie.

"What legend is that, Penny?"

"The old castle—you know—."

"I don't know that I do. It was besanded, of course. The church was buried, too. You can get to it easily. Go through the village and across the golf links. But stay on the footpath, and mind the golfers."

They laughed. She disappeared to get Ernie's breakfast, and they were soon, three of them, all engrossed in their breakfasts. Penny spread marmalade on a piece of toast she had no room for and wondered what Ernie was thinking. She liked him best of the lot. He was human, and he didn't put on airs. Her story had made him thoughtful.

"Your breakfast will get cold," Penny said gently.

"Oh, yes, you're right." He smiled at her.

"Ernie takes forever to eat," commented Eloise. "His mother always made him eat everything on his plate, and he never got over it."

Ernie let this pass, but he picked up his fork and paid close attention to his bacon until Eloise began to answer a question James was putting to her about her accent. "Oh, I'm French, though I've been in the U.S. since I was a teenager. My family left France during the war," she said quickly, as if that explained everything. The brusqueness in her tone suggested that she didn't want to talk about it. "Tell me about Coventry. What is there to see there?"

While James described Lady Godiva's gallant ride naked on a horse through the streets of Coventry, Ernie found his voice again. He put his knife and fork down carefully and said quietly to Penny, as though nothing else had happened or been said since she had finished telling the legend. "You tell a good story. You think there's some basis in fact? Tell me more about that."

"It seems likely that the Welsh kept their ways, and perhaps had dances, maybe religious rituals, out on the green below the castle. When you're at the castle, you can look down and see a maze on the plain below that's near the river. These mazes are very old. Possibly even the religious ritual was matriarchal. It feels to me like a fight between a warrior culture and a culture that was more matriarchal. The singing and dancing of the fairies, and the anxiety the warriors felt about it. They wanted to kill what turned out to be 'bodiless' and to disappear, but these fairies had the power to bestow a vengeance that was natural, i.e., Mother Nature got even.

"It reminds me of the Artemis legend, too. Another matriarchal legend. Actaeon, with his hunting weapons, trespasses on the goddess's sacred grove when she's bathing naked with her nymphs, and so he's punished by being turned into a deer and his own hounds kill him. The hunter becomes the hunted. You can see Artemis as Mother Nature. She has her weapons."

Ernie had forgotten his breakfast entirely. His tea cup had not yet had even a drop of tea in it. His sausages were sitting in congealing fat. Penny found his attentiveness to her endearing. Why did he have to be married and to a woman who obviously enjoyed embarrassing him as often as possible in front of other people?

"You've given this a lot of thought," he said. "Do you work such thoughts into your poems?"

"Sometimes," she said.

"I'd like to read them." The man was a treasure. Perhaps his wife could go home, and he could stay another week by himself.

"I have my most recent book with me. Would you like to borrow it today?"

"Very much. My wife walks more than I do. It would give me something to do. And you've made me curious about this castle. Eloise, let's find that castle right after breakfast. Penny has whetted my appetite." Eloise looked up. Her breakfast was eaten, her plate cleaned even of all traces of grease. "Use your appetite first on your breakfast, beloved, and then we'll go hunt castles." She stood up.

At this moment the front door bell rang, and Penny heard Evelyn hurrying to get it. Penny looked at her watch. It was 9:15. Uh, oh.

"Oh, am I late? I'm so sorry. I'll get a quick shower and be right out. Toast is fine. I don't need eggs. Are you positive you don't mind? Eggs, then, and one piece of bacon. All right, then, one teeny sausage." Evelyn walked back to the kitchen, and for some reason Eloise sat back down again, and turning to James, said, "Is that your wife? We heard she went out for a swim."

"Yes." James sighed, looked down guiltily at his clean plate and empty toast rack, and picking up his cup, drained it. "She'll kill me when she finds out I ate a whole breakfast. Even the cornflakes."

"Over my dead body," said Evelyn. She quickly took up Penny's, Eloise's, and James's platters, stacked them, glanced at Ernie's, which was still half full of food, and marched out as though to begin some war of her own on food wasters and late breakfast comers. "I won't tell her if you won't," Evelyn threw back over her shoulder to James.

He smiled and looked at Eloise. "I know I'm overweight, but my new wife—we've been married eight days today—."

"I won't tell," said Eloise, and turning to Penny, "Tell me again how you get to the castle?"

Penny explained, and was well into the contemporary legend of the war between the golfers and the holiday makers when Christine suddenly appeared from behind Penny in a silk turquoise dress that clung to her very handsome figure in all the right places and tended to become, if not the conversation piece, the distraction from whatever conversation had been going forward.

"Oh, Jimmy," she said, "I hope you haven't been eating." Eloise stared at her. Penny noticed that Eloise had started toward the lounge, but stopped now, whether because horrified or fascinated.

"I have," he said meekly, giving away every bit of his guilt in those two words. James had volunteered everything he'd said he didn't want her to know. Did he like his Prussian to hound him? Enough was enough. Penny hated hearing other people's family fights. She was getting out of here.

The genuine interest of the psychiatrist had touched her. But with two married couples on the point of war and Evelyn looking like she might march in with a butcher knife, she thought of her chalk cliffs with affection. Only the rock roses to talk to. Only the Gower wind to deal with.

"You didn't eat that big breakfast, Jimmy, not after you promised me?" Christine was looking at this plump man, who had been eating cornflakes for forty years, with his bald head and his persisting air of a gay bachelor, as though she despaired of ever shaping him up. She is right to doubt her powers, thought Penny. This man acts meek, but he will win in the end. She'll never change him. She thinks she has him by the short hairs, but she's wrong. She'll never outwit him.

"No afternoon nap today," said Christine. "Little boys who overeat have to get lots of fresh air and exercise." She was giving him that fixed look, and he was beginning to sweat, though it couldn't be more than 65 degrees in Evelyn's dining room.

"This is disgusting," said Eloise, but, though she stood up again, she couldn't seem to leave. "Ernie, I'm going to get my jacket and take a little walk. I'll meet you by the castle in half an hour." But she stood there, riveted to the two lovers' fight.

"Please! Darling Christine," said James Hampton III, "I do so want my afternoon nap. You may spank me," he said. He gave her an intense stare. "Just let me have my little nap. All good little boys want their naps. Please, Mama, dear."

"Not today," said Christine. "Jimmy's been very bad."

"I can't believe this shit!" said Eloise. But she still didn't move.

Penny caught a look partly of sorrow and partly of worry on Ernie's face.

He picked up his fork and looked directly at Eloise. He seemed to put every ounce of love, attention, and common sense that he was capable of into his next words. "It's nothing for you to worry about, Eloise. I'll catch up with you. I've almost finished eating."

That seemed to get through.

"Oh, good. There's hope," she said. "Yeah, see you folks later." In an entirely different voice she said to Penny, "Great legend. Can't wait to see the castle," and to Christine: "He ate every bit of his breakfast like the good husband he is, and he deserves for you to treat him like an adult." She flounced out, walking so fast through the house that it seemed only seconds before they heard her slam a door in the back where their bedroom was.

"What's her problem?" asked Christine. She moved Eloise's tea cup and sat down where Eloise had been sitting, across from James. She reached over and got the clean cup from the other place setting and poured the last cup of tea from her husband's pot.

"She's upset because I'm a slow eater," said Ernie.

"You're slow, and James is a fool," said Christine.

"Yes, I'm a fool, dear," said James. "But this good Gower air has whetted my appetite." He looked with boyish appeal to Evelyn, who had marched in with Christine's teapot. Then looking at Penny, he said, "Mrs. Trueblood's breakfast is the best in Great Britain. Plus," he added, looking steadily at Christine again, "I need energy to explore this castle we've been learning about. I might get so tired even you would think I needed a nap."

For cat's sake, thought Penny. I will lose my breakfast for sure. "I'd better be going," said Penny. "I want to get out on the cliffs today." She turned and walked fast back to her room and would have slammed the door if it would have slammed, but it wouldn't quite close.

She was ready in five minutes and, for the second time in two days, left before she told Evelyn goodbye. Good grief. She hadn't come to Wales to listen to this garbage. She forgot all about giving Ernie her last book of poems to read.

FOUR

When she arrived at the library, it was nearly ten. She took off her backpack, leaned her stick against the wall of the library building, and got her diary out. She'd write herself into a better mood or she'd never get a good poem today. Usually Evelyn's guests weren't this intrusive.

When Lucy drove up in her small, very old, perfectly preserved green car, she did feel better. Lucy was seventy. The car looked fifty. Lucy had retired from being a school librarian in the Midlands, moved to Gower, and taken this part-time library job.

It hadn't been until the summer before that she had gotten to know Lucy Straley. She had been looking for new detective authors, and they had gotten into conversation about their favorites. Lucy had recommended Amanda Cross, an American writer of feminist detective fiction. Up until then, Penny hadn't known that there was such a genre. She was also surprised the Gower librarian knew about such things. Lucy didn't announce herself as a feminist to everyone, but she worked on people and situations quietly and saw them change, she said. Penny herself hadn't noticed much change in Gower people, in comparison with the villagers of Riverdell, but she liked to hear what Lucy had to say.

"Good morning, Penny. You're in early. Been waiting long? I'm a few minutes late."

"No problem."

"I hate to be late, but there was a German woman in the post office trying to mail a package. I was behind her trying to get my pension and pick up my paper. Helen always gives such good, fast service, but there was not much she could do with this German woman. Now there's someone who needs to have her consciousness raised."

Penny piled her stick and backpack onto a chair and pulled up another one near enough to Lucy's desk so they could talk, as Lucy went around setting things out, rearranging the books on the tables in the children's corner, checking in and then re-shelving some that had been put through the slot while the library was closed. She handed Penny a book. "Here's another author you might like. She takes some getting used to, but she's splendid. A compatriot of yours."

The word *compatriot* was beginning to have bad connotations for Penny. "Paretsky! I've this very morning heard from my friend in Riverdell about her. Great! Yes, I'll take her. Let's see—I got two yesterday. Can I take out one more?"

"Two more," said Lucy. "You have four tickets. What did you think of the Grimes?"

"I didn't get very far. I watched the telly with Evelyn. That Christie was on, with Jan Fisher—."

"Oh, did you enjoy that?"

"Yes, as much as I got to see. Evelyn's latest B and B couple arrived in the middle—two Americans. By the way, that German woman who held up the post office line—she's with us, too. She and her very British husband are newlyweds. He must be forty, and she's older, I think."

"She takes very good care of herself," said Lucy. "I've seldom seen a woman who has given as much care to every aspect of her appearance, including staying healthy. A perfect physical specimen. Yet here she is on Gower, where the wind blows, and it rains often, and she dressed for the French Riviera. Unfortunately, no sensitivity at all to Helen or the rest of the customers waiting behind her. A narcissistic woman if I ever saw one and probably being used by her new husband."

Penny thought of James. Yes, he was manipulative. But Christine definitely got her licks in. "She infuriated everyone at breakfast," said Penny. "It only took her five minutes, and we were all ready to kill her, except maybe for the psychiatrist."

"Oh, you've got a psychiatrist? Is he the American? I'd love to talk to him. They're said to be so caught up in Freud's ideas of family drama. I'd love to have a chance to ask a real one what he thinks. Could you talk him into coming to the library? We'll be open tonight. Seven to nine."

"I doubt it, Lucy. He hasn't admitted he's a psychiatrist yet. I like him the best of the bunch. He's down to earth. His wife is French and off-putting. He acts protective of her, and she's very rude. He ends up doing whatever she wants him to. She and the German woman almost came to blows at breakfast, and I left Evelyn in a real dither. Usually Evelyn's guests are so tepid as to be offensive. But these two couples! Fortunately, the Americans leave tomorrow, and the newlyweds in a few more days—next Tuesday, I think. Whew. I'm frazzled by one scene at breakfast. I'll be a basket case by Tuesday."

Lucy sat down at her desk and began hunting through her cards for overdue books.

"Probably it's the German woman," said Lucy thoughtfully. "Like putting the cat among the pigeons. She's uncomfortable with everything and everyone who is not busy adoring her. All that dressing fit to kill covers up a great hunger to be loved for herself, but I wager she never has been, and now, even if she were, she probably wouldn't recognize it or be able to take it in. She's constantly unsettling the people around her by expecting out of them an inordinate amount of attention and consideration, right?"

"Good analysis," said Penny. "You observed a lot in a short time."

"Fifteen minutes. Plenty of time to study someone. She was going to insure her package but couldn't decide for how much. Then she investigated every special service the British postal service offers. Made up her mind fourteen times and then changed it. Helen is constitutionally unable to be rude. I think she'd die or quit her job before she'd ask people to take their business elsewhere or step aside until she'd helped the rest of us."

"I watched a very similar scene yesterday in there. What finally happened?"

"Oh, the German woman flounced out—didn't even post the package. Said she'd go back to the Swansea post office again where they understood how to post a package. She couldn't have said anything that would have hurt Helen more. She'll probably fret over that for weeks. I could have throttled that woman myself. So many people still hate the Germans, and then the Germans you meet seem determined to keep that hatred alive. We should have been able to get over this old World War II stuff a long time ago. Some people were worried about German reunification; said they'd never trust the Germans, that a Prussian was still a Prussian and always would be."

"The American's wife being French originally probably doesn't help either," said Penny.

"Oh, she's French? No, the French are very bitter still. The British were bombed, and that was bad. But the French were occupied, and some died in concentration camps, too—plus the torture of the French underground when they could catch them. Yes, if she's French, she could easily be rubbed the wrong way. She'd likely resent anyone with a German accent."

"That explains why, as soon as Christine began talking—and she has a thick German accent—Eloise started acting funny."

"She's the psychiatrist's wife?"

"Yes. The presumed psychiatrist's wife. He has a nice chair-side manner that got activated when Eloise began to act rude. He talked to her like she was a child who was having trouble remembering how to behave."

Lucy laughed. "From what you say, she was. Do you think psychiatrists are sometimes attracted to people who will be 'patients' for them all their lives? I've wondered about that."

"Could be," said Penny. "Not always. But a lot of people are drawn to psychotherapy in the first place because of difficult childhoods, and they may be only one step ahead of people still acting out their childhood traumas. It does fit those two."

"Bring him around tonight, if you can. I'm dying to meet an American psychiatrist."

"If I can. Oh, Lucy, here I am trying to forget these holiday people I have to live with against my will, and you are lining me up to bring them to visit you."

Lucy laughed again. "Not all of them. The German woman was kind of interesting, but not enough to see a second time. But the psychiatrist, and even his wife, that would be a real treat."

"It's true he reads. He asked to read my book. I forgot to give it to him. Here comes a customer. I'm going to check out this Paretsky. Have you got that Christie that was on TV?"

"It's out, but I'll hold it for you. Here you go. I think you'll like this gutsy, high-spirited American. Have a good day out on the cliffs. If you get a poem, let me read it. I love your way with words, Penny. I've read your first book on Gower four times."

How could she not love this woman? She was calming, sensible, accurate in her perceptions of people, and she liked to read her poetry. "That helps," she said. "Maybe I'll make it to a poem today yet."

"Of course, you will. Cheerio!" sang Lucy as Penny headed out the door. Then she turned to the gentleman standing in front of her desk with his four books.

When Penny got back to Evelyn's about three, she was feeling much more tranquil. The cliffs, the sea, the gulls, the wind, and the little wild flowers had had their healing effect. She had begun to slip into her Gower mode: writing, ranging around the cliffs, indulging in food and detective fiction, and visiting with her favorite Gower people. She believed in as much whimsy and pleasure as possible when she was encouraging the Muse, and as few aggravations.

Harold was in the lounge with Evelyn, and they were having a cuppa. "Have you had a good day, Penny?" asked Evelyn. "Want a cup of tea?"

"Sure. Hi, Harold, nice to see you. Are you still walking up a storm?"

Harold stood up. He was tall for a British man and not good-looking. He had a long face and a large nose, with drooping jowls. He looked like a sad Basset Hound, but he was amiable and always neatly dressed in a worsted sports jacket and wool pants. A widower who coped well with being on his own, he was about seventy-five, vigorous, opinionated, would talk your arm off if encouraged, and when Penny was in the mood, she did encourage him.

"I am," he said. "My morning constitutional, five miles along the cliffs, rain or shine. Keeps me fit all day. Are you enjoying being on Gower again?"

"Oh, yes. I've been out on the cliffs, too."

"Which way did you go?" he asked.

"I got as far as Big Tor. The tide was in, so I went down to the Gower Store and got an ice cream." She looked at Evelyn. Evelyn didn't think the Gower Store existed for anything besides ice cream, but Penny found other things there: maps, guides to footpaths, stationery with water color scenes of Gower.

Evelyn nodded her approval as she handed Penny her tea.

"I don't suppose you were up at the top, at Stanley's store?" Harold asked.

"No, not today."

"What a terrible thing for Stanley."

"Why, what happened?"

"The Prussian!" Evelyn exploded. "She has been up there and

knocked over a whole make-up and perfume display. Stanley had just got it in, and half of it broke."

"The woman who's staying here was buying perfume," explained Harold, "and she gave a bottle a jerk when she couldn't get it loose, and the whole thing came over—some splashed on her. She was fit to be tied. Stanley was trying to get up the glass, and his daughter was mopping her off, trying to. She was unbelievably rude. You'd hardly credit it, even in a German woman. Her husband right there. He could have just offered to pay Stanley for the lot, but no—."

Evelyn interrupted. "Penny, all the money they have. Stanley probably wouldn't have let them pay, but they didn't even offer. More tea? I can make a fresh pot."

Penny said no, thanks. She sat back in her chair. One human being, no matter how unhappy with herself, shouldn't be able to get a whole village into a dither.

"She insulted John, too," added Evelyn with evident relish.

"Who's John?"

"He's a poet, like you." Harold was eager to explain. "He comes around, usually later in the summer when most of the holiday crowd is gone. Maybe you've seen him. He's tall, roughly dressed. He sleeps out on the cliffs. I see him up at Stanley's when I'm picking up the paper for Evelyn and me."

"Yes," said Penny. "I did the other morning. He was having coffee outside and was writing."

"It's true he doesn't look like much," said Harold. "He's a nice bloke though. He writes poems that rhyme. He says he'd like to meet you."

An earnest amateur. Not on your life, thought Penny. "So what did Christine do to upset John?"

"After making this total mess inside the shop, she decides it would calm her down (as if she was the one needed calming) to have a coffee. She'd said she did want to buy Evening in Paris perfume if Stanley could find it when he picked up the mess. The nerve she has.

"So she sits down. Most of the tables were empty. I was leaving with my papers. She goes over to John's table—he likes to sit and write over his morning coffee, kinda private, don't you know? So he can concentrate, right?"

Penny nodded.

"So she says, 'Mind if we sit here?' He looks up, kinda surprised, but he's a good bloke, and he says, 'No, ma'am.' So she takes a cloth out and whisks the table off, gets dirt and water all over John and his papers, and then she sits herself down. That fat husband of hers—."

Evelyn objected. "He isn't fat, Harold, stout. He's sweet, though I can't believe he likes her. I can't fathom it. A nice gentleman like him."

"Anyway," said Harold, "so they talk loudly, and John decided to move, and, when he starts packing up, she says, 'Do you mind telling me what you're writing?'

"So John mumbles something."

"'Don't mumble,' she says. 'I can't hear you. What do you write?'

"'Poetry,' says John. 'Doggerel, I call it.' Though he's putting himself down. It's very pretty stuff.

"'Rhyming verses,' John says.

"'Is this possible?' she asks. 'Everywhere we go here we meet poets—writers of *doggerel*.' She emphasizes the *dog* in *doggerel*, looks disgusted. I wanted to tell her not to be so rude.

"'So where are you staying' she asked. 'We have a poet with us at the Pobbles House,' she says, 'an American.' As if that was a dirty word.

"'Nowhere,' says John. 'I stay where the Spirit moves me. Gower is holy to me. I sleep with the rabbits. The seagulls nest near my bed.' That's John for you.

"'How disgusting!' she says. 'Seagulls are so nasty.' She wrinkles her nose.

"'I do,' he says, kind of gruff, and then he stalked off, mad as hell. I never saw John get so mad. You know he doesn't look like much, but he gets on with everyone here, except—."

Penny filled in: "Except for the German woman. What is it with you Brits? Can't you forget World War II?"

Then the two of them were off for twenty minutes on the German bombing raids during the early forties. Harold had pulled people out of bombed buildings, when it was possible. Evelyn had worked with Hal in Bristol. They had had to send their five-year-old son away to a safer place in the north of England until the war was over.

Penny listened, her eyelids drooping. Finally, she stood up. "You'll have to excuse me. All that good Gower air has made me sleepy. When is supper, Evelyn?"

"Six all right?"

"Fine. Wake me at quarter of, if I'm not up. Now don't let Christine get you two off balance. She's a mess, granted, but no point letting her upset you. You should know better at your age."

They both stared at her, astonished, she knew, at her directness. She never was sure what effect she had when she said exactly what she thought to Brits, and she'd probably never know. They, including Evelyn, remained inscrutable. Neither one made an answer to that, but Evelyn finally remembered her manners and said, "See you later then, Penny. Have a good rest."

FIVE

As it turned out, Penny didn't sleep a wink that afternoon. Into the world she found peaceful and untroubled had come this woman who disturbed everyone around her. Usually the Gower folks were placid and predictable. Now they were going off the walls.

If she wrote to Cathy and walked her letter up to the post box near Three Cliffs Store, it would go out at seven a.m. It was hard to be prompt answering letters at home, but here her few duties became pleasures.

She told Cathy about the disrupting presence of the German woman and her insipid husband, the contemptuous response of the French woman, and her pleasant chat with the psychiatrist husband. How glad she was to talk with Lucy again. She wished Cathy luck in keeping cool and told her she had already checked out her first Paretsky.

She felt better. She told Evelyn, who was making an apple pie, where she was going. Harold was out in his yard, pottering among his roses, and waved her off. She reached the post box ten minutes later. Not again. But it had to be. There in the parking lot near Three Cliffs Store was the Rolls Royce. It could be someone else's. She walked quickly over to the post box. In case it was the newly marrieds, she would scoot back to Evelyn's.

"Hallo, Penny! Good afternoon!" It was James, emerging from the shop carrying a newspaper. "Lovely day we've had."

"Yes," she said. Letter mailed. Now to get out of here quickly.

"Like to join us for afternoon tea? They have Welsh cakes today."

The man had learned entirely too much about her. "No, thanks, I'm due at Evelyn's for supper. See you later. Enjoy your tea." I'm being far too nice, she thought, to someone I want to leave me strictly alone. I never learn. She waved, smiled, and almost got away, but then Christine emerged, wearing a sea-blue, slinky dress, with heels of the same color, and carrying a small plate piled high, yes, with Welsh cakes. "Good afternoon, Penny. Come have a Welsh cake with us."

She sounded insincere, but maybe it was the best she could do. If Penny hadn't disliked the woman so much, she might have been tempted. The thought of Evelyn's apple pie helped.

"Thanks. That's nice of you, but I need to get back." Fortunately, she had a good excuse. Besides, these weren't Evelyn's Welsh cakes—they were made commercially. A pleasure she could forego. Too much lard and not enough butter.

Christine was headed toward that poet—the one she had already upset earlier that day. John was looking aghast at Christine as she steamed over to the table where again he had spread out his things and had been writing away.

There were people sitting at all the other tables, but several had space for two more. She wanted to leave, but she was caught up in the drama of these two so totally different people, though both were narcissistic. Poets had to be to some extent—she knew she was—but she tried not to let it get out of hand. Here they were about to clash, and she was standing there gawking, admit it, curious. She knew it was going to be awful. But still—.

"You're finished with this table, aren't you?" asked Christine as she set down her plate. John picked up his half-empty milk bottle protectively as if afraid she might carry it off and throw it away, and set it nearer the book in which he was writing.

"No," he said, and set his body in a mulish pose. Christine began to flick a small towel she had produced out of her pocketbook over the table. John didn't move.

Ah, he's going to fight, Penny thought. Who will win? Stanley's daughter emerged from the shop with a tray, set down their cups in front of them and a pot of tea, and was going to dash off, when James asked her if she'd bring out some ginger nuts and gave her a pound coin. She disappeared quickly, probably alert to the storm brewing, and Christine, folding her skirt carefully under her, sat down on the bench she'd whisked off and inspected first, and then turned back to John. "How long have you been occupying this table? All afternoon?"

John looked surprised but didn't answer. Not one for quick repartee. Clearly uncomfortable but feeling territorial. The mulish look returned.

Christine called out again to Penny: "Come have a Welsh cake, Penny. Have you met the other poet? He writes doggerel, he says, whatever that is."

She had fallen right into this one. John looked over at her and beamed. "Oh, hello, you must be the American poet. So nice to meet you. Stanley's always talking about you, and that man—who lives near where you stay—."

"Harold Austen?"

"Oh, yes, Harold. He likes my verses, he says, and he thought I'd like to meet you."

Penny smiled. A compulsive human habit. When would she learn?

"Oh, yes, he's mentioned you. Nice to meet you, too." You lie, Penelope Weaver! "But I've got to run. Bye, all," and she was waving her way out of there when Christine picked up the milk bottle John had forgotten about as he talked to Penny and poured some into her tea.

"That's my milk!" growled John, and then he looked up at Penny, embarrassed. "I was still drinking it," he said, plaintively. "I hadn't finished it."

"Your—." Christine looked genuinely horrified. She rose where she had been sitting, grabbed up her cup, and flung the tea and the cup toward some flowers that were part of a garden border and just beyond the concrete where the tables were. "I can't take this!" she shrieked. The cup landed on the flowers and didn't break.

Penny heard Christine mutter the word *filthy* over and over as she stepped over the bench, still very careful of her skirt, and bending over, crying, headed for the Rolls Royce.

James III had a difficult dilemma. He was being handed the ginger nuts, and a whole plate of Welsh cakes was about to go to waste. He made a quick decision, glancing uneasily at John, whose glowering look had intensified. James tucked the package of ginger nuts and his paper under his arm, took a quick swig of his tea, grabbed a handful of Welsh cakes, looked over at John, and said, "Sorry." He pointed to the change from the pound coin, which was now lying on the table, and said, "Get yourself some more milk, and have some Welsh cakes."

Then James walked toward his car, not that distraught, Penny noted. He had his cookies. This was not the moment to chat with John, not that she wanted to. When John had scooped the change off the table and gone into the shop, she took her chance to make a graceful exit and turned back toward Heatherslade Lane and Evelyn's delectable apple pie.

Again Evelyn talked her, against her better judgment, given the fights going on between and among the guests and the stack of interesting books waiting for her on the dresser in her room, into watching another detective movie. This one was set in the Caribbean and was by an author she'd never heard of. She did it to keep Evelyn company as she coped with her fractious guests. Evelyn was already fretting about Friday's breakfast—how she'd get them all fed and herself ready for Harold by ten. Penny realized she had been thinking more of her own escape the past two mornings than of Evelyn. She offered to do the washing-up after dinner, but Evelyn wouldn't hear of it. She was relieved when Penny said she would let the other guests know how important it was to Evelyn that they breakfast on time.

The apples in the pie had a wonderful flavor. The crust was flaky and light. They had New Zealand lamb chops, new potatoes, and fresh peas. A perfect meal. She wanted to help Evelyn with her guests, but some instinct told her trouble was brewing and nothing she did was going to have any effect. She had, in the last twenty years, learned to trust her gut reactions more than she had been able to do in the first thirty or so years of her life.

She'd said to Evelyn, "The only real cure will be when these guests are all gone."

Penny dried the dishes for her. They got back into their conversational ambience of other summers. Evelyn chatted about her grandchildren. She asked Penny if she could help her figure out how to visit New York.

When they settled in the lounge, Evelyn had the channel changer and agreed to keep it on this channel. About 8:30, as they were settling into their movie, the bell rang, and the outer door opened. Someone knocked at the lounge door, and Evelyn got up, unconsciously handing the remote control to Penny. Ernie and Eloise walked in, exuding the good mood they were in.

"We've eaten at that perfect little restaurant in the hotel right on Oxwich Bay. Beautiful! Thanks so much for suggesting it. The best steak and kidney pie I ever ate," said Ernie.

"And so many sailboats out. The view was magnificent. What a great day it was," said Eloise. "I think Gower is my favorite place in Wales now. We'll come back to Gower next time, won't we, Ernie? I like it much better than Snowdonia."

If anyone had made a careful study of Evelyn's character, he or she could not have hit more precisely on the thing most likely to please her. Evelyn was Gower proud. She believed that all the beauty of Wales had been cooked down to an essence and that essence was the Gower peninsula. She listened to visitors describe other places they had been in Wales, as patiently as she could, like someone who knows how to cook an excellent English roast beef and Yorkshire pudding dinner hearing its American cafeteria version praised. Evelyn knew that once they saw Gower, they would stop praising Snowdonia.

"What are you watching?" asked Ernie.

Penny explained.

"Mind if we join you?"

"Oh, no, of course not," said Evelyn with more than her usual enthusiasm. "Can I offer you a cup of tea?"

"No, that's fine," said Ernie. "We had wonderful coffee, too, at the Oxwich Hotel."

So the four of them settled down to untangle the mystery, Evelyn and Penny catching the other two up on what had already happened.

At nine the bell rang again, and Evelyn went to get it. Stanley hesitated to come in, seeing that Evelyn's guests were in the lounge, but she offered him a cuppa and urged, "Come in. We're enjoying this murder."

Stanley found a seat quietly and inconspicuously. Evelyn reappeared with a tray, tea cups, the tea pot under a cosy, and a plate of Welsh cakes. Penny wondered where she'd find room to eat anything else, but she'd better not refuse when the gods offered Welsh cakes for the second time in one day. So they all had a cuppa. Everyone was in a good mood, and so far they were all watching the telly.

At 9:30 they heard the outer door open. As absorbed as they were, they all looked toward the lounge door. After a warning tap, and before they could have heard Evelyn call "Come in," in came Christine, who had fully recovered her poise but seemed more subdued than usual. James followed, the expansive one tonight. "We're just back from a beautiful drive all around the peninsula. The sun came out just as we got to Worm's Head. What a striking view."

Evelyn smiled and poured them tea, brought two more chairs, Stanley helping, and again they all settled their attention on the screen. Penny still had the remote, but all she knew how to do was change the sound, up or down. She resolved to hang onto it and keep the sound up. She slipped it down out of sight into the cushion of her chair and leaned slightly so as to hide it. She saw Evelyn looking in her own chair and on the lamp table next to her. Penny decided to pretend she'd forgotten she had it. The movie wasn't that good, but it had become a matter of principle. Did they all get to finish the film, or would Christine and James disrupt them?

"What is it?" asked Christine. No one said anything. Finally Evelyn, again vainly looking around, answered, "It's a murder Penny and I picked out. I forget the name. It's almost over. Would you like a Welsh cake?"

Wrong move. She hadn't told Evelyn about the incident with John. Evelyn had no way of knowing that Welsh cakes might be emotionally charged for Christine.

"No," said Christine, looking right at Stanley, "I never want to see another Welsh cake as long as I live. They're half lard, aren't they?"

Stanley said nothing, perhaps not realizing she meant to slight his Welsh cakes. Evelyn was startled and looked aghast. Everyone liked Welsh cakes, in her experience, even foreigners. Perhaps Christine had guessed that slighting Welsh cakes was, in Evelyn's mind, tantamount to blasphemy? Christine couldn't have done anything much more offensive if she had said that Gower was ugly.

Meantime, James was smiling blandly. It was clear who had eaten all of the Welsh cakes he had made off with that afternoon. He reached over and took two of Evelyn's, as she said, firmly, to Christine: "I use fresh butter in mine. It's my grandmother's recipe. Are you sure you don't want to try one?"

But Christine shook her head. "I hate tea with milk. Have you got any lemon?"

Evelyn leapt up and took off for the kitchen.

"Is anything else on?" asked Christine. Penny thought smugly of the control hidden in her chair. Thank the goddesses the knob was broken. Amazing how oblivious this woman was of the effect she was having. Couldn't she see they were all, except for occasional distracted glances at her, glued to the telly?

"I think I read in the paper that there was a good news analysis program on at 9:30. Couldn't we see? I haven't seen any news in a week."

You've been too busy making news, thought Penny. If you only knew the waves of gossip you've stirred up on Gower. But Christine was not to be daunted by being ignored.

"Murder mysteries depress me. They remind me of the war. I can't watch them. Can't we even see what's on the other channels? James, check channel three." James leapt out of his chair and moved up to the screen, blocking everyone's view. He tried all the knobs but produced only snow and a louder volume.

Evelyn returned with a plate of cut pieces of lemon. Christine helped herself, but she didn't thank her. Instead, she said again to James, as if no one else were present, "Try three."

"The knob's gone that changes the channels," James said.

"What have I done with the channel changer?" Evelyn said. She stood up, looked in her chair and all around it.

Eloise erupted. "Mr.—. I forget your name. But if you could move, please? We're all enjoying *this* program."

"James, at least turn down the sound. I can't take this suspense. Everybody stand up, and we'll find the channel changer. It must be here somewhere." James pretended he hadn't heard her orders. He sat back down and began to watch the movie again.

Christine said again, "Everyone stand up." No one stood up. Stanley would have probably, but he looked toward Evelyn, and she had gone back into the kitchen, probably to see if she'd left the remote in there. Stanley looked at Penny, who smiled but didn't move. Then Stanley's British politeness did him in. He rose and began looking into the seat of his own chair, Christine helping by turning over the cushions. When Evelyn returned, everyone but Penny had been routed. Penny couldn't see the screen or hear much as they were all talking at once. Yet she refused to be this woman's victim. The others were all incredibly annoyed; James was embarrassed.

It was Eloise who got Penny up. "I know you wanted to watch this, but none of us can now. Let's look in your chair."

So Penny rose, and at that instant Evelyn remembered. "Oh, yes, I gave it to Penny when the Rosewoods came in. I knew she was so interested. She loves murders."

Not for much longer, thought Penny. She looked down herself and felt in the cushions, pulled up the remote control, and handed it to Evelyn. "Sorry, I forgot. I was too caught up in the program," she lied.

Evelyn handed it right to James, and they all sat down. "Try three," said Christine.

Eloise said, "This rudeness is unpardonable, madam," and stalked out. Evelyn hurried after her. Penny wanted to retire, too. After all, she could have had a perfectly happy evening in her room all alone and enjoyed a book. Why was she even sitting here? Maybe the evening could be salvaged since Christine now had the news, and the British love their news. The angriest one of those present had gone to bed.

"Don't worry," said Ernie to Evelyn when she returned. "She'll be fine. We have to leave tomorrow, and we wanted to get up early and have a walk before breakfast."

"Oh, that reminds me," said Evelyn, once more settled in her chair. "If you don't mind, Friday is my day to shop. My neighbor Harold"—she nodded in the direction of his house"—is good enough to take me into Swansea. We need to leave at ten. So, if you'd have your breakfast again at 8:30, it would help. I get up at 6:30 and unlock. You can go out as early as you like."

Ernie smiled as if to compensate Evelyn for the channel changing conflict. "You're very good to us. Yes, we might go out as early as seven, and we'll be sure to be back by 8:30. You can depend on it."

"I want to get in a swim, too," said Christine.

"Oh, do be careful of the high tide. It's at 7:30 tomorrow," said Stanley.

Christine nodded, but Penny couldn't tell if she'd paid any attention.

"I can serve you and Mr. Hampton up until nine," said Evelyn, looking pointedly at Christine, "but after that, it will only be toast. Is that all right?"

Evelyn's learning to draw boundaries, thought Penny. Will wonders never cease?

Christine turned back to her news without answering. But James replied for her. "That will be fine. I've promised Christine to walk myself before breakfast so I'll work an inch off my waistline before I sit down to your delicious breakfast, which I have so much trouble resisting, and put it right back on." He laughed. Christine did not.

Evelyn smiled at him, enjoying his flattery. Funny, how we all get trapped, all the time. It's so hard not to play these games.

James and Christine had apparently played themselves out once the regular BBC news began. They excused themselves and went off to bed to their newlywed entertainments.

Once the news was over, Ernie said, "I'd better be getting to bed, too." He stood up but didn't look eager to leave.

Evelyn turned off the telly. "I was sorry your wife was upset. This Prussian woman is so hard to please. I'm afraid your wife was offended."

"It's always hard for her to meet anyone German and be civil," said Ernie. "You see, her mother was in the French Underground and was arrested by the Gestapo when she was only three years old. She doesn't remember her mother. The Underground got Eloise out, first to England, then later to Sweden by boat. But her mother didn't escape. She was one of many millions who died in the death camps. It is hard for her to forgive the Germans. We are both Jewish. In the U.S. it is easier to forget about it. But here—I think she thinks of it more when she's in England. Christine upset her at breakfast.

"It's not rational. She knows it's not rational. But don't worry. We had a good day. She loved the old castle." He looked at Penny. "Your legend was perfect medicine. It got her mind off Christine and the Germans. We walked all the way to Oxwich and enjoyed the hotel dinner so much—a lovely day—and then had fun riding the double-decker bus back and walking across the golf links.

"No," he said kindly and firmly to Evelyn, "you mustn't worry. It's something that happened a long time ago. Nothing to do with you." He looked around. "Any of you." He looked toward the door out of the lounge. "Not Christine and James's fault either. It's—she's touchy. We've really enjoyed Gower, but we have to leave by ten to catch our plane in London. Breakfast at 8:30 is perfect. Thanks, Mrs. Trueblood, for everything."

What a peacemaker, thought Penny. I wonder how many times he has had to make that speech to cover for his wife's rudeness. She smiled at Ernie, and then she remembered her book. "Oh, Ernie, you still want to read my poetry? Or is it too late?"

"No, no. I'd love to. Give me something to read in bed." He waited in the hall while Penny went in her room and got it for him.

"You can give it to me at breakfast," she said. "I'd like to know what you think."

"Thanks, Penny. You're kind."

Penny picked up suddenly some great weariness in him that he hadn't shown before. People did this with her, trusted her with knowledge or a side of themselves they didn't ordinarily show. It always touched her.

She smiled. "I hope you like these poems. See you at breakfast." She walked back to the lounge thoughtfully.

Penny had planned to bid the others goodnight, get in the bathroom ahead of Evelyn, and put herself to sleep with the Grimes, but when she got back, Evelyn and Stanley were full swing into discussing the German woman.

"She drives me up the pole!" said Evelyn. "I wish she was leaving tomorrow."

Penny said, "I'm going to warn you, Evelyn. I expect her to be late for breakfast. She enjoys upsetting people. Did you notice how she got us all upset and then left, with kind of a smug air? I would do just what you said you'd do. Leave her toast and juice and cereal, and a pot of tea."

"But the tea will get cold."

"Put the cozy on it. Go shopping. It isn't worth it, letting this woman upset you. She will be gone in—how many more days?"

"Four," said Evelyn. "They leave Tuesday morning."

"Do the minimum. Let her have toast. I won't try to watch any more movies. I've learned my lesson."

Stanley laughed heartily, but Evelyn protested. "But you're a guest, too, and the Rosewoods. It isn't right. I can't believe her manners. It's like I always say: people don't behave except when you get back to the white cliffs of Dover. Then you're all right." She must have realized she'd omitted her American friend from her world view. "You're all right, Penny. I don't know how you are at home." Penny raised her eyebrows. "But you're fine here. But that Prussian."

"You should have seen the way she acted up at my shop today—twice. Both times she upset everyone around her," said Stanley. "But I blame her husband, too. He could do more to control her. He should certainly offer to pay for the damage she does."

They both consoled Stanley about the ruined display. He said the

58

manufacturers would cover the damage. People in other stores had also been complaining about the display. It was too flimsy, too hard to get the perfume out. "But," and he turned to Penny, "what worries me most is her effect on the other customers. You saw how rude she was to John, and he's a very steady customer."

They were both looking at Penny. Why couldn't they talk about something else? But she did, briefly, tell them the second John story and said she'd felt bad for John.

"He was fit to be tied," said Stanley. "You know he always sits out there, and I'm proud to have him, his being a poet and all. He says she spoils everything for him. He can't think or write, and he has an ulcer. Not even all the milk he drinks will help if that woman upsets him. So he bought some extra milk and food for the weekend. I told him I thought they were here through the weekend, then leaving. That's right, isn't it, Evelyn?"

"Yes," she said. "They leave Tuesday. If you see him, tell him it'll be all clear by noon on Tuesday."

"Oh, I think he'll stay away awhile. But I don't like it."

"I wish he'd get a haircut," said Evelyn. "I don't mind him sitting there, but he could look tidier."

"He's just John," said Stanley. "He's the way he is, Evelyn, isn't he? Neither you nor I nor even Penny here"—he smiled—"will ever change him, will we?"

Penny said, "He's in the good British tradition of the eccentric. I respect that. Don't you, Evelyn?"

"His hair and his wrinkled clothes drive me up the pole," said Evelyn. "But I still like to see him out there."

"Right," said Penny, "and he'll be back once the Prussian is gone. Not to worry. Listen, I'm turning in. Nice to see you, Stanley. See you at breakfast, Evelyn. Wake me at quarter of eight."

"Fine, Penny. Good night." She turned back to Stanley. "But what I say is—."

Penny closed the lounge door and went into the bathroom. A quick shower and to bed.

SIX

Penny had gotten well into the Grimes before she finally yielded to sleep about one a.m. It did help her forget everything else. When she couldn't make her eyes stay open, she turned out the little bed lamp and snuggled under the duvet. She was asleep in seconds.

Something—was it someone crying out?—woke her in the middle of the night. She sat up in bed. What had she heard? The house was silent. Maybe she had been dreaming. Yet she had the distinct impression that someone had called out, and a part of her could still feel some appeal, as from someone urgently asking for help.

She got out of bed, pulled on her robe, switched the bed lamp on. 3:30. She heard nothing else, but she'd check. She opened her door quietly and listened. Still no sound. All the rooms were off this same hall. She moved near each door, walking very quietly and listening. No sounds came from Evelyn's door, which was near hers and opposite the bathroom. Nor from the Rosewoods', which was down at the end of the hall on the right.

She stepped near the Hamptons' door, which was on the left. A faint murmur of voices. Someone sobbing? Christine? Maybe. Under behavior like hers, there must be a lot of pain. Good for James. There was a flow of sound that on the whole sounded like whatever had been upsetting to whomever was being soothed. Relieved, Penny went back to the bathroom, peed, and went back to bed. She was soon asleep again.

But this was not to be her morning to sleep in. Very early—six?—she heard voices in the hall. She opened her eyes enough to see that light was coming through the curtain already, but it wasn't anywhere near time to get up; she turned over and fell asleep again.

She groped her way to consciousness again, aware that there had been a lot of noise nearby. The clock said 6:30, and she heard the outer door closing and someone walking away. Christine going swimming? She dozed again. Then the clanging of the milk bottles roused her. She might as well give up. This time she heard Eloise: "Mrs. Trueblood, your milk is here. We're going for a walk."

Penny stood up, looked out her curtain, and, yes, there went Eloise and Ernie, going toward the cliffs. Were they truly happy together? Few people were, she'd decided. It must be the hardest relationship of all to achieve: a happy marriage, a genuine balance of power, with real love sustaining it from both sides. She believed it was possible, and she still fell in love. As long as she was engaged in loving, she figured she was healthy, even if nothing had yet worked out. But, as a friend of hers had once put it kindly years before, "There may be a few surprises left in your lucky grab bag." She had been right. There had been. Perhaps there might be one or two more.

The Rosewoods didn't look harmonious. There was a stiffness, a careful separation between their bodies. There's as much conflict in their marriage as with Christine and James, she thought. They hide it better. I'm glad I don't have him on my hands. Eloise can have him. Ernie and Eloise turned right and toward the top.

She got back in bed and reached for her diary. She wished she weren't so tired, but once she was out and about, she'd forget that she had had only about five hours instead of the eight or nine she treated herself to when she was on vacation.

A knock on her door. "Come in. Oh, hi, Evelyn. Thanks. How did you know I was up?"

"No surprise. Everyone else is up. I didn't see how you could sleep, even if you had wanted to. The way that French woman yelled, too, as if I didn't know the milk was here, but now they're out for a walk, and Christine has gone for her swim, and soon James is going for a walk. Penny, would you mind terribly having your breakfast early? I'm so afraid these others are going to be late."

"No problem," said Penny.

"Thanks, Penny. About 7:30 then?"

"Sure."

Evelyn retreated, and Penny took her cup of hot tea off the dresser gratefully. Another cold morning. Evelyn's shopping day. She'd do her part, not dawdle too long over her tea.

Penny met James in the hall as she was walking toward the dining room and her cornflakes. "Good morning, James."

"Oh, hello, Penny. I hope you slept well?"

"Fine, yes." Why tell the truth? Nor did she want to admit to having listened at his door.

"And you?"

"Not so well. Christine was upset in the night, doesn't like it here, wants to leave. I finally convinced her that we shouldn't leave; today would be better. We're going to Rhossili and Llangennith. We want to see that haunted house you told us about, try that shop with cream teas, and have a look at the Church of St. Cennydd. I'd better get stepping. I've promised Christine to walk for a whole hour, and I need to be back by 8:30." He looked toward the kitchen door behind which Evelyn's pans were clattering and the tea kettle coming to a hard boil. "Don't want to delay the shopping," he added conspiratorially.

"Oh, no," said Penny, smiling, and waved him off. She settled to her cornflakes. She never ate them in the U.S. Or white toast. Never had bacon and eggs for breakfast. But here they were part of a routine she loved.

Maybe she'd get another poem today. The newlyweds would be at the other end of the peninsula, and the Rosewoods, gone.

It was nice having breakfast alone, too. She hadn't had a big enough dose of thinking time yet this morning. She liked to be whimsical. Which way would she go first? Maybe she'd catch the bus to Oxwich and when she headed back, the tide permitting, walk along the beach.

She was finishing her sausages and starting on her toast when she heard the splat of the post coming through the front door and Evelyn walking to get it.

"A letter for you, Penny," said Evelyn and picked up her platter. "Do you have enough toast?" Evelyn stood waiting.

"Oh, yes, fine. This is from my daughter Sarah, the one who just got married."

"She was awfully young, wasn't she?" asked Evelyn. "Mind if I sit down and have a cuppa with you, Penny? I'm shattered. I do hope they all get back at 8:30."

Penny smiled. "Yes, she's young. Sure, Evelyn, have a seat. Remember, if they're late, it's their problem. They'll get cold toast and lukewarm tea. Serve them right."

"Oh, Penny. Should I? I need the money from my B and B people."

"Of course. Why should you get in a swivet? They're all spoiled."

"The men are all right. It's the women."

"Evelyn, the men's problems don't show as much, but they're rude, too, or they wouldn't tolerate wives who are. This letter from Sarah was written on the first day of their honeymoon. She says they've already had their first fight and made it up. I doubt they'll stay married very long."

"Oh, Penny, what a shame! She's only nineteen, isn't she?"

"Yes, but very worldly wise. When she was fourteen she told me that she knew more about the world than I did. I think she got married to cure herself of marriage. I did that, though I didn't know it at the time."

"Penny, my stars!"

"Yep, I do think so. They've lived together over a year. They fight all the time. She's not very happy. She's doing what she needs to do to get on with what she's truly interested in. She's exploring love and marriage first."

Evelyn didn't comment except to say, "I'm so glad I had Hal. We had such good times. Young people these days give up too easily."

"It's different today, Evelyn. Everything's being reexamined. We're living through a period of domestic wars. Those that would like to be married, like me, can't find anyone who wants them."

"You will, Penny, you will, though if I were you, I'd stay on my own. It seems to suit you." Evelyn gathered her cup and rose, as if she had listened quite long enough to rather disgraceful ideas. "I'd better get back to work. I hope those others come back soon."

Evelyn disappeared into the kitchen. Penny poured herself another cup of tea and returned to Sarah's letter.

Penny heard the front door open and men's voices: James and Ernie. They sounded at ease with each other. Interesting. 8:30. Evelyn would be relieved. She heard Evelyn telling them, "Yes, I can serve you now. Go right on in. I'll have your tea ready in a minute."

Penny quickly poured herself a full cup from her pot in case they had any ideas about borrowing her tea. As she emptied her teapot into her thermos, James came into the dining room. James smiled smugly. "Great morning, Penny. Brisk and cloudy still, but I think it will clear. The moor is very beautiful."

"The moor?"

"Oh, no, that's wrong. Stupid me. What is it you have in Gower?"

"Chalk cliffs," said Penny firmly. Why did he act stupid?

"Christine isn't back?" he asked, as though Penny—like his mother?—would know everything.

"I don't think so." She resisted adding, "I don't keep track of your wife for you."

He seemed relieved. Was James one of those men who want to be married but don't like the person they have talked into playing the role for them? He clearly lusted after Christine. She was gorgeous, but she was too perfectly dressed for Penny's taste, not even a smidgeon of anything carefree or natural.

She didn't envy him living with Christine. In his relief that he could eat his breakfast in peace, not threatened by Penny, she detected a human being she might even like. She might like Christine, too, no matter how infuriating she was, if she could glimpse her vulnerability,

Evelyn bustled in with his tea, and James beamed at her. "Mrs. Trueblood, I am ravenous, and your lovely big breakfast to look forward to." Evelyn fell for him, with less skepticism, much less.

"I'll be right in with it. You enjoy your cornflakes," she said in the tone of a mum to her precious boy.

Penny watched James across the table. Yes, he overfilled his bowl, poured milk, and liberally sprinkled sugar. The cornflakes were perched on the rim of the bowl, ready to fall over like soldiers being crowded up onto their own city walls by an army that had breached them, ready to jump to their death rather than surrender. She wasn't able to observe how he handled his spoon though, as Ernie came around behind her and sat down next to her. He set her book of poems between her place setting and his.

"Penny, I congratulate you. You are a marvelous poet. What a feeling for language! How you capture the beauty of Gower. Thank you so much."

Penny was so pleased that she found it hard to answer, and then he was so close. How did she get into these situations? Were they all ganging up on her so-susceptible heart? She didn't even like them that much.

64

"Thanks, Ernie. I'm glad."

James looked up from his cornflakes. She had missed his sleight of hand again. The cornflakes had receded, and not one had spilled. James could attend to details when he wanted to. "May I borrow your book, Penny? Christine and I will be here a few more days. Ernie was telling me how beautifully you write."

Evelyn, entering with James's platter, chimed in. "She's much better than that poor old sod up at the top."

"John," said Penny, cringing to be compared with a "poor old sod" and his rhymed verses. Thirty years of writing poetry, and to be compared with the amateurs.

She handed James her book. A photo of Three Cliffs Bay was on the cover and the word *Gwyr*.

Ernie poured his first cup of tea. "Is it okay if I ask you a question?"

"Sure."

"You spoke in there about the 'leyline' of your life. What do you mean?"

This was awkward. He was so close.

"You know what Socrates said?"

"What?"

"That, when he asked the poets to explain what their poems meant, they said they didn't know."

"Should I not ask then?"

She looked at James and watched as he put several pieces of sausage and egg on his fork and popped it in his mouth.

"It's always okay to ask," she said, "but poets often say more than they understand. I can talk about leylines, as long as you understand that the poems may say and *know* more than I do."

"I understand that," he said quietly. She was sure then that he was a psychiatrist. An *iatros*, a healer, who helped people heal enough to live in relative peace within their own minds. Yet his questions had a certain urgency. A healer in need of healing?

"I see my life as a path, that is, when I'm doing what I feel I need to be doing, I feel like I'm on a holy line. A leyline is a line between two ancient holy sites. So a leyline for me means that I'm traveling the road I need to."

"Fascinating," said Ernie. He still hadn't touched his juice, made much headway on his tea, never mind about the cornflakes, but, when Evelyn appeared with his platter, he moved his cereal bowl to the side and smiled as she set it down. She looked concerned but collected the unused bowl and disappeared.

"How do you interpret spraining your ankle as Mrs. Trueblood told us you did last summer?" asked James, giving away that he was not as silly as he projected he was.

"Actually, I interpret that—I fell hard and really twisted it—as due to feeling rebellious because I did have a sense of where my leyline was taking me, but I was afraid."

"Very interesting," said Ernie, so quietly that it felt too intense to look at him. She could tell he was moved. "You mean you think your unlucky fall was, in truth, a form of luck, a good thing, overall?"

"Exactly," she said. "It sounds strange."

"It is unusual. Usually people who have accidents attribute them to persisting bad luck. They say, 'I always have bad luck.' You're saying that your fall was essentially a good thing—an unfortunate incident which you could have avoided if you had followed your intuitive sense of where you needed to go, and that normally you have few accidents because you do follow this sense?"

"Yes."

Evelyn reappeared, looking fit to be tied, and said, as she collected James's plate and looked incredulously at Ernie's, which he hadn't touched yet, "You gentlemen don't happen to know when I can expect your wives for breakfast, do you?"

The outer door opened. Evelyn dashed back through the kitchen and into the hall. "Oh, so glad you're back. Did you see Christine?"

"No."

"I'll have your breakfast ready in about ten minutes."

"Fine. I'll take a quick shower and be right out."

Ernie was asking her something. Eager to finish this conversation before his wife came in? Penny looked at her watch. 8:50. These women were cutting it close. A hundred to one, Christine would be very late. Would Evelyn stick to her guns? She turned to Ernie. "Sorry. I wasn't listening."

"What other incidents have convinced you that you live a charmed life?"

Ordinarily she would have enjoyed answering, but Evelyn was in a swivet. She sensed an urgency in Ernie, as if this was a life and death question for him. Why?

"Actually, Ernie, as much as I love to talk about this, I know Evelyn wants to get ready for her shopping trip." She said this loudly so as to be heard in the kitchen. "When I talk, you don't eat."

"I don't have to eat." He looked at his plate. "I'm not used to eating a big breakfast."

"You'll hurt Evelyn's feelings, if you don't. She hates for food to be wasted. The British are contemptuous of Americans who waste food. They have never had that much to waste."

Ernie picked up his fork. She'd reward him by answering. "Other incidents? I have had problems, disappointments, things going wrong. But I have had my car develop a flat tire in my driveway or in a service station where I had stopped for gas. I seem to have the opposite experience from someone who is accident prone. Even when things go wrong, they aren't as bad as they could be, and they're usually fixable. My life is relatively accident free, or 'accident unlikely.' But when something does go wrong, I try to fit it into my view of myself and my life."

"Very interesting, indeed," said Ernie. Then he bent to his food. The intensity of his interest, aggravated by their sitting so close, had quieted, too, to her relief.

Meantime James was eating toast and looking through her poems. Evelyn arrived carrying a teapot as Eloise came in from the lounge door. "Super," said Evelyn. "I'll bring your breakfast in a minute. Will you be having cornflakes?"

"No," said Eloise, "no cornflakes." Evelyn whisked the bowl off and disappeared. Penny saw Eloise look with amazement at Ernie assiduously eating and James reading her poetry book. She seemed unsettled. Was this behavior that she didn't usually see? Was she jealous of Penny?

"So what have I missed?" she asked.

"We have had quite a lively discussion with Penny," said James, "about her beautiful poetry. You've already read it, but I—."

"No," said Eloise, looking at Penny. "I went right to bed last night. But Ernie said it kept him up late reading it. He couldn't put it down."

Her compliment was sarcastic.

"It's a lovely book," said Ernie. "Pity we have to leave today. I think you'd like it, too. There's quite a lot about the old castle and Oxwich, and some of the other places we've been."

"It's too bad we have to leave," said Eloise, but she didn't sound sorry or interested in poetry. Evelyn appeared with her platter and vanished again. She'd be up the pole if Christine didn't heave into sight soon.

It was 9:10 and no Christine. "Cold tea for Christine," she said loudly.

"Sorry?" asked James.

"Your wife will miss her breakfast."

James looked at Eloise busy eating and Ernie, who had speeded up. Spurred by her American loudness?

"She should have been back," said James and stood up. "I'll go see if she's coming."

When he left, Eloise said, "We were going to leave at ten, remember, and we still need to pack."

"I remember," Ernie said, and they ate in silence.

"I hope I'll be seeing you people again. I'm going to go out for my day's walk soon. It was nice to meet you. Have a good flight home." How trite it sounded, but she couldn't very well say, "I'm relieved to turn you back to your wife and make my getaway."

"We'll look for your books to be reviewed in *The New York Times*," said Ernie, as if making one last effort to let her know he valued her, her writing, and her earlier openness. But he sounded glib and insincere.

Evelyn appeared carrying a glass of juice, a rack of toast, and a teapot covered by a cozy. She set them at the place where James had been sitting, arranged also clean silverware from a nearby drawer, and smiled at Penny.

"You did it," said Penny. "Great!"

Evelyn couldn't exult yet. "I hope she comes in soon, but I won't be able to cook a big breakfast. I have the shopping."

"Right," said Penny. "Now if you folks will excuse me, I need to get ready, too."

SEVEN

You never step into the same river twice, thought Penny, as she headed out, walking stick in hand, thermos of tea in her backpack, with a rain-coat (it was still cloudy), and her notebook, plus her mystery in case she got stuck somewhere and had nothing to do. She needn't have worried, as it turned out.

She had waved Evelyn off with Harold; looked into the dining room where Christine's teapot was stone cold by now. It was nearly ten. The Rosewoods were in their room packing.

James hadn't returned. He must still be looking for Christine. She had been warned several times about the tides. Surely she had been careful. She was so inconsiderate that Penny hadn't expected her to be on time. Still it was more irritating behavior than usual, even alarming, that she hadn't yet turned up.

Christine was James's problem, thank goodness. She decided to go to Oxwich by bus. She loved that wide bay, the low dunes near it, and the long flat-topped, green, green Oxwich point.

She was chatting with Helen after she had bought her stamps and posted her letter to Sarah, the P.O. being empty, when James suddenly appeared in the open doorway. He looked dreadful, very white. Plump, pink, high-spirited James had had a bad shock.

"What's wrong, James?" asked Penny, leaving the counter and walk-ing over to him. She talked in a normal voice, sensing James needed grounding help. He acted barely aware of his surroundings.

"What's wrong, James?"

"I—. Oh, Penny. It's Christine. She's dead."

"Dead?"

"Penny, what shall I do?"

Helen had come out from behind the counter. She hurried back behind it again and brought out a straight chair. "Get him to sit down, Penny. I'll call the constable."

James let Penny help him sit down. He put his head in his hands like a child. "She's dead. Oh, Penny!"

"There," she said, observing herself playing his mum. It might help him cope. Was Christine dead, or was he simply discouraged because he couldn't find her? He did act like someone who has seen a dead person. Had she drowned after all, in spite of Stanley's warnings?

"The constable said he'd call Swansea. There's an Inspector Morgan who usually handles things like this for Gower. He should be here in about thirty minutes," reported Helen.

"Nearest police station is thirty minutes away?"

"No," said Helen. "We have one in Reynoldston, but we don't have too many problems like this here. The Reynoldston man is down in Llangennith about a robbery, but he'll make sure we get help from Swansea."

Penny turned her attention back to James. He was bent over, still holding his head. Good, get more blood to his head. He had looked awfully white. She put her hand on his shoulder and waited until he looked up. He didn't look quite so white. Good.

"Tell me what happened, James. Helen has called the police."

"I was looking for—. Oh, Christine! My darling!" He broke off and buried his head again. He was crying now. All to the good. Here she was, calm and calming. Good in an emergency. She thought of Proust saying that the "face of true goodness," such as the faces of those who spent their lives in acts of practical charity, was often "brutal." She knew how that felt. She did feel brutal. She saw no point in allowing his own mawkish self-pity to overwhelm the man, so, yes, here she was guiding him through a great grief, because, in spite of everything—she couldn't do it otherwise—she loved him. "James, you went out looking for Christine," she continued, when he lifted his head again.

"I looked all along the cliffs, and then I went down to the place where she likes to swim."

"Is it on this side or the other side of the Three Cliffs?"

"The other side."

"Yes, that's Three Cliffs Bay."

"I didn't see anyone swimming. Then I saw her, lying on the beach, and I hurried over. She was dead, Penny! My beautiful Christine. It's horrible. We have to get her away from there."

"We will, James. Don't worry. Try to relax." So she must have been foiled by the sudden tide change or the undertow, but why wasn't she carried out to sea?

He bent his head again and sobbed openly.

Penny walked back to Helen. "Any chance you could close the post office for half an hour until we can get him settled back at Evelyn's?"

Helen looked startled but rallied. "I—I—guess so. The police may do it anyway to keep a crowd from gathering in here. The poor man needs a little privacy. Wasn't he the husband of that Prussian woman? Is it her?"

"Yes," said Penny. "She's dead, he says. I think he's right."

In close to thirty minutes Detective Inspector Kenneth Morgan knocked on the P.O. door.

A crowd of a dozen people had gathered outside after Helen had put up a sign and let the door's blind down. The word of anything unusual spread quickly in a village. The Prussian had made herself extremely disliked in a very few days. Penny could imagine the villagers saying, "It serves her right."

Kenneth Morgan had a reassuring presence. Penny liked him immediately. He had on a neat white shirt and a dark jacket but not the usual police headgear. He was tall, well-built, his brown hair greying. His brown eyes met hers, and he smiled. He had come in a little four-wheel drive vehicle that he had pulled up right to door. She remembered. They couldn't easily drive down to Three Cliffs Bay. There was only a path through the woods.

"Where exactly is the body, ma'am?" asked the Inspector, speaking to Penny, having taken in quickly that James was distracted. He felt easy to talk to, and, in some quiet way, very respectful of her, as though he and she were the adults in the situation and bore equal responsibility for managing it. She wasn't used to this in a man, especially not in Wales.

"It's on the beach at Three Cliffs Bay. Not Pobbles, on this side, but Three Cliffs—the beach on the far side of the cliffs."

"I can get there in my four-wheel drive, but we'll have to get the body out by boat. I've rung the coastguard. Can you stay here for awhile? I'll take the man—what's his name? What's your name, sir?"

"Hampton. James Hampton, III, sir."

"Mr. Hampton, you say your wife is dead. Are you very sure? I don't like to bother you, but if she is, we'll need you to identify her."

"Oh, Christine!" wailed James.

"He's sure she's dead," said Penny. "I'm Penelope Weaver, and I'm staying in the same guest house—Mrs. Trueblood's. It's not far away. Do you think it would be all right if I walked him back there and gave you the address and phone number? He'll be okay, but he's in shock."

"Let's keep him here for now. Earlier I asked them to send an ambulance out from Swansea, hoping she was alive. The ambulance men can check him out, be certain he's all right. If he is, they can take you back to Mrs. Trueblood's. I'd rather have you both right here for now. In fact, I may need you to identify her. He's not in very good shape for a rough ride down the slope." Inspector Morgan smiled.

"You want me to ride down there with you?" she asked, astonished.

He smiled again, pleasantly. He had a nice smile. "You've got it, love. Let me talk to Helen a minute." He went behind the counter and consulted with Helen in a low voice. Penny heard him telling her to have the ambulance men keep an eye on Mr. Hampton and check his blood pressure. He returned to Penny and James, who was still sitting slumped over.

A siren. The ambulance had arrived. Morgan had not used his siren as he approached the village, but the ambulance men perhaps enjoyed impressing the villagers. Fifty or so people were milling around the P.O. and chatting. Evelyn would have enjoyed the occasion. What was she thinking? Poor Christine was dead.

"The ambulance blokes can see to Mr. Hampton. I'll ask them to wait until we get back. Can you come with me now?" He stood looking at her, seeming to like what he saw. She had her hand on James's shoulder.

"James?"

"Penny, what will I do?"

"You sit here for now, James, and collect yourself. I'm going with Inspector Morgan, and these ambulance men will stay with you. They'll make sure you're okay. You've had a bad shock."

He was docile, despite being distraught. "All right, Penny. I'll stay right here. You go with the inspector, help them get Christine out. Penny, it's so horrible."

"I know. I'll be back very soon." The ambulance men had been let in by Morgan and had already begun to talk to James.

"Come along, love," said Kenneth Morgan, and Penny followed him out the door, thinking to herself how she did love the way British men called you *love* when they didn't even know you.

Penny was curious how he would get even a four-wheel drive vehicle down to the beach. There were paths from the castle down, but they were so deep in sand, it was hard to walk them, much less drive something through them. The only other path she knew was down from Park Mill, where Gower Store was, and it was through the woods and very narrow.

He did, in fact, take the road back to Park Mill and follow the path she had found yesterday that went from the road, along the little river, and then onto the beach. The tide was still high, but as they emerged from the woods, they saw a crowd gathered down near the water. Penny sat beside him. She was well-buckled in, and he was a good driver, took the footpath slowly.

Once on the hard packed sand of the beach, he went faster, and she could see the coastguard boat anchored off shore. They were soon at the edge of the crowd. "Please stay here," Morgan said. "I'll need to move these people out of the way. They have no sense, don't think about how they make it hard for the coastguard folks to work. The S.O.C.O. people will have come with the boat. We have to treat it as a crime scene in case somebody did for her." He came around to the back, opened a compartment behind Penny's seat, and got out some stakes and a coil of rope.

"Did for her? You mean murder, Inspector?"

"It happens," he said. "Usually it's a drowning, but we have to be certain." He smiled. "Please call me Kenneth. I grew up on Gower, and I hate being called Inspector. I'll be back in a few minutes."

"All I know is what I've learned reading detective fiction," she said. He nodded and walked off. She didn't say, "Everyone hated this woman, and a lot of people will be very glad she's dead." Suddenly she had a premonition. It was she, not some little old Jane Marple or Maud Silver, who would be assisting the police with their inquiries. She had a role, like it or not.

She sensed suddenly that someone *had* killed Christine. She remembered her sobbing in the night, wanting to leave. That probably added to James's guilt, too. He could have killed her. She aroused conflicting passions in him. He got sex sometimes, but no love, and she wouldn't play his mum the way he wanted her to. He made mums of other women wherever he went—to compensate? He was terribly upset, but he would be if he'd killed her, too.

She checked her intuition that she used when she read detective fiction. Did James do it, she asked herself. The answer she felt was no. Apart from James, who had already made her his mum, there was Evelyn. She couldn't abandon Evelyn in this grisly business. A part of her protested loudly: No! This is my vacation. I'm going to write. But something else was firmly descending onto her shoulders: a new role: detective.

Then this man Kenneth. She could already feel the hold he had on her, though she didn't understand why. They talked to each other as though they had always known each other. There was that book she had read years ago called *Seeing Things*. One of the women had had a lover. They had felt like they'd been lovers for six hundred years, through several incarnations. That's what she felt about Kenneth, like she had known him six hundred years. She suddenly felt naked and vulnerable there on the beach, familiar to her from so many walks across it, as she sat in the small vehicle. There were no barriers between them and no power struggling. They were so straight with each other. Trust was in place instantly. She had met him twenty minutes ago, and already they worked as a team?

She had been looking toward where the crowd had been. She could see a woman in a white coat and three uniformed men waiting, too, one holding a camera, as Kenneth worked with his stakes and rope to make a large square around Christine's body. The people, most in swimsuits, had gone back to their family parties nearby or were standing respectful but curious at the rope barrier. Christine was now visible, face down, her healthy, voluptuous body of no use to her any more. Something was awkward about the body's position. It looked unnatural. The man with the camera began taking photographs from every angle.

Kenneth walked back to her. "Would you come over now, love. I need you to identify her."

She went willingly, though with a sense of dread, too. As she walked with him, she thought of her carefree days and evenings, reading and writing, being whimsical. Would she ever get back to that? Some intuitive voice answered: "Yes. Do this now. This is right."

Christine, her blonde hair matted, was wearing a bright blue bikini, the one Evelyn had disapproved of. It was the color of the robe—where was the robe? This was definitely Christine. What she dreaded was seeing her face. She waited while Kenneth looked again carefully at the ground all around the body. The curious had already walked all over the wet sand. There didn't seem to be any clue to help them understand what had happened.

Then Kenneth lifted Christine's body by the shoulders and turned her over. The people watching gasped audibly, and Penny sucked in her breath. Christine had wet sand all over her face. It gave her a terrifying look, like a mask. Her open eyes bulged out and showed through the sand in places. Eerie.

"Joyce, we'd better let you get the sand off," said Kenneth. "Sorry. I forgot to introduce you. Dr. Townsend here is our police pathologist in Swansea, and these men are Bert Jones and Frank Thomas, the two best men of our crime scene experts. This is Miss Weaver. She knew the deceased, a Mrs. Hampton, we think. Miss Weaver has been staying in the same guest house in Pwll-du. You know, Evelyn Trueblood's? The husband, James Hampton, III, who found the body, is in the Pwll-du post office. The ambulance men are checking on him. Naturally, he has had a bit of a shock. Now, Miss Weaver, what do you think? Is this Mrs. Hampton?"

"Yes," said Penny. "I'm sure it is. She had a bathing suit like that and a robe she wore of the same color. The robe should be somewhere down here. She also had a big towel with her when I saw her leave this morning."

"Good point. We'll look for them. Now, Joyce, we'll let you do what you need to, and then get Mrs. Hampton taken back to Swansea."

Bert and Frank carried a stretcher up, which they set down near Christine. Dr. Townsend bent down to make her examination.

"While you do that, Joyce, Miss Weaver and I will check the nearby rocks for her bathing robe and towel. That might give us a clue as to what happened, though I'm not optimistic."

Penny followed Kenneth away from the body and the pathologist. She wasn't as squeamish as she once had been, but she definitely preferred not to watch.

"Any ideas where to look first?" asked Kenneth, and there was a lilt in his voice, not only the normal lilt of a native Welshman speaking English, but as if, despite the gruesomeness of their task, he was happy to be with her, to go clambering over the rocks together. "Let's wade the river," said Penny. "If I'd come swimming, I'd have put my things near the Three Cliffs, on those rocks, and then walked down this way."

As they approached the rocks, the sun broke through. Penny looked at her watch. It was almost eleven. A lot had happened to her between ten and eleven. Am I on my leyline right now, she asked herself. She got a resounding yes.

"I see something," said Penny. Sure enough, among some rocks, about midway up the pile, was the bright blue robe, carefully folded. In a pocket they found an expensive woman's watch, two one-pound coins, a bottle of suntan lotion, a small mirror, a comb, a lipstick, and a tube of liquid makeup.

"Her watch?" asked Kenneth.

"I think so. Definitely her robe. She wore some kind of flip flops, too. I don't see them or her towel."

"She may have been wearing the shoes, put the towel down nearer where she was swimming. I'd hate to climb over rocks like these in bare feet."

"But where?"

"She looks to have been in the water for awhile and drifted back in. The water could have carried the flip flops somewhere else. Some of those people might have picked them up, the towel, too. It's eleven now. Mr. Hampton found her—when would you guess?"

"Maybe quarter of ten? He had to walk back to town. He got to the post office shortly after ten. Helen called right away."

"We'll see when Joyce places the time of death. Let's go back." He picked up Christine's things and put them in a plastic bag. "I don't see anything else here."

When they reached the cordoned off area, Christine's body had been moved to the stretcher, face up, and the sand cleaned off. Yes, it was the Prussian all right, her eyes decently closed now, a worried look on her face. Death had taken her by surprise. Her unhappy life had continued right into death. Her hair was matted and untidy. Even so she was beautiful, more so now than in life. The perfect look was gone, the supreme effort to control everyone around her. She was vulnerable and finally fully human but too late to benefit from that state.

Penny noticed the marks on Christine's neck, as Dr. Townsend was saying, "We think she was strangled. There are bruises the shape of finger marks on her throat, and you saw her eyes." She was right: someone had not been able to take Christine a minute longer.

"Dead for probably two hours, maybe as long as four and a half. I'm estimating time of death as roughly between 6:30 and nine. I'll know more after the post-mortem. She was left in the water, perhaps with the hope that the outgoing tide would carry off the body. It brought it back instead. I'll be back in touch this afternoon. Where will you be, Kenneth?"

"Call me at the post office, and I'll keep Helen informed about where I am. Thanks, Joyce." He signaled to Bert and Frank, who picked up the stretcher and headed for the boat. "We'll leave the cordon for awhile," said Kenneth.

EIGHT

Life was certainly paradoxical, thought Penny, riding with Kenneth along the narrow highway that threaded its way the length of Gower on the southern side of the peninsula. They were passing Pen Maen Inn, where she had several times taken refuge during the rain and had a cup of coffee or splurged and had a bar lunch.

My favorite schedule in my favorite place doing my favorite things has been disrupted. I am not ranging the cliffs and writing. I am riding in a four-wheel drive. I am watching someone turn over a dead body and identifying it. I'm not reading detective fiction. I'm living it. Furthermore, I'm very interested in the investigating officer. All in one hour? Life has turned me upside down, and I'm blissful?

Kenneth drove through the village and slowed for the crowd of a hundred outside the post office. He stopped and cut his engine.

People surged over. Stanley, who looked white, called, "Inspector Morgan! Is it true? The German woman?"

Kenneth looked at him steadily, unsmilingly, and said, "She's dead, Mr. Jones."

"Drowned. I tried to warn her."

"Maybe drowned. Maybe not," said Kenneth. "Did you know her?"

"Not really. She came in the store."

Other people were pushing up and calling out, "Is she dead?"

Kenneth faced the crowd. "We've had a death down at Three Cliffs Bay," he said. "A visitor, name of Christine Hampton. Now you folks can help me by going home unless you have anything to tell the police about what happened. Naturally, her husband is distraught, and we're doing what we can for him. Now, folks, go on with your life. Not a thing you can do, and I've told you all I know now."

Not strictly true, thought Penny. It was undoubtedly murder. Who?

Probably before nine a.m. Christine had left at 6:30. Couldn't have been earlier than 6:45 or so. Had she died when they were eating breakfast? Or before, seven to 7:30? Christine infuriated people constantly. She created potential murderers around her wherever she went.

She'd better think about James. When Kenneth reached out his hand to help her down, however, she wasn't thinking about James. There was already a spark between her and Kenneth, and it was going both ways. He looked at her directly and happily. His eyes were so alive and so kind. "May I help a very astute American lady down from my horse?"

"Thanks. Your horse?"

"It has horsepower. It's why we Brits drive on the left side of the road, so we can mount our horses on the correct side. Will you come in with me, madam?"

He opened the door, as Helen unlocked it from within, and let her precede him. Again that sense that they were equals; that however solemn and terrible things were, he was happy. He had turned back, still holding the door. "Mr. Jones? You may be able to help us, too." No one else had come forward, but Stanley Jones had waited for a directive and now followed her in.

James was still sitting in the same place, still slumped over. The two ambulance men were standing quietly near him. James looks no worse, but no better, thought Penny. I've never done this before, helped a man I scarcely know, who is an imbecile, cope with his overwhelmed feelings. She thought of Lucy saying, "Any one of us can be overwhelmed at any time." True. Meantime, she was struggling with a different set of feelings, which she couldn't even settle down to enjoy. She had James to think about. Kenneth was counting on her. She knew that, too.

James looked up; he seemed more remote than before. He focused on her, ignoring the others, much as a child will ignore everyone until his mother returns, whatever they offer him. He didn't look at Kenneth, seemed oblivious of the ambulance men. Kenneth motioned for them to come over and consult with him.

"Penny!" said James. "Did you see her? She's dead, isn't she? Is she?"

"James, yes, Christine is dead. The coastguard police have taken her body into Swansea. They are good people, and they're looking after things. Don't worry about that. I'm so sorry, James. Are you okay?"

"I—I don't know, Penny. Can we leave now, go back to Mrs. Trueblood's?"

"I'll ask, James."

She walked over to the three men in a huddle with Helen. Stanley was standing uncertainly near them, looking worried. He probably wanted to leave but couldn't until he'd said his say. Penny heard one of the ambulance men saying, "His pulse is very regular now. I think he could go. We can take him back and the American lady." He looked at Penny.

"Miss Weaver," said Kenneth.

"Call me Penny. I'll be happy to go back and stay with him. Evelyn is in Swansea doing her shopping. I have a key, but she had left the house unlocked, I think, the back door, because some of the guests hadn't gone yet, and James was still out. I'll stay there with him, make him some tea."

"I tried to get him to drink some, but he wouldn't," said Helen.

Stanley shifted his weight, glancing at James uneasily and then at Kenneth.

"If you men will take Miss Weaver and Mr. Hampton back to Mrs. Trueblood's, then I will take Mr. Jones to the station to get his statement. Helen, you close soon, don't you, anyway? Why don't you go on and take your lunch break. I want a minute with Mr. Jones, and then we'll be off and leave your post office to get back on its normal schedule. Your satisfied customers have all gone home for a bite but will be back at one, I'll guarantee. You might as well take a little rest. Thanks for letting us barge in on you."

Helen smiled faintly, and, nodding, disappeared into her living quarters at the back of the store, and Penny took one of James's arms, while one ambulance man helped him up and the other held the door.

How can I be so sad and so happy all at once, Penny wondered. Here is this so human, so foolish James, looking to me as his savior, which I am not. At best, I'm a friendly person who is irritated but not contemptuous. His temporary savior wants to be involved in a murder investigation so she can flirt with the inspector. Pray the gods he is not otherwise committed. She already seemed to know that, whatever other women were in his life, she had a place.

Then he smiled when she nodded goodbye, as if he were claiming her for another time, in another place, when they could say to each other what now only their eyes said: "I know you. I know I can count on you. More. Later."

When they returned to Pobbles House, Penny was glad Evelyn wasn't home. The sight of Penny arriving in an ambulance again would "shatter" her. Bad enough that James was out of it because of grief, and she herself was unable to concentrate because the old familiar erotic attraction was taking her over.

They got James into the house and seated him in one of the lounge chairs. While James was brooding, she would make them a cup of tea. She thought she could find the tea things and make some sandwiches.

Evelyn wouldn't mind, though she did guard her kitchen like an artist protecting her workshop from careless hands. But Penny knew where she kept the bread. As she was opening the refrigerator, having filled the electric teakettle and turned it on, the outside kitchen door opened. She turned, startled.

Eloise, with Ernie behind her. "Hi, Penny," he said.

"You're back? Or haven't left?" asked Penny. "I thought you had a plane—."

"We did. We do," said Ernie. "We were half-way to Cardiff, where we turn in the car, and realized we left our clothes bag in the closet. We must have wanted an excuse to come back." He smiled as if they shared a secret.

Eloise had gone back to their room.

Penny closed the refrigerator. Speaking in a low voice, she said, "We've had something bad happen, Ernie. Christine is dead. James is in the lounge. He and I just got back. He found her on the beach, where she'd gone swimming."

"Dead?" asked Ernie. "The German woman? Drowned? She went swimming...she was late. We left here about 10:15. She wasn't back yet. Dead?" He looked worried and, for someone whose profession was helping people cope, very ill at ease.

"Maybe not drowned," said Penny, remembering how he and James had been out before breakfast and had come back together, Eloise still later. "Maybe murdered." She watched his reaction.

He repeated her words, looking at the floor. When he looked up, he had pulled himself together. "Why do you say 'murdered'? Surely, a swimming accident? She went out alone."

"I identified her," said Penny. She turned away from him to turn off the teakettle. "The pathologist found bruises on her neck. It looked like she had been strangled. I'm sure that the inspector who's investigating will want to talk to you all, Ernie. You may miss that plane, after all."

Ellie walked in, a clothes carrying bag over her arm. "That's all we forgot. We'd better dash. Bye, Penny."

Ernie stood still near the back door. Penny couldn't read him. He was lost in his own thoughts. Had he heard her or Eloise? He was suspended, like when he'd ignored his food at breakfast.

"Ernie, let's go," said Eloise. She moved around him for the back door. "We've lost two hours. We'll barely make it."

Finally, Ernie looked at Penny. "Whatever has happened, I'm sorry. She was a difficult woman to be around, but I feel bad she's dead—"

Eloise was turning the door handle, but at the word *dead* she stopped and came back into the kitchen. "Who's dead?"

She looked at Ernie, but it was Penny who answered. Ernie didn't act guilty, but he acted strange. How would Eloise react?

"Eloise, Christine is dead. The police think she was murdered."

A look of surprise and shock crossed Eloise's face. "The German woman? The one we all hated?"

"Yes," Penny said quietly. "The one we all disliked. But don't talk so loud. Her husband is in the lounge. He's having a hard time. I'm making him a sandwich and a cup of tea. It would be good if you stayed and talked to the police. I'll fix you a sandwich, too."

Eloise listened very carefully, but it was hard to read her. Possibly she'd prepared what she would say, but she had seemed surprised. Eloise turned to Ernie. "Should we? We have non-refundable tickets. We'll lose over $1000. Couldn't they telephone us?"

Ernie said firmly, "Penny, it's nothing to do with us. We only came back for our clothes. I do have to get back. I have patients. I'm a psychoanalyst. It's hard for me to leave people even for three weeks." He looked at his watch. "It's after twelve now. Our plane leaves from Heathrow at five. We'll be lucky to catch it now. I'm happy to pay for phone calls." He got out his wallet and handed Penny a card. "Give this to the police. We'll be home this evening by U.S. time, and I'll be in my office tomorrow. I could even come back if that's needed, but right now we need to get home."

Eloise moved to the door and went out. They did seem awfully eager to leave. She couldn't detect any guilt, but she picked up how ill at ease they were. Ernie seemed more concerned about making their plane than about his patients. She had a powerful intuition to keep them a few more minutes. She had gotten Ernie to eat his breakfast. Could she delay him?

"I'm worried about James," she said. "I guessed you were a psychiatrist. I hadn't imagined analyst, but you did remind me of friends I have at home who are analysts." He smiled fleetingly as though he'd like to hear more about her analyst friends.

"I know you're pressed for time," she went on, "and I'm sure your patients need you. But I've got a man here who's deep in shock. I'm the only one grounding him, by allowing him to see me as his mother. I feel in over my head, Ernie," she went on. "I've never had to deal with someone this distraught. If you could take fifteen minutes to chat with him, it would help me enormously. The British aren't oriented to psychological stuff like we are. They haven't found anything wrong with him but shock. His pulse is okay again, so they haven't taken him to the hospital, but he's barely coping. Could you?"

She hoped she had conveyed her need of his help. She was counting on the openness to her that he had showed when his wife wasn't present. She was being manipulative, but it felt like the right thing to do.

"Fifteen minutes? If we drive straight to Heathrow going the speed limit on the motorway and turn the car in there, pay the extra charge. Twelve-thirty now. We should be there by four. Okay. Take me into him."

Penny felt the tension go out of her body. She had done it. "I'll take you in and get back to the tea. A cup of strong tea and a sandwich may help, too. I wouldn't tell him you're a shrink. It might alarm him." She flicked the kettle back on and then led the way through the dining room into the lounge.

James was still in his stupor. Penny had seated him so he could look out the window. Now she said gently, "James?"

He turned his eyes from the window and looked at her with the eyes of a very sad child. "Penny! Oh, Penny! She's gone."

"James, remember Ernie? He came back because they forgot some of their clothes. He'll talk with you a minute while I get the tea. He feels bad about Christine, too."

"Christine, my darling! Why didn't we leave when you wanted to?"

Penny knew he'd eventually feel guilty about that. She nodded to Ernie and glanced out the window at the Rosewoods' car, with Eloise waiting in the driver's seat. She wished fervently that Kenneth would come now. Then she saw his little vehicle loom into view. Perfect timing. Had he felt her sense of urgency or had she felt his? No matter. They were operating as a team. She hurried to the kitchen where the kettle was on hard boil. She flicked it off. Where was the tea?

She was hunting in Evelyn's cupboards when there was a knock at the back door. Kenneth, and they were alone. Not for long, and in a crisis, but alone.

He smiled. "I thought you'd be in the kitchen. I wanted to see you first."

There was so much gladness in his eyes. She dropped her eyes, felt a rush of nervousness, not usual with her. She reminded herself that erotic feelings took away one's ease with the beloved in the beginning. Her awkwardness would be revealing. They were now both conscious of what was happening. She had to pull herself together. Oh, you gods, help! Athena, where are you?

"I'm so glad you're here," she said. She didn't sound as nervous as she felt. "I've delayed the Rosewoods, but they're on the point of leaving again." She heard a horn blast. Eloise? "You should talk to them, Kenneth. They were both out walking this morning early, during the time Christine died. Christine was infuriating to be around. She upset everyone. Not so much Ernie, Mr. Rosewood, who's a psychiatrist, by the way. He's in there talking to James." Another horn blast. Only an American.

"They fly home from Heathrow today and were going to leave." She smiled and whispered, "I tricked him into staying. That's her on the horn. Maybe you could ask her to come in? I'm making tea. You don't have any idea where Evelyn might keep her tea, do you?"

He walked close to her. She could feel the magnetism between their bodies.

"I'll help you look for the tea," he said, holding her eyes with his, "if you'll promise to let me take you out to dinner as soon as we get a breathing space." He was standing right beside her at the counter and reached up to open a cupboard. He was about her height. She stared at his hands as they lifted things and moved them. He had the right hands.

They'd been used for manual work of some kind. She'd always wanted the hands of the man she loved to have worked.

"Is that a deal?" he asked softly, using, unexpectedly, an American idiom.

She was breathless. Without speech.

He was so close, the hairs on his arms brushed hers as he lifted down the tea and set it in front of her.

"Yes," she managed. She was still staring at his hands, resting quietly on the tea tin. She couldn't look at him. "Thanks." She summoned her courage. Why was it so hard? She looked into his eyes. They were so open, so filled with love that she trembled and again felt speechless. He put his hand on hers, lifted hers, and put it on the tin of tea.

"Make tea," he said. "I will see you later." He strolled toward the door into the dining room.

NINE

When Penny finally got cheese sandwiches made and found some of the condiments the British call "pickle" in Evelyn's refrigerator to go with them, she carried everything, including the tea in Evelyn's big pot, into the dining room. Then she returned for cups, saucers, small plates, and a new pint of milk. Evelyn would kill her for not putting it in the small pitcher she used when she served Harold his mid-morning cuppa, but she wasn't going to ask Kenneth to find anything else for her. The way he had found the tea tin had left her barely able to function.

She laid plates and spoons, found the paper napkins, and walked to the door into the lounge. It was only love, which is, after all, a good thing. Relax. Take this one step at a time. She had an unspecified date was all. He had his work cut out for him with this case. That date might be weeks off. Be calm, dear heart.

James was the first to notice her. She felt sure both Kenneth and Ernie were aware of her, but they were talking quietly. Ernie sat in one corner of the couch under the window that faced into the lounge, and Kenneth was on a chair near him. James looked less pale and more focused on the present. He even smiled at her. "Oh, Penny. You're still here. I'm so glad. Do you think I might have a cup of tea?"

"Of course, James. That's what I've been doing. I've made some sandwiches for us, too. Come on in."

"Oh, Penny. How did you know I was famished? I told Christine I wouldn't eat—. Oh, Christine! You're gone!" After having stood up brightly enough, he sank back down again, whether overwhelmed with grief or guilt, Penny wasn't sure. Probably both. Christine had always wanted him to skip lunch.

The other two men seemed to be in some kind of a contest to see who could ignore her the longest, so she walked over to James and put her hand under his elbow. "Come on, James. A cup of tea will do you good."

He allowed himself to be led into the dining room and sat down at the first seat he came to, which was where Penny usually sat. She poured him tea and seated herself opposite him. She decided she'd ignore the other two, though she could see them well enough. They were grown-ups. They could certainly come in and collect their tea and sandwiches.

James helped himself to two sandwiches and several pickled onions and began to eat. A good sign. She didn't know what Ernie had said to him. Sometimes the key thing a therapist did was to listen. In any case, James was coming out of his extremely distracted state. The food would help. She handed him a cup of tea. If you'd been given a bracing cup of tea every time you'd had an upset of any kind all your life, merely drinking a cup must have powerful and calming effect. She marveled at how many situations the British solved with a cup of tea. James looked up at her gratefully, a little too gratefully. She needed to signal that she would temporarily play his mum, but only temporarily. What could she say?

Evelyn! He had adopted Evelyn already. Evelyn didn't think he was a silly ass, and once she got over the fright this was going to be, she'd make a great mum. If it was true that a "little boy" man didn't care who played mum as long as someone did, she should be able to hand him over to Evelyn when she got back.

"James, I think you should probably stay here awhile, maybe a week longer? Until we see what they might need you for? When Evelyn gets back"—she looked at her watch—"in a couple of hours, you can ask her if she has anyone else coming in. She's good at looking after people. She was great to me when I sprained my ankle last summer."

He was looking at her with interest. He clearly liked the idea of staying where the breakfasts were so delicious and so plentiful. Perhaps it was beginning to occur to him that he could now once again eat whatever he wanted to. Or maybe, she thought, as his eyes filled with tears, he'd never be able so freely and indulgently to enjoy his food again. Christine had touched his stomach and his conflicts about food, if not his heart, though perhaps for all practical purposes they were the same.

"I'm sorry, Penny. The tea is good, and the sandwiches, but they make me think of Christine. She didn't think I should eat lunch after I'd had that big breakfast, and I did eat a big breakfast today. Why does everything have to be so terrible?"

"It is terrible, James. But Christine would want you to pull yourself together and eat now. It's a good sign that you can eat. The tea will help, too. Okay?"

He smiled blearily and dutifully returned to his cheese and pickle, even reaching for a third sandwich and smiling sheepishly, guiltily at Penny as he did so. She nodded.

Two sandwiches left. She could make more. The two men didn't act like food had yet entered their minds.

As she was gazing at the other two men, the front bell rang. Penny rose, but Kenneth looked at her as if he had never once stopped thinking of her, his eyes again conveying so much without words. She was sure the words, when he said them, would be extravagant, flattering, delicious. What he said liltingly, in his Welsh accent, was, "I'll get it, Penny."

Eloise. Penny heard her saying, "Oh, hello. I'm Mrs. Rosewood. I'm checking on my husband. We're leaving to catch a plane. Ernie, what's keeping you? It's nearly one o'clock."

Ernie stood. As Eloise approached him, Kenneth following her in, he said, "Mr. Morgan, Inspector Morgan, this is my wife, Ellie. We were planning to fly home today, but given what you've told me—."

"Ernie, we can't stand here talking. Planes don't wait."

Kenneth looked at Penny, and she gestured toward the tea pot. He turned back to Ellie. "Mrs. Rosewood, I think the best thing for all of us to do would be to join Miss Weaver and Mr. Hampton for a spot of lunch and a cup of tea. We need to talk. You see," he said, and indicated that they should proceed into the dining room, "we've had something bad happen, and we want to understand all the circumstances around it. You and Mr. Rosewood are important to our investigation."

Ellie erupted. "Investigation? You want to know that the woman was offensive and manipulative? I see no reason—."

James turned in his chair but didn't seem to take in that Ellie was talking about Christine. He turned back to his nearly consumed cheese and pickle and helped himself to more tea.

"Mrs. Rosewood," said Kenneth, gesturing toward James and putting his finger on his lips as if to warn a thoughtless child to be more considerate, "Mr. Hampton's wife is dead. This is hard for all of the people involved, but especially for Mr. Hampton. We'll be investigating Mrs. Hampton's death very intensively for the next few days. Your husband says he feels that he could arrange to stay a little longer. If you leave now, we would wire Heathrow a subpoena to ask that you return. You won't be able to get through customs, you see, not when we don't yet know whether it was an accident or"—he paused—"if it was deliberate. If you will both cooperate now, you should be able to return much sooner. Please have a seat. I will call the airline and explain that the police have detained you to help with inquiries into the death of Mrs. Hampton. They may give you new return tickets without charging you."

Ellie hadn't moved. She was staring at the back of James's head. "Why don't you come out and say you think it's murder," she said acidly, "instead of beating around the bush."

This time James did understand. He leapt up. "Penny? Murder? Was Christine murdered?"

Penny also stood up. Everyone was looking at her. She decided on partial truth. "It's very possible, James. We'll find out soon enough. Now finish your lunch. I'm going to make a few more sandwiches for the Rosewoods and the inspector here. Sit down, James. Everything is being done that can be done. You'll help most now by finishing your lunch." She placed a sandwich each on the two clean plates.

James seated himself, looking very worried. Penny took up her plate and gestured to Kenneth to sit where she'd been sitting. She lifted the nearly empty teapot and the empty sandwich plate.

Ellie hadn't moved. Now she turned to Ernie. "Ernie, this is ridiculous. Your patients—"

Kenneth was looking steadily at Penny, his eyes full of gratitude and, yes, love. What else? She ran for the kitchen. Sandwiches. Let her keep focused on that. This man caused desire to flood through her merely by looking at her. If they had to wait weeks to have a date, what was she going to do? You couldn't win. Life was always doing this to her. Stirring up her wanting.

Why did he have to have such powerful eyes, why did he so clearly already respect her and on such brief acquaintance? Was it obvious to everyone else? Fortunately, they were all pretty distracted. No, *fortunately* wasn't the right word. Christine was dead, James's grief was real.

It was sad and terrible, yet her hormones had unceremoniously plunged her into the full pitch of desire.

She set the empty sandwich plate down on the counter and moved to collect and fill the teakettle. Suddenly, she heard the door between the dining room and the kitchen swing open and someone was behind her. She turned around. Kenneth was inches away. She was so startled, she almost dropped the kettle. He reached for it and turned toward the sink, not quite nonchalantly, but certainly not as though all his senses had exploded all over his body like hers had. He was a long time filling the kettle. Maybe he was having trouble with control, too.

He walked around her and over to where the kettle got plugged in. He flipped the switch on. "I've come to help," he said. "Do you want me to slice cheese or bread?"

He looked right at her, amused. "Cheese or bread?" He looked in her eyes, and moved closer. She couldn't speak. He murmured, "I want to help you make lunch. Don't worry. We'll manage this lot and us, too. You're angry?"

She shook her head no and tried to smile. The things her body was doing. Messages were flying places where she hadn't realized she had sensation. A general wake up. Holy cow.

"Penny?" he asked.

"Umm?"

"Penny, look at me. Are you happy?"

"Umm," she said, without opening her eyes.

"Penny—" Then he was kissing her, his lips firm and warm, his tongue speaking all his astonished longing. Her knees felt trembly. She was weak. She'd fall. He held her tight and then gently removed his tongue and kissed her on the lips again. He said again, "Penny, look at me."

She looked.

"Penny, don't worry. We'll find a time." He smiled. "Now, bread or cheese?"

She laughed, made a growling noise at him, and turned to the refrigerator. When she turned back, she said, "Here's the cheese. I'll do the bread." She moved over to the counter where Evelyn kept the long loaf of white bread in its box as the teakettle began its hard boil.

Kenneth had not eaten. He had stood at the dining table awhile asking them some basic questions about time and place. She had contributed as she could, being the only one, besides Evelyn, who had been in the house during the relevant time.

Once Kenneth had learned when they'd all left the house that morning—Christine at 6:30, the Rosewoods at seven, James at 7:30—and that James and Ernie were back at 8:30, Ellie a little before nine, neither Evelyn nor Penny having left at all, he seemed to have what he wanted from everyone, except for Ernie. He urged James to get some rest; allowed Ellie to resettle herself in the bedroom that she and Ernie had vacated, and asked Ernie to go with him down to the station in Reynoldston, where they could call the airline, Ernie could call his office in New York, and he could take Ernie's statement. "I will need to talk to the rest of you later," he had said. He drank a cup of tea standing up. Ernie didn't eat or drink any tea. Ellie ate several sandwiches, and James had two more.

"The postmistress has agreed to let me use the post office after she closes," Kenneth had told them. "We're having some renovations done at the station, and this will be more convenient for you. Miss Weaver, since you were here all morning until just before ten, and so are out of it"—a vague phrase which must mean she couldn't be guilty—"could you come down to the post office, too, at eight this evening and listen in? You may be helpful to us."

"Sure. Eight should be fine. Evelyn and I eat about six, and we can probably feed James for dinner, too. I'll ask Evelyn. But is it okay for me to listen in?"

"I'll ask my Sector Inspector," said Kenneth. "I think I can fix it, assuming none of the witnesses object." He looked around at the others. "I think they may be glad you're there. You're not as scary to them as I am." He smiled. Penny saw that Ernie and Ellie were nodding.

Then James excused himself. She watched him walk off, lightly and gracefully despite his bulk, his body language no longer conveying tragedy, suggesting rather that the pieces of Humpty Dumpty were getting reassembled.

When Ernie had followed Ellie out to the car to carry things in, Kenneth helped Penny clear the table. "I'm going to leave you the washing up," he said, beaming, "but after we talk to all these people, if you'd do me the honor, I'd like to take you out for a pint. If the pubs are closed, for a walk on the beach."

"I expect the beach will be there all night," she said. "We may get tired."

"We may," he said, "and I will be considerate. If you want to come right back here and get in your bed, I'll bring you right back and carry you off tomorrow night instead."

She turned to the sink. She'd wash up the dishes. No, there wouldn't be hot water. Evelyn turned off the heater during the day. She'd boil some in the kettle. "I'll tell Evelyn to expect me late," she said. Something strange is happening to me, she thought. She focused on running cold water on the plates. Would she ever be tired again?

He came over and put his arms around her. "Happy?"

"I think so," she said calmly. "It's hard to concentrate on these dishes with you stirring me up."

He removed his hands slowly, lifted her braid, and kissed her neck. "I'll let you work," he said. "I have work to do, too. Tell Evelyn that I'll see you back safely. You have a key? Aye. You are a love." Then he popped quickly out the back door.

She felt limp but managed to unplug, fill, and replug the kettle. Five minutes passed before she realized she hadn't turned it on. Fortunately, on British voltage, heating a teakettle took only two minutes.

As she was plunging her hands into soapy water, she thought how another of her stereotypes had bitten the dust. She'd never expected to fall so hard for a policeman. Far too often she'd get people pegged, only to have them slip loose from their moorings. She had to admit it made things interesting.

A friend of hers had once described her life as coasting. Since age fifty, Penny had given up all notion of coasting or closure. She tried to keep up, and that wasn't easy. Her job seemed to be not to win, not to finish, but to cope.

She didn't want Evelyn coming home to a mess. When she'd finished cleaning up, it was three o'clock. Penny sat down at the little kitchen table and indulged in a rare cup of instant coffee.

TEN

"Penny, what are you doing here on this gorgeous day? Why aren't you way to the other end of the peninsula?" Evelyn had her arms full of groceries and more hanging in a string bag over her arm as she came in the back door. Harold was right behind her, also laden down with a sack of potatoes and plastic bags full of groceries.

"Hello, Penny, what's keeping you indoors on a day like this?" he asked.

Penny jumped up and began helping Evelyn empty the bags. She set the groceries on the counter. "Evelyn, a lot has happened. Let's get all the groceries in and then sit down, Harold, too, and have a cup of tea. I have a lot to tell you."

Harold was doing most of the hauling, so Evelyn turned automatically to fill the kettle. "What's wrong, Penny? Are you all right?" She looked at Penny's feet as if expecting she'd sprained an ankle again.

"I'll tell you. Let's have our tea here in the kitchen. I'm not the only one in the house. James is back in his room, and Eloise is still here."

"My stars, Penny, didn't those Americans leave yet? Where's Christine? Did she get her breakfast all right?"

"I'll explain," said Penny.

Evelyn was searching in her cupboard. "Penny, I can't find the tea. Did you—?"

"I did," said Penny. "Here." She could never again think of a tea canister without certain other associations.

So they settled around Evelyn's tiny kitchen table, sitting in a huddle and waiting for the tea to steep. Evelyn's kitchen table had no room for elbows, barely for the cups and the pot.

"Christine's dead," said Penny, watching Evelyn's face carefully. She was very vital and sturdy for seventy-five, but it would be a shock.

"The Prussian?" asked Evelyn. "My stars." She grew pale.

"The Prussian," said Penny.

"Good riddance," said Harold emphatically and then he looked embarrassed.

"She was hard for all of us," said Penny, keeping an eye on Evelyn, "and that's part of the problem. James found her on the beach of Three Cliffs Bay this morning after you left for town. It looks like someone killed her. They can't say that publicly yet, but that's where things are. I've given James and the Rosewoods some lunch. The inspector—he knows you—Kenneth Morgan? He's based in Swansea but grew up on Gower."

Evelyn nodded, still pale. "He used to be our constable."

"He asked the Rosewoods to stay a few more days, too. So they're still here. Ernie has gone with Kenneth to call his airline and office in New York. The others are resting. Everything's more or less under control. James is naturally pretty upset, but he's coping. I did make myself at home in your kitchen, Evelyn, in order to take care of him. I hope that's okay?"

"Of course." Evelyn seemed very abstracted. She poured tea into their cups with the milk she'd already poured in them and took a few sips of her own tea. Penny waited.

Then she looked up at Penny. "I'm glad you're here, Penny. I'm getting too old for upsets like this. What should we do now? I hate to say it, but I'm like Harold. If someone had to die, I'm glad it was the Prussian."

"We don't have to do anything at the moment," said Penny. "Kenneth has things well in hand. Later, after supper, he'll talk to each of us. We'll each make a statement. He wants me"—could she say this with a straight face?—"to sit in while he interviews people, so I'll go down to the P.O. after supper. I might be late tonight—is that okay?"

"You have your key," said Evelyn. "We'd better not leave the house unlocked if there's a murderer hanging around. Penny, how terrible. On our nice Gower, too."

Penny didn't say that the murderer might be locked in with them. Let Evelyn think for the moment that it was someone "out there," someone they'd never met or even heard of, which, of course, it might be, though if she was living the classic British detective novel, which this felt like, of course the murderer would be one of them.

It could have been one of her breakfast companions, or Stanley, Helen, or Harold, or that poet—any of this small group of people whom Christine had infuriated.

She'd advise James, the Rosewoods, and Evelyn to lock their bedroom doors. Hers wouldn't shut, much less lock. But she could scream. She could do what her friend Cathy did when she was alone at night: she could borrow Evelyn's broom and plant it, on the path from her bed to the door, with her hiking boots, her walking stick.

Harold drew her back to the present by saying, "I may have been the last person to see her alive. I was coming back through the village this morning about quarter of seven. I know I was home before seven because I had time to boil the kettle and make my tea before the news came on at seven. I saw her in that beach costume of hers. I even said 'Good morning,' but she wouldn't answer me. I'm sorry I said 'good riddance,' but those Prussians—they never change. They'll do anything. Look what they did during the war. She asked for it, if you ask me."

"I don't want to worry you, Harold, but you'd better come down to the post office tonight, too, and give a statement." Penny finished her tea. She was thinking she'd better ask Evelyn if she'd feed James tonight when Evelyn said, "Shouldn't I make a statement, too, Penny?"

Penny was startled. Evelyn wasn't likely to have throttled her house guest, even if she could have slipped out between 6:30 and 7:30. After that Penny had seen her there.

"What you could do is come down with Harold about eight to the post office, and he could take yours, too. You may have noticed something. Let me ask you this. Are we having fish and chips tonight, your Friday night special?"

"That's what I was planning." Evelyn looked around at the groceries she still had to put away. "What time is it, Penny?"

"It's four."

"My stars. I'd better get moving. I was going to make a pie."

"Evelyn, would it be okay if James ate with us? He can have half of my fish, and maybe you can do some extra chips. I think it may soothe him to stay right here for supper tonight. I told him I'd ask if you could keep him a few more days after Tuesday. Could he stay until Friday?"

Evelyn stood up and put their cups in the sink. "Certainly, Penny. Poor man. No. No one else coming in until next Friday. I'll make him a cup of tea when he gets up. You and I can each eat half of a filet, and he can have a whole one—how's that?"

"How about splitting it three ways, Evelyn?" asked Penny. "I love your fish and chips, and I'm willing to share with James, but he's lucky to be so well looked after. You and I need the protein, too. He polished off five cheese sandwiches at lunch."

"My stars," said Evelyn. "He does love to eat." She smiled to herself and was putting cans away with enthusiasm, no doubt looking forward to pleasing James's palate.

Harold had been standing at the back door, waiting for a chance to speak. "I'll be off, then, Evelyn. Want to go have a pint at the club. I learn anything, I'll let you know, Penny, and you can tell the inspector."

"You can tell him yourself after supper," said Penny. "See you about eight?"

"Yes," said Evelyn. She was getting out a pastry board and sifter. You couldn't hold the woman down. Harold vanished, closing the back door quietly behind him. Suddenly Penny was exhausted. The house was still quiet. Maybe she could catch a nap. Evelyn had things in hand again.

"Let me know if I can do anything," said Penny. "I'm going to lie down. What a day."

"You like detecting, Penny." Evelyn smiled. "Here's your chance. Did you like Kenneth? Now there's an eligible bachelor for you. Nice as pie. What did you think of him?"

Penny blushed. Evelyn always guessed. Had she thought she could fool her? "I like him, Evelyn."

"I knew it," said Evelyn. "You've already written him a poem."

"No." Penny laughed, "but I might. We have a date after we do these statements tonight. I might be a little late. Evelyn, he is nice."

"Of course, he is. A little wild though. Comes of riding all around in that four-wheel drive of his, I expect. Don't let him move faster than you want to, but, Penny, he is lonely, and there's no one around here smart enough for him. Go sleep. You'll need it." She grinned wickedly and turned back to her pie crust.

At seven that evening Evelyn's phone rang. Penny was doing the washing-up. She had her hands in hot, soapy water and listened to see if she could figure out who it was. James had returned to his room. The

Rosewoods had gone out for dinner but had promised to turn up at the post office at nine, so Kenneth could get Ellie's statement. She could tell it was Kenneth on the phone by what Evelyn was saying.

"Terrible! I'm quite shocked. My stars. Yes, Penny's here. She has already told Harold and me to meet you down there at eight. I'll try to think of everything I can . . . Certainly. She's helping me wash up. I'll get her."

Evelyn was grinning. "It's for you, Penny. Your beau. 'Helping the police with their inquiries.' That's not what they called it in my day." She put her own hands in the soapy water as Penny walked slowly toward the phone. How did people learn so much about her so quickly? But why be embarrassed? She liked the man. He was available. She was available.

These years she knew who she was, and she was doing for herself most of what she had once asked of a husband. She earned her living, provided her roof, had learned to defend herself in arguments, take care of her car, draw lines and make rules for her kids. She liked sex, but there were other priorities: time to write and good companionship; control over her time and her house. It was company she wanted, if it could be found, with sex, without too many demands other than the normal human ones. It did bother her that this was happening so fast. It was fun. She definitely wanted to be with him, but was he as trustworthy as he seemed? You had to keep an eye out when your senses were reeling. If it was going to be a major love affair, she wanted to be sure.

"Hi, Kenneth."

"How'd you know it was me?"

"I guessed."

"How are you, love?" His voice alone set her off. Here we go again. Rats. How can I even argue with the man?

"I'm fine. I'll see you at eight."

"Love, do you think you could pop down at seven. I'd like to get a statement from Helen, and yours, too, actually, before the others come. Please?"

"Kenneth, are you sure you need me to sit in on the interviews. Is it really all right?"

"No doubt about that," he said. "I do need you, love. I've fixed it with my chief, and I'll clear it with the others. It helps me a lot. I definitely need you," he said in a very unambiguous way. "So seven then?"

Penny looked at her watch. "It's seven now, love." That slipped out. These British men! Evelyn laughed in the kitchen. "I'll come as soon as I can. Maybe ten minutes?" She looked at Evelyn, who was waving the dishpan she was rinsing out to indicate that the chores were done.

"Super," Kenneth said. "Listen, think hard for me about everything you can remember from this morning."

She laughed.

"Before ten." He laughed, too. "Say, from 6:30, when Christine went out, until James came into the post office. The pathologist is sure she was strangled. She estimates death occurred between eight and nine. The post office opens at 8:30 in the morning. I've talked to Helen and the Three Cliffs Store owner, Stanley Jones. He said he opened on time at seven and was in his store from then on, with lots of people in and out. He says he didn't see any of the people from Evelyn's. We know that James and Ernie were in his store between eight and about 8:20. He says his daughter must have waited on them. We'll talk more when you get here."

"All right."

"See you, love. Ta."

"Bye, Kenneth. I'll be right down."

As she hung up, it hit her. *Cennydd. Llangennith. Cennydd* was the Welsh for Kenneth. *Llangennith* meant *Kenneth's church.* The old saint from fourteen centuries ago had founded a church there. She loved the legend of how the saint, as a baby, had been abandoned on Worm's Head Point, had been fed by seagulls, then had lived a saintly life. Perhaps Kenneth was a modern saint in the way he dealt with people—difficult ones, crowds that some wouldn't have been able to manage so lightly and easily. To be so competent, serene, and sexy all at once probably meant he'd been through hell, as she had, and come out the other side. And he liked her. She moved in a daze into her room.

He was so eager to have her there that it seemed inconsiderate to take time to dress. She'd had a shower before supper. She brushed her hair and braided it, remembering that kiss on the back of her neck. How would she concentrate?

But did she want it to slow down, she asked herself, as she let herself out the front door and locked it. Yes and no. It was hard to keep up, but if things slowed down, it would be pure torture. But, if it was as good as it seemed, going slowly wouldn't hurt, was wiser.

ELEVEN

It took Penny five minutes to walk to the post office when she walked briskly. How could she fall in love and solve a mystery all at the same time? She had trouble thinking when Kenneth was around; and when he wasn't there, all she wanted to do was think about him. The more her erogenous zones came to life, the more her ability to think was derailed.

How had she gotten herself into this? Plus, someone not yet known by them to be a killer, if alarmed that the truth might come out, might kill again, might kill her, if she were helping, or Kenneth, or even Evelyn.

Suddenly, she felt again, powerfully, that sense of a new destiny entering her life and changing it. She had a visual image of herself walking back to where the body had been, looking for additional clues. She was good at finding things. Then she had another flash, of herself listening to people. That, too, she had been good at in the past, in other connections. Her intuition was insisting that she would solve the mystery and prevent another murder.

She suddenly saw a third scene: Evelyn standing in her kitchen making a pie, and a figure without a face coming up behind her with hands moving in as if to choke her. No! Not Evelyn! Kenneth could take care of himself. So could she. But Evelyn wouldn't be as able to defend herself. So she might save Evelyn. Nothing had ever before felt so important to do exactly right, felt so truly life or death, while at the same time being so hard.

She had reached the main street and turned left to walk along the broad sidewalk that led into the village. As always, she admired the pink to yellow rose bushes blooming in one particular garden. The British were devoted gardeners, and they had the ideal climate for roses. What was there about pink and yellow together that so touched her? She didn't know. She'd read that plants responded to affectionate messages, and so, as she passed them, she said aloud, "You're gorgeous, as always," and then to herself, since you are in this mess now, up to your ears and a lot depends on you, do the best you can.

Okay, Kenneth, she thought, as she stood before the door of the post office, its shade lowered, and knocked softly, here I am. Ready to be your partner on two fronts.

                ✑

Kenneth opened the door as if he'd been standing beside it waiting. "Hello, love," he said with the fullest tide of love in his eyes she had yet seen. "You made good time." She glanced quickly around the post office. No sign of Helen. They were alone again. Could she do this?

He walked over to a table he had put in the middle of the room, took a seat behind it, and motioned to her to take one of the two chairs in front of it.

"I know I can be disconcerting," he said, and she found herself smiling into his eyes, returning the messages his eyes sent her, even feeling hungry for more, foolish though that was, if she was going to be able to help him. "You disconcert me, love," he said. "But I will attempt to focus on these interviews and not make life harder for you by kissing you between times." He grinned. She was speechless.

Even when she felt speechless, she had learned she could usually say something "Thanks. I'll do my best, but it helps me if we stay on an even keel." She paused. "I'm worried, Kenneth. I have this hunch that whoever it is may kill Evelyn next."

He looked solemnly at her. "Maybe I'd better stay up there." He laughed. "No, not what you're thinking. Not at Evelyn's. Next door with Harold. He's an old acquaintance."

"Okay, that would work. Even on Evelyn's couch. You've probably realized that the murderer could be in with us. Harold says he saw Christine going to swim when he was walking home through the village before seven this morning."

"Good. Now . . . " He moved his papers around and got out some clean sheets. He set his tape recorder between them. "Let's get your statement, then Helen's. She has no objection to your being present. I'll make notes. Then you can look it over, note any discrepancies or questions. Later, when it's typed, you'll need to come to the station and sign it. We're establishing times, places, alibis, people who could verify these.

I'll also ask everyone how they felt about Christine and what they think happened. It's not standard procedure, but people give themselves away sometimes in their fictions. They inadvertently reveal the truth."

Penny was relieved to work on the problem with him. Her hormones were behaving rather well. There was a low humming in her body, like a low grade state of being aroused, but not major flaming up. "Sounds good. Ask away."

She told him how she had been wakened each time someone went out that morning, her room being close to the front door. She went through the rest of the breakfast comings and goings until she got to the post office, and James came in.

"Anything unusual happen the day before? In fact, go back to when you first met the Hamptons and the Rosewoods. I can use your impressions to check against the others. If you hear them tell something different than how you would have told it, make a note, and we'll talk later. Most people sooner or later reveal everything you want to know about them, don't you think?"

She smiled. She had read that idea in Proust and had adopted it. "Have you read Marcel Proust?"

"Of course! One of my favorite books, his *In Search of Lost Time.* And you?"

"Oh, yes. I'd love to talk with you about it later." She went back to her arrival, getting to know the Hamptons, how Christine had seemed to offend all of them, even the poet John.

"I wonder where he was this morning?" said Kenneth. "I'll have to hunt him down."

"You don't think he did it?"

"Love, I don't think anyone did it so far. I'll have to talk to everyone who might have seen or heard something this morning."

Penny nodded. "I understand. It's a process, and we've only begun. We were all offended by her. She upset the usually placid Gower people, Evelyn, Stanley, Harold, Helen—she was very rude twice in the post office here. Helen was doing her best to please her and no possibility. She flounced out twice after holding everyone up.

"She was like an invasion all by herself, and she reminded them of the German bombing of World War II. I was irritated, too, and Evelyn was fit to be tied because she couldn't get her to eat her breakfast on time. Christine must have been very unhappy in an incurable way. She was stuck. You know how some people are stuck and some are still growing?" He nodded.

"Yet even though James wasn't even getting the sex he wanted, he acted like a kid let loose in a candy store and told he can have whatever he wants. Whatever she did that annoyed him, and despite her getting her way all the time, he still acted more happy than not. You know, like some animals who are so sure you're not going to hurt them that they aren't troubled when you step on their paw by accident. They seem to know you didn't mean to hurt them. He was like that. She was enjoying spending all his money, and he was having a ball."

"An American expression meaning?" asked Kenneth.

"Having a glorious time," said Penny.

"What do you think happened?" asked Kenneth. "Guess."

"I think it was someone who was bothered already. Possibly she met this person down there and further infuriated him or her. Whoever it was may have meant to scare her, and it got out of hand. My best guess would be someone staying at Evelyn's, but not James." Could that be true?

"That leaves Ernie and Ellie."

"True. They're the ones acting the strangest. Either one would fit my vision." Oops. It was out. Would he think her crazy? She had had some men give her a wide berth after she'd told them of certain psychic experiences she'd had.

"You mean you actually saw the Rosewoods in a vision?" He was suddenly very alert.

"What I saw—it was like a dream, probably a premonition—was someone about to choke Evelyn. Not fat like James, no face. No clear gender."

"You're joking. You actually saw this?"

"Umm."

"When?"

"Walking down here. I told you I was worried about Evelyn."

"Do you often have these visions?"

"I've never had a strong visual one before. I'd been thinking about Evelyn maybe being in danger, and suddenly I saw her standing in the kitchen and these hands about to strangle her."

Kenneth broke into her reverie. "Never visual, but you've had intuitions before? Are they usually accurate?"

"Usually. They can be wrong. My wishes can interfere. When I want something very much, the premonition acts a lot like a wish fulfillment dream. But a good intuition, one more likely to be accurate, has a very spontaneous quality. It appears suddenly out of nowhere."

"Like this one did," said Kenneth.

"Right," she said, startled. "Right."

"We can't rely on it," he said. "We'll still need evidence, but it may help us like a hunch helps. I also have a hunch it's someone who was staying with Evelyn, and I don't think it was James either. The time of death is wrong for his doing it when he found her, though he was out and about earlier."

"But I doubt James, the James I know," said Penny, "could kill her and return to eat a big breakfast and not seem the slightest bit ruffled."

"But you said he ate a huge lunch."

"True, but he was in his normal state at breakfast, not in the state he's still in—shock, grief, despair. I grant you the man manages to eat whatever's going on."

"Let's think about the Rosewoods. I like the man. I've got his statement here. Tell me what you think. He's bringing his wife back at nine."

Penny read it. Everything fitted. He was honest about his wife's distaste for Christine and her bitterness toward Germans. He said the two of them went out at seven and walked toward Pwll-du, away from the Three Cliffs area. Then she wanted to go farther on her own when he was ready to turn back. She could walk faster and enjoyed walking more, so she took off, wanting to go all the way to Pwll-du Head, and he walked back to Three Cliffs Store slowly, went in there and bought a paper. James came in the store to get a paper, too, and they got back at 8:30. Unfortunately, his wife was late by twenty minutes.

"This is right, the part I know," Penny said. "I was surprised that the two men had become companionable. The wives certainly weren't. If she went to Pwll-du, she couldn't have murdered Christine, because she was back so soon after he was. Maybe someone in the Pwll-du area saw her. What now?"

"Evelyn can confirm that you were there the whole time, 6:30 to nine?"

Penny laughed. "Yes. She decided to wake me up at seven. If I'd gone out, she'd have noticed. I'd have had to pass through the front hall or the kitchen. She'd have seen me. Do I seem like a murderer?"

He blushed. Good. Maybe he felt speechless for a change.

"Only of the plans I had before this morning. You've had an impact, Miss Weaver. Nothing is the same," he said, looking up, only after he'd said all this.

"Is that bad?"

"No." He smiled. "It's good. But I'm glad you have an alibi for this morning. I don't want you being made a scapegoat. I'm worried enough about John. I hope he's got an alibi."

"You know him?"

"Very well."

"You like him?"

"Not that much, but he's harmless. A sad soul. People love to hang things on the lone eccentric, the one who doesn't fit, and from what you tell me . . . "

"His bulk doesn't fit in my vision image, if that helps."

"It's possible it will somehow. It's nearly eight, and the others will be turning up. Let's get Helen. Be right back, love. Like a cup of tea?"

"Sure."

"Helen spoils me. She told me she'd have a pot ready. I'll be right back. Don't go away." He gave her a deep, searching, affectionate look that told her she'd never get away from him. Nor want to.

TWELVE

They had barely finished Helen's statement, brief, terse, and corroborating Penny's when there was a knock at the door. Penny looked up. Kenneth was talking to Evelyn at the door.

Helen vanished into her apartment. Helen's mother lived with her and could verify that she had been with her until 8:30 when she had opened the P.O. as usual. The shortcut down to Three Cliffs Bay was directly across from the P.O., but Helen hadn't noticed any unusual comings and goings down that path. She'd been too busy to look out much. She gave Kenneth a list of people who could vouch for her having waited on them between 8:30 and ten.

Kenneth turned back to Penny, pushing the door closed. "Are you ready for the next customer, love?"

She smiled. No kisses between interviews, but his speech was flirtatious. She nodded to him.

Evelyn and Harold came in together. Harold was talking fast. Was he nervous? "No, no, Evelyn, you first. I can pop right over to the club and pop right back when you're ready to go home. I know you'll want to get right back. That all right, Inspector? Ladies first? I like to keep the ladies happy. That all right with you, Penny? My, you look official. You're the Inspector's right hand man—woman, I mean. I can't get it right. Evelyn would like to get this over with." He moved closer to Penny and said, conspiratorially, "If you have any pull with the Inspector—"

She smiled at him, amused. Kenneth was watching them. When Harold finally stopped talking, he said, "Is that all right by you, Evelyn, to go first? Are you both all right with Penny sitting in?"

"Of course," Evelyn said and took the chair next to Penny. She also seemed ill at ease. Funny how people could be completely comfortable in their own living rooms or kitchens, but set them down in some semi-official situation, and everything became strange, even the post office where they had come nearly every day for years. Of course, a deposition was a solemn undertaking.

"I'm all nerves, Penny," Evelyn confessed. "Do help me if I forget something."

"I can't do that," said Penny, "but I am to make a note if I think of anything as you talk. Don't worry, Evelyn. You'll do fine. Answer his questions as best you can."

Kenneth had said goodbye to Harold, closed and locked the door. He again took his seat. He had put on his jacket when he went to get Helen. He looked the part of the serious and trusted village constable—a person you could be comfortable with, yet the jacket made you feel respectful. It would be hard to be afraid of him for very long. Yet Evelyn didn't seem to know what to do with her hands.

"How are you doing, Evelyn? Relax. This won't be so bad."

"I'm shattered, Kenneth. To think, a murder right here on Gower, one of my guests. And that nice man. He's in a state. I'll do my best to help. I hope I can remember everything. It has been a long day, and my memory's not as good as it once was."

"Not to worry," said Kenneth comfortably. "I'll just write down what you say, and you can read it over. If you think of anything later, tell us. Give us your impressions about each of the guests you have had with you the last few days, and then we'll go over the events of this morning. Start with Mr. and Mrs. Hampton."

So Evelyn, slightly more at ease, began to talk of the newlyweds, how they had fought at times and been real lovey-dovey, too. She had found them harder than usual because they didn't always have their breakfast on time, and then they would come back in the middle of the day; Christine had wanted to borrow her iron, which she hadn't wanted to lend, so she had ironed one dress for her, but then Christine had asked her again. Plus, she never knew what they'd have for breakfast. Christine had gone out early for a swim several times. They were very awkward about the telly, not agreeing even between themselves on a program, and then the night the Rosewoods came, the Prussian had thrown a real temper.

"No one liked her," said Evelyn. "Those two wore me out. I said to Harold, when we were driving into Swansea this morning, 'I'll be so glad when next Tuesday comes, and they leave.' He said she was a Prussian through and through. You'd never change her. I wasn't even that sorry to hear she was dead. I mean, I didn't want her to die, but, once she was dead, I thought, better her than someone else, Penny, say, or anyone—"

Kenneth was smiling, to encourage her. "I get the feeling she rubbed everyone the wrong way," he said. "Is that what you mean?"

"Oh, yes. I could never see what James Hampton saw in her. She dressed beautifully but was so ugly inside, so thoughtless. You couldn't get through to her. I feel sorry for him. He's all torn up. He's better off, but he can't see that."

Kenneth took her over the morning. She had been wakened by people talking in the hall. That was about six. Penny made a note: "Me, too—who?" So Evelyn had gotten up before her usual time. She had let Christine out at 6:30.

"She was wearing a bathing robe?" asked Kenneth.

"Yes, a bright blue one, to cover up the suit, which wasn't enough to cover her."

"Bikini," said Penny. She managed to keep a straight face.

"I guess," said Evelyn. "She was married. She had no business wearing such a skimpy suit."

"What kind of mood was she in?" asked Kenneth.

"Her Prussian mood: I'll do what I want to. She said she'd be back for breakfast, but I didn't believe it. If I'd said anything, it would have been water off a duck's back, so I didn't bother."

"What did you do between 6:30 and seven?" asked Kenneth.

"I went on into the kitchen and had my bran flakes and juice. I like to eat early when it's shopping day, and all those breakfasts to cook. Then I started cooking the bacon. I cooked enough for five people. I figured, if any was left, Penny and I could have it in a quiche later. At seven, when the Rosewoods went out—I was trying to keep things quiet so Penny could sleep—but that Mrs. Rosewood—she's a French Jew, you know—she yelled that the milk was here. So I told Penny she could eat early. She was awake. That would get her breakfast taken care of."

Evelyn said she had left with Harold for town at ten, and they hadn't gotten back until after three.

"Tell me, Evelyn, have you any idea who might have done this? Between us. You're a good judge of character," said Kenneth.

"I can't figure it out," Evelyn said. "That Prussian was maddening. She even upset that poor sod who hangs around Stanley's store and writes poetry."

"Yes, Penny mentioned that John was upset. Do you know where he is, by chance? I need to talk to him, too."

"Stanley said he was trying to avoid that Prussian, so he took off over to Oxwich, until this Prussian left. She made his ulcer act up. I don't blame whoever did it. If I had to guess, I'd guess that poor old sod did it. Maybe he felt he couldn't get any peace and quiet with her around, so he up and killed her. If he did it, you can be sure she provoked him."

Penny could tell this bothered Kenneth. He cut her short and changed tack. "We know that Harold was out this morning, too. Do you have any idea when he went out or got back?"

Evelyn hesitated. "Most days he goes out at nine and gets the paper on his way back and brings me mine, and we have a cuppa about 10:30. On Fridays he does his walk earlier. Usually goes out at six. He wasn't back when I let the Rosewoods out at seven."

"How could you tell?"

"Harold always gets his milk in right away. He likes to say 'good morning' to the milkman, so he watches for him. But he hadn't gotten his milk in yet at seven. I was getting mine."

Penny made a note that Harold had told her and Evelyn earlier that he was back well before seven. Why would Harold lie?

Kenneth thanked Evelyn, and saw her to the door. Harold would come back after taking her home.

"Bye, Penny. See you later. You have your key, so I won't wait up." She glanced at Kenneth.

Penny smiled. "Right. Thanks, Evelyn. You'd better get some sleep."

"Yes, I'm shattered. Bye now." ~

"Nice landlady you have," said Kenneth. "Doesn't quite trust John, but she likes you very much. You told her we had a date?" His eyes were alight. Yes, even looks were a problem. He was clear across the room, and they were alone again.

"I did," she said. "Evelyn likes you. She says you're a little wild. Do you think you could practice being circumspect?"

He looked startled, as if to say, me? Wild? "If that will make you happy."

"I don't know about happy, but it keeps me functional," said Penny, looking down at her notes. "You have quite an effect even at twelve feet."

He moved closer, looked like he was going to scoop her up and hug her but thought better of it, and went behind the table again. There was something to be said for tables. "I'll be circumspect now and wild later." He grinned. "Any thoughts on what we've got so far?"

Penny focused her mind back on the two interviews. "I think Helen's out of it, though it's possible she observed something in that 8:30–ten period that she hadn't yet realized is significant. Or it may be that the murderer didn't come back this way but walked back along the cliffs. Two things in Evelyn's statement. I remember, too, being waked at six by voices in the hall. We could find out whose voices and what they talked about? Then there's a funny discrepancy between when Harold says he got back and Evelyn's observation that it was after seven, as he said to me and Evelyn this afternoon that he'd come back and made his breakfast and was listening to the seven a.m. BBC news. Something's fishy there."

"Good you noticed those things. I'm glad I asked you to sit in." He grinned, gave her a long, erotic look, and then said, "Whoops, circumspection!" and shifted to his usual placid look. "Let's ask Harold about that. Want a warm-up on your tea?" She nodded. "I'll be right back, love."

He returned carrying a plate of Welsh cakes and digestive biscuits and two fresh mugs of tea. "You do manage to charm all the women into fussing over you," she said. "How did you know I liked Welsh cakes?"

"I didn't," he said. "I like Welsh cakes. The biscuits are for you."

"You're like that, are you?"

"No. You may have all the Welsh cakes and all the biscuits, too, if you will . . . " He stopped and stared at her, as if willing her to guess what he was thinking.

"You're bribing me?"

"No, tempting you."

"I'm already tempted. I'm trying to stay rational. How about sharing the Welsh cakes and the biscuits?"

"You are a very smart woman, not easy to tempt."

"Tempting has come and gone. We're working on sanity now."

"Oh, it's like that, is it?"

"Yes, your eyes are giving me looks that qualify them to be described in a novel as 'bedroom eyes.'"

"Are they now?"

"Could you very sweetly bring a little circumspection into their behavior until we get all these depositions done?"

"I could sweetly do that and many other things," he said, not changing his look but, if anything, turning up the intensity.

"I won't be able to look at you," she said. "Please?"

"My love, I will do as you request. I will behave perfectly."

A knock at the door. Penny sipped her tea while Kenneth jumped up and let in Harold.

Harold strode in, nodded to Penny, and took a seat. "Glad to help, Inspector. This is a terrible thing." Kenneth let him talk some. "Want to keep things as easy for Evelyn as I can. She and I aren't spring chickens any more. We both came here, moved into our bungalows twelve years in September. Hal was a great friend. She's had a time adjusting to his being gone. I try to help out."

Penny smiled, thinking of his faithful carrying of Evelyn to town every Friday and also to the doctor. She knew, too, that he'd been right there when Hal was ill, and Evelyn was visiting him every day in the hospital. She liked the man even though she didn't know him that well. She felt he sometimes talked to keep from being known. About his deep feelings she couldn't guess. Did Evelyn know him any better? Maybe.

"That Prussian woman was plain rude to Evelyn. It burned me up. Evelyn works so hard. At her age, she's going from morning to night. She loves doing for people and keeping up her garden, but that Prussian barged in when she wasn't wanted. Then when she was wanted, for breakfast, so we could get off to town on time—. That's partly my fault. I like to get back by three, get my chores done, and go down for a pint, Constable, oh, sorry, it's Inspector now.

Kenneth nodded. He hadn't asked a single question yet. "Tell me, Mr. Austen, what time did you go out for your walk this morning?"

"My constitutional? Let's see. I got up at 5:30, had a cup of tea. Headed out right on six. I wanted to get back by quarter of seven and make my breakfast so I could eat it while I watched the seven o'clock BBC news. I did the circuit to Pobbles, along the cliffs, and then back through the village. I was having my cornflakes when the BBC came on."

Kenneth didn't act surprised. "Did you see Christine Hampton while you were out? She went that way about 6:30."

Harold seemed startled but adapted quickly. Why had that startled him, Penny wondered, since he himself had told her he had met Christine when he was coming back.

"6:30, eh? Oh, I met her coming through the village. It was on that lane that goes down to the footpath. I think it was about quarter of, could have been twenty of, when we met. She wouldn't even exchange a greeting. I was home by ten of, maybe quarter of. She could have been walking slowly."

The more he talked, the more Kenneth and Penny exchanged looks that said, "Can't seem to get his lie fixed to suit him, can he?" Penny wondered if Kenneth would mention the milk.

His next question was: "How much did you actually talk to Christine Hampton?"

Again Harold seemed baffled by the question. "Talk to her?"

"Yes," said Kenneth. "You speak as if you knew her well."

"Not well," said Harold. He acted ill at ease for the first time. "But I know her type. I've met Prussians before, and I know what they did to London during the blitz. I was in the Civil Defense, and we'd go around every morning and pull people out of the rubble. You couldn't get some people to go into shelters. Terrible, it was. Bodies, pieces of bodies. People still alive but going to die no matter what you did. I hate the Germans. They aren't our enemies now, but they should never have let East and West Germany get together again. Never trust a Prussian."

Kenneth let him run down and then asked again, "How much did you talk to this German woman?"

"Talk to her?"

"Yes."

"I heard a lot about her. I went over for a cuppa the day after they arrived. We were having our tea, and they came in. We didn't talk much. The husband seemed all right, a good enough chap, off his head about her. Soon as she spoke, I knew she was Prussian. She was stuck up like every Prussian I ever met. I didn't want to talk to her."

"You said you spoke to her this morning, and she wouldn't talk to you. Can you explain why you spoke to her today?"

Harold smoothed his hand over his head, although every hair was in place. He stared down at the table, then looked up. "Not so easily. Hard to explain. To be polite? Sometimes you feel like saying 'good morning' even when you don't especially like a person. No reason to let her rudeness influence me."

"Mr. Austen, we've been thinking it might be good for me to stay nearer to Evelyn's house. Sometimes, one murder sets off another. We don't know who killed Christine, but I'm concerned that Penny, Evelyn, and the other guests might not be safe. If you have a spare room, would you mind if I stayed with you a few days? You wouldn't have to worry about my meals, but I could keep a better eye on Pobbles House."

"Like that, is it?" said Harold. "That would be fine. I'm used to it just being me, and I thought I could protect Evelyn, but why not? You want to bring your duds up tonight?"

"I think so, yes, if you're certain it's all right. We have a murderer on the loose, possibly among us. We can't be too careful."

"Right-o." Harold acted a bit dazed. Could he be the murderer? Had he killed Christine? Had there been some conversation that had set off his rage at the Germans?

Kenneth asked a few more routine questions and then let him go.

Then Kenneth turned to her. "What do you think?"

"He's lying, and he's very uneasy, but I can't understand why."

"I can't either. I thought I knew the man, but now I'm not so sure I do."

THIRTEEN

The next day being Saturday and Kenneth not needing her help, Penny decided to give herself an emotional break from both Kenneth and the case and take off on a walk. She would, however, go down to Three Cliffs Bay and look around, in case there were any clues they had missed. She'd awakened with the feeling that she should go back there. She hadn't slept much.

Kenneth was going to hang around Evelyn's. He and Harold would fix Penny's bedroom door so it could be locked. Kenneth wanted her safe behind a lock. Evelyn and James had talked non-stop through breakfast, and the Rosewoods had eaten early and left for the day. Kenneth had promised them an estimate on how long they would need to stay in the area. He had taken their passports and hoped he wouldn't have to detain them long. He also had other paperwork to do in his office in Swansea later that afternoon.

He had so quickly become large in her consciousness that Penny wanted time alone to think about it. Too much, too fast. She found herself cutting through the playing field for the village children and then along a footpath to the library. She wanted to talk to Lucy. She might have a fresh perspective on the murder. Did she know Lucy well enough to tell her what was going on with Kenneth?

She'd been hit before, as if by a ton of bricks, by love, but this felt different. He acted as madly in love as she was. Possible? How could it have happened so quickly? Why did they trust each other so much? They had scarcely met and, though they were already working together easily, they hadn't had time yet for getting acquainted, talking about ordinary things.

Maybe he was playing around. Maybe he treated all single women he met, who acted the least bit susceptible, like this. She wanted to believe that it was different for him, too. He had told her the night before that he had been idealizing finding a Welsh woman, not an American, and settling down. Moving out of his flat in Llangennith and buying his own cottage there when his thirty years were up. He acknowledged that Penny was having a big effect on him, that it was all a little alarming. She could scarcely remember what it had been like before she met him.

What was it Lucy had said once, that when you found someone it would work with, and it wasn't wishful thinking, you would know. She had undergone a major life change in the last twenty-four hours. What next?

She was still a poet. She was out for a walk on Gower. Her stick, her hiking boots, her knapsack with some biscuits and tea in it for lunch. She had several hours on her own and not even another date planned with Kenneth. But her thoughts were full of him. His kisses came back to her. His hands at her waist. His tongue . . . .

They had had their pint at the Pen Maen Inn, then leaving his car in the car park when the inn closed, had gone walking, their arms around each other's waists, down to the sea by the path that led first to the old castle. He had had his flashlight. No one else was out. The pubs had closed at eleven.

They found a comfortable place in the dunes not far from the castle. He spread a blanket he had thought to bring along. The castle ruins were dim shadows against a sky behind them where a moon was rising.

The sea spread itself ahead of them. How many times she'd looked at it, aching with love that seemed doomed never to be answered. Its gold look, when the afternoon sun caught it just right, had seemed like the golden liquid love itself. Now it was silvery where the brighter stars and the moonlight were touching it. Lights winked over near Big Tor in the caravan camp on the hill. But more than the lights, she noticed the huge blackness around them. She'd never felt so safe. Only the stars could see them. She had longed so for everything he might want to do to her. Her body was like a violin, precious, beautifully made, but hidden in a closet for years. All those love fantasies, but no one touching her body, waking it up.

"Penny," he said. "I'm going to kiss you."

"Hmmm," she said. She yielded to his lips, clinging to him in her ecstatic helplessness until his tongue released her, and she collapsed into a happy heap, turning her face into his stomach, wanting to cry and laugh, and not being able to do either. Finally, she whispered—he had lifted her up and cradled her head against his shoulder, and tucked the blanket around her tenderly—"Oh, Kenneth, you make me feel so good. Why is it so good, Kenneth? I don't understand."

"We were ready," he said. He clasped her to him. They lay quiet a long while, comfortable, his hands stroking her face, moving over her, then kissing her when she thought she couldn't wait any longer. The wind reached them, but they had the blanket for warmth. Between kisses they talked of what they wanted for the rest of their lives. He had five more years until he could retire. He wanted to grow a garden and have a milk cow; make cream cheese, and sell it. Have more time to read. She hoped to give more time to writing. She wanted to be able to live wherever she wanted to for six months out of the year.

"In Wales?" he asked, lifting himself up so that he could look into her eyes. His eyes looked very happy, shining with love and peacefulness. How could she not say, "Maybe in Wales."

He had kissed her again. Then he had said, "We've had a long, tiring day, love, and, as beautiful as you are, you need your sleep to stay beautiful. Plus, I don't want to overwhelm you. We're moving pretty fast for two people who have known each other for one day. So we should wrap you up in this blanket and throw you in the sea."

He quickly flung the blanket around her and lifted her in his arms. She knew she weighed one hundred and seventy pounds. Her middle age had padded her in breasts and thighs, around her belly. But how easily he had lifted her. He couldn't weigh much more himself, maybe two hundred, and he was a little taller. She felt the hard bands of muscle in his arms. He was all muscle.

"You wouldn't do that!" she protested.

"I wouldn't?" He kissed her nose where it stuck out of the blanket.

"I believe you would," she said, "but no doubt you'll think ahead to the problem of getting me back home, a poor, wet, chilled American, not used to the British custom of swimming in fifty degree weather with a forty mile an hour wind blowing, and you'll decide to wait until it's warmer."

"I might," he said, starting to walk through the dunes, his feet awkward in the deep sand, downwards toward the sea. "Then again . . . "

He stopped and kissed her again, this time on her eyelids. "I can see the stars reflected in your eyes," he said. "You have wise eyes, grey like Athena."

"I also have powerful intuitions," she said, "and I pray to Athena when I'm in a spot, and she turns up every so often. So beware."

He laughed and set her upon her feet, adjusted the blanket around her shoulders, and put his arm around her waist tightly. "Let's go look at the sea in the moonlight before I take you home. It's a lovely night and I promise not to throw you in tonight, but one night we'll go swimming in the sea by moonlight. It's a pleasure you wouldn't want to miss."

She shivered, suddenly afraid. Why? Because it was happening so fast? Did one fear pleasure? Very intense harmonies were scary? You had to get used to them? She hadn't had so much pleasure all at once in a long time. He seemed to understand her and her body so well, as if, without being aware of it, she had sent him all the messages he had needed. Possible?

So, the tide retreating at something like one in the morning, they had walked together by the same sea where they had come together fourteen hours earlier and found Christine's body. Christine had lost her chance, and they had theirs. Briefly. It's all brief, she thought, as they walked along, arm in arm, without speaking, letting the silver edges of the waves spread up the beach toward them, falter, fall back, and disappear, leaving flecks of foam silver, too, in the moonlight.

She had been scarcely aware of turning the stile gate, but there suddenly was Lucy's little green car and the library. Yes, she needed to talk to Lucy. Her head was spinning with all that had happened. She didn't want to change it; she didn't have to understand it. But she wanted to be wise. To have a mind other than her own listen and react. Say, "Great!" or "Are you sure?"

As soon as she entered, she wished she hadn't. The poet John was piling books into his knapsack. He and Lucy looked up. How much she wanted to see Lucy, and how much she didn't want to see John.

"Good morning, Penny," said Lucy and handed John the last book.

He was watching Penny. "Good morning, Miss Weaver," he said stiffly.

She didn't say "Call me Penny." She didn't want him to get any more familiar than he already was. She merely nodded. Then she remembered that Kenneth did want to talk to him, for his own protection at the least.

"John was planning to hide out until the German woman left," said Lucy, "and I've told him she's dead. He can return to his favorite haunts."

"You heard then?" asked Penny.

"I'm sorry, Miss Weaver," said John. "I think death is terrible. So final. But she was a very bothersome woman. I'm glad she can't bother me any more."

"No," said Penny, "unless she comes back to haunt you." As soon as she said the words, she wished she could take them back.

John dropped the book he had been holding. It was one of her favorite books: *Gower Legends*. Penny stooped down and got it for him.

"Why would she do that, Miss Weaver?" John asked, as he took the book.

"I don't know why I said that. Don't worry about it. I was thinking about her having been murdered."

"Murdered?" he asked. He turned pale. She thought he was going to pass out.

Lucy's head jerked up from the filing she'd started. "True, Penny? I thought it was a drowning."

"Probably not," said Penny. "There's an investigation going on that assumes she was killed deliberately. But"—she turned to John—"the detective, Inspector Morgan, does want to talk to you."

"To me? Why to me?"

She wanted to joke, "to make sure you didn't kill her," but John was not in a joking mood, nor could she imagine him in one ever. Here was one certifiable case of a man with no sense of humor. He was weak and without defenses where most people have some strength, some reserves of pride or something. Even James had guts. This man left her utterly cold.

"Why me?" he repeated, in a cloying way. "I haven't been around here. I've been over in Oxwich. I walked over to bring back my library books. I just learned that this German woman was dead. What have I done?" Was he obsessed or guilty?

Penny told herself to be clear and patient. Lucy looked worried.

"The Inspector is talking to everyone who had significant interactions with the dead woman. She made a lot of people angry, so he wants to hear their stories." Why should he be excused from the problems the rest of them had now?

"I wasn't angry at her," said John.

"You left town to avoid her," said Lucy, as though surprised he couldn't admit to any anger.

"Not because I was angry," John insisted. He had a stubborn look on his face. "I have to go. It's nothing to do with me. Tell the Inspector it wasn't me. I wasn't angry at her."

Lucy decided to take a hand. "It's a routine investigation, John. They're talking to a lot of people. Penny, didn't Inspector Morgan talk to you, too?"

Penny flashed on his face in the moonlight bent over hers. Talk to me, yes, he did, she thought. She couldn't help smiling. When she looked up at Lucy, light danced in her eyes. "Yes, of course, he is talking to all of us," she said. "If you'll stay here, John, I'll call him. He's at Evelyn's, and he can come round. He'll probably want to see you, too, Lucy. He's checking all leads, to try to understand."

She looked over to where John had been. He was gone. The man could move quickly when he wanted to. She felt like running after him, but that probably wasn't appropriate. "Can I borrow your phone, Lucy?"

"Of course."

"Hi, Evelyn, it's Penny."

"Oh, hello, Penny. Is everything all right?"

"Fine. Listen, tell Kenneth that John, that poet—he wanted to talk to him—he left the library in a hurry and may be heading back for Oxwich or toward Stanley's—I'm not sure. Get Kenneth on the line, and I'll look and see which way he went." She put down the phone, rushed out the door, and saw John loping across the golf links. "He's going a good clip across the Golf Links," she said to Kenneth when he came on.

"Who, love?"

"That poet, John. Didn't you want to see him?"

"Eventually. He'll keep. Let him go. You all right?"

"Yes." She smiled. She had never felt so all right. "Yes, very all right."

"That's the main thing," he said. "Harold and I have about got your door fixed. I forgot to ask you if you'd have dinner with me tonight. Will you?"

"I will," she said. "What time?"

"Six?"

"Sure. Tell Evelyn not to cook for me, okay?"

"I will, love. Maybe she'll coddle James a bit tonight. You should see them."

"I can imagine," she said. "I'm going to walk awhile after I leave the library. Probably get back at four. I'll be waiting for you at six."

"Great. Ta."

He rang off. When she looked back at Lucy, she was smiling. "Ah ha, the Inspector has asked you to dinner?"

Penny glanced around the library. No one else. "Yes," she said. "It's moving rather quickly, Lucy. To be blunt, I'm worried."

"You don't look worried. You look quite happy, relaxed, gleeful. Sit down and tell me what you're worried about."

"The speed mainly. I only met the man yesterday."

"You're both about fifty, right?"

Penny nodded. "I am. He acts like he is. I don't actually know."

"Kenneth has had some pain, same as you. An earlier marriage didn't work out. No kids. He has been on his own about ten years now. He's a real treasure, Penny. I wouldn't worry. If it feels good, that sounds like a good sign to me." She smiled and went back to checking in books.

"Are you saying, because we've both been through a lot of pain, that we're able to make up our minds quickly? Read people better?" Penny looked toward the door, but she still had Lucy to herself.

"Probably," said Lucy. "Sounds like a good theory. Don't you think, as we live, we get so we can sense what people are like more quickly. You and Kenneth are both real grownups. So hard to find. So hard to be a grownup. So few of us around." She laughed, affectionately, easily, playfully, at herself, at Penny. "What a good thing that you and Kenneth found each other. He's a lovely man. One of my very favorite people. So free of the impulse to stereotype, to fit women, or anybody, into a pegged hole. Very open to what happens, as it happens. I think it's great you two like each other. Perfect."

"Did I say that we liked each other?"

"You didn't have to," said Lucy. "You shine with it. It's coming out your pores."

"Is it?"

"Yes." Lucy laughed in that warm and affectionate way of hers.

"Oh, dear."

"Not to worry," said Lucy. "Most people don't notice things the way I do. Kenneth would have noticed."

"John?"

"Oh, dear me, no. Very distracted by his own worries. Most people are. Pretty much, you can trust the people who will be able to tell what is going on. I bet Evelyn is pleased. She admires Kenneth Morgan. Always had a lot of respect for him, likes to coddle him, when he'll let her."

"She's maybe going to worry about my virtue."

Lucy laughed loudly and happily. "Your virtue! It's that bad, is it? Good goddess, Penny! You two do move quickly."

"No, no," Penny protested. "Not yet, but it's coming. You think Evelyn will kill me?"

"Not if you marry him. Though common law would be all right with her, too. Evelyn believes in loyalty. She's not much with bed-hopping."

"Neither am I. Loyalty's important to me, too."

"Evelyn's no prude, Penny."

"You sure she can handle this?"

"If it's as good as you say, Evelyn will be delighted. She has a lot of affection for you, Penny, and for Kenneth. If you two are happy, she'll be happy."

"Thanks, Lucy. That helps. I'd better get out on the cliffs, write this man a poem."

"By all means. We must keep that Muse busy. You're still an important poet."

"Thanks, Lucy. I needed that. You don't think I'm a fool then?"

"I do. I think you're a great fool. A very lucky fool. Go on with you. Let me know when I need to worry about your virtue."

As it turned out, though she had never wanted so much to write, she didn't write a poem that day. Her new love feelings for Kenneth having settled a few notches deeper because of Lucy's happy response, she decided to follow the path to the right of the golf links, which she had seen John taking, not because she wanted to catch him but out of curiosity. A narrow dirt road led into the area where there were many summer shacks.

Evelyn had told her that some of these flimsy houses had been there since she was a girl. Her family used to rent one and come down for a few weeks in the summer. She walked past the water tower, keeping it on her left. She had heard that John lived in one of these empty houses in the winter. She wondered if he might hide there in the summer, too. She had a hunch that he wasn't going back to Oxwich, and that he was going to hide. John was scared. Why was he so intent on not talking to Kenneth? If people were inclined to scapegoat him, why didn't he take his chance to clear himself?

John did get up very early. Harold said he'd met him sometimes when he walked before breakfast. Maybe John knew something, had had another scene with Christine and killed her? Unlikely. He had acted surprised when she'd told him Christine had been murdered. Yet he had acted very ill at ease.

Penny came to a cluster of twenty or so summer cottages, some dilapidated, some repaired. Once, at a distance, she thought she saw John, but, if it was he, he vanished into a shack. When she got closer, there was no sign of him.

She didn't find him that morning, but she did find something else. She walked on over to the castle and down to the beach through the deep drifts of sand among the dunes, and made her way across the little river, carrying her shoes, over to the roped off area where Christine's body had been. The ropes were still there. She wasn't sure what she was looking for exactly, but she continued to have a strong sense that she should be here.

Then she saw it, right next to one of the stakes, washed into a ripple in the sand where the tide had tugged at the stake: a little bright blue stone. She picked it up. It was a sapphire—with a blue fire in its depths when it caught the light. It was beautifully faceted. A real jewel. Christine's?

It looked familiar. She'd seen a stone like this on someone's hand. But where was the ring and why was this stone here now? She wrapped the sapphire carefully in a napkin she'd had in with her lunch and tucked it into the pocket of her backpack. If only she could remember who had worn the ring it came from.

FOURTEEN

As she walked along the slatted boards of the walk that led to the main footpath through the golf links, through the village, and home, she tried to follow the strands. If John had done it, would he have ambled so casually into the library? If he bore no responsibility, why had he run off? Harold seemed more sinister, too. It bothered her the way these people, after fifty years, still hated the Germans. Christine was the real scapegoat. It was very confusing. Why had she imagined that she had a role to play?

When she knocked on the lounge door, Evelyn's cheerful voice called, "Come in." James and Evelyn were having tea. "Penny, have you had a good day? Where did you walk to?" Evelyn asked, as if it had been a normal day.

"I've been over to Three Cliffs Bay and around the dunes near the castle," she said and, as Evelyn stood up, "and I'd love a cup of tea if there's one left in the pot."

Evelyn said, "Sit down and talk to James."

Penny wished she hadn't mentioned Three Cliffs Bay, but James didn't seem perturbed. Had he heard her? He looked better, more present, less distracted. He was neatly dressed in a dark suit and tie, and a perfectly ironed shirt—Evelyn's doing? He seemed ready for whatever came next.

"How are you doing, James?" she asked.

"Pretty well, Penny. I wanted to thank you for staying with me yesterday. I was in a daze. Evelyn has been looking after me today. It is hard, you know." His voice faltered. "But doing tolerably well."

She nodded. "I'm glad. It's all any of us can do, try to cope with what Life turns up." She thought of all the raging happiness that Life had turned up for her, and James had had his happiness taken away. That slightly pompous air that James had had before all this had happened was returning now.

Was he enjoying his status as a bereaved person? Maybe he hadn't been that bereaved? The man was so infantile, and yet intelligent in a canny, manipulative way. She had been so sure James was innocent, and yet?

Evelyn had returned with her tea and poured some more for James and herself. "Have a Welsh cake, Penny?" She gestured toward the plate. "My stars, they're all gone."

James smiled guiltily. "Sorry, Penny, I hadn't known you'd be coming. I can't resist Mrs. Trueblood's delicious cakes. She spoils me, Penny. She has been so very kind."

"Never mind, I'll make some more, Penny," said Evelyn. "I can offer you digestive biscuits?"

"No, no. I'll be eating dinner soon. Kenneth told you?" She hadn't meant to mention this in front of James. Her happiness seemed too big to bring into this room in which the restraint that grief imposes was still large.

But Evelyn was attuned to her need for privacy, also to James's need to remain center stage and relatively unperturbed, so she said, "Yes, I know, Penny. I'm doing an evening meal for James tonight. It helps him not to have to go out looking for his dinner. Let me know when you'll be here."

"I will," said Penny. "I'll go take a nap now. When do you turn on the hot water? Is a shower at five possible?"

"Yes, Penny. It's on now."

"Great." She stood up.

"Penny," said James. "Will you be seeing the inspector?"

"Yes. Why?"

"Would you tell him I don't feel like talking yet about Christine. Maybe Monday, if that's all right?"

"Tell him yourself. He's coming here at six, James." Was James afraid of Kenneth?

"I can't, Penny. I feel so bad." He sounded fake. What was going on here?

Evelyn said, "I don't mind telling the inspector you'd like to wait until Monday. I'll probably be seeing him when he comes."

Evelyn to the rescue. The man was well enough to eat all the Welsh cakes and converse normally with two women. Why couldn't he give his own message? It might be important for Kenneth to know that James was scared to talk to him. She looked first at Evelyn and then at James. "James, the inspector is trying very hard to find out who killed your wife. We're all trying to help him. We've all had our turn: Evelyn, Harold next door, the Rosewoods. Even the lady in the post office. All the pieces have to be on the table before he can see how to solve the puzzle. The inspector won't be unkind. The sooner you feel up to talking to him, the better. He and you had worked out a time tomorrow?"

"We had. Tomorrow at two."

"Why don't you see how you feel tomorrow? We all want to get this over with quickly. The Rosewoods can't go back to America until the inspector lets them. If you possibly can—."

"All right, Penny. I'll see how I do tomorrow. I feel so dreadful. I can't think properly. I can't even remember what happened exactly."

Evelyn jumped in, soothing, reassuring. "James, you're so much better today. By tomorrow you'll be more fit. The inspector's very understanding. Do your best. I was nervous myself. My stars!" She laughed. "If I can do it, you can, James."

He looked at Evelyn, reassured, as a child is by his mother's presence in a dark room. "All right, Penny, I'll wait and see. I hope I'll do what he wants. I will try."

Penny smiled at him. She'd been tricked into playing his mum again. "I'll see you both later. I'm off to have a shower and a rest." And a little peace of mind, she thought.

Kenneth took her into Swansea that evening to an Indian restaurant where they served wonderful curries. After the initial checking in with each other, they had ended up talking mostly about the case.

Kenneth smiled his complete enjoyment of her as the tall, turbaned waiter set down a platter piled high with a mound of rice, with curried beef over it, dhal to one side, with a little container of thick yoghurt, and a sprig of coriander for garnish.

"Lovely," she sighed. "I love curry. How did you know?"

"I guessed," he said, "but so far I've been guessing quite well about you. The more I learn about this case though, the more baffled I am. I brought you here so we could forget it for awhile—"

She held his eyes. "You trust me to help you as you think out loud? Do I mind? No. I'm thinking about it, too."

"You're perfect," he said. "You're right with me all the time."

"It's not hard. We've gotten very quickly attuned to one another. It feels good. I always wanted this."

He moved his leg and let it rest against hers and took her hand. Her left hand. It meant he couldn't eat, but his food wasn't there yet. Fortunately, all she needed was her right hand. "Don't get me so excited I can't eat."

"Is this too much?"

"No." She took a mouthful of curry and rice. "Delicious. Want a taste?"

"Umm." He took his fork and she moved her platter toward him.

"You're right. Good, as always. I'll let you try the eggplant when it comes. My all-time favorite, though the beef is my second favorite. Where were we?"

"You wanted to think aloud about the case."

He poured more wine in her glass with his free hand.

"Right. So these people we've interviewed so far? It may not be any of them. I'll have some people tomorrow from Swansea help me make the rounds of the caravan camp and the summer cottages, the people most likely to have seen anything or been at the beach. Not many holiday people go down before nine, but several left early from Evelyn's. I think our puzzle will be solved by understanding what was going on with those folks, Stanley, Harold, the lot. By Tuesday I'll have to decide whether to turn it over to the Major Crimes Department. If I can get a handle on it, that won't be necessary, and I can send the Rosewoods home. How does James seem to you?"

His platter had arrived. As good as her beef was, she was glad she would get to taste his eggplant. Penny waited for the waiter to leave, Kenneth having assured him that the food was delicious and the wine top quality. "I think James is recovering too quickly. He wanted me to ask you to delay your meeting with him until Monday."

Kenneth lifted his eyebrows.

"I wouldn't carry his message, and then he said he'd wait and see. He's nervous though, says he can't remember very well."

Kenneth nodded. "What he forgets may be as significant as what he remembers."

"The man is really infantile but canny."

"I know," said Kenneth. He pushed his platter near hers. "Try the eggplant."

"Lovely! I had it once years ago. I've tried unsuccessfully to make it, but this is close. Yum."

Kenneth withdrew his hand so he could use both knife and fork in British fashion. "He's the most likely. He was out early, and he didn't meet up with Ernest Rosewood until nearly 8:30. Plus, he found her, though Joyce doesn't think anyone did it as late as quarter of ten. He could have killed her and gone back to discover her. He's so histrionic it's hard to tell what he's feeling, and he acts terrified when I ask even simple questions."

"Some father problem, I'm betting," said Penny. "He loves to be babied. Christine didn't though. She demanded that he indulge her. The man loves to eat, and she was always on him, wanted him to skip meals. She held sex over him, too. They had some, I could pick up, but not as much as he wanted. We all heard her innuendoes—pretty sickening."

"So he's a mama's boy who found himself a sex-mama. But his sex-mama rationed sex and food."

"While spending all his money."

"He didn't seem bothered by how she spent his money?"

"Not one whit," said Penny. "He loved it. He bought her new clothes, laid on big dinners, with champagne."

"They were newlyweds. Was he a virgin?"

"Apparently not. I bet not very experienced, though. She'd been married before. She told Evelyn he had, too, when young. What got me was how happy he seemed, despite the fact that she was always on him about something, and you couldn't make Christine happy."

"People are sometimes happy when they have no cause to be," he said. He took a sip of his wine and held her eyes. "I have cause. I think I have cause. But my happiness is out of all bounds in relation to what I know about you. If you browbeat me."

"I couldn't. I haven't got it in me."

"But if you did, say—" His eyes were intense. "I'm so far gone, I'm not sure I'd notice."

"You'd notice. You'd take action. You'd dump me in the ocean. Your feelings are strong, but you can fend for yourself. You're testing me right now. You want to know how I feel."

"I do." His eyes didn't move. She looked and looked into them. The soul was visible in the eyes, she'd heard. His soul seemed visible in his.

"I trust you," she said, "as much as I ever have another human being, and I don't know why. I don't understand very well how I feel or why. It's a lot to get used to. I'm scared sometimes. Will you continue to like me as you learn more? I've scared a lot of men off. I'm so unconventional. I take such risks."

"Two reasons why I like you. Why don't we take it as it comes?"

"Okay. Now eat."

He laughed. "You're bossy, too."

"Sometimes I am. I've needed to be. So are you."

"Touche. Let's talk about James. It's possible he killed Christine. But you don't think so? Your instincts are better than mine here. I'm inclined to trust your finely tuned intuition, though we still have to gather evidence. The times have to work."

"Right." She wasn't eating very fast, though she was hungry. "Remind me: who had the opportunity?" She took a big bite of beef and rice.

"All right. At seven the Rosewoods went toward Pwll-du. They separated, and he came back. She kept on toward Pwll-du, he says, and she confirms. He went in the store about eight, and he met James there."

"The men got back at 8:30. We're depending on the Rosewoods' word that they went toward Pwll-du and that she kept going when he turned back."

"Right."

"So he had a possible hour or so, and she had one and half, nearly two. She got back about ten of nine."

"Could a person go very far away from Three Cliffs and get all the way back there and then to Evelyn's in the time we've got?"

"I don't think so. If she kept going, she wouldn't have had time to get to Three Cliffs or he to get there and then back to the store. He said they'd gotten pretty far before he turned back."

"I'll ask him again," said Kenneth.

"She would have had to come back along the same road, if she went to Three Cliffs. Why would she want to find Christine? My impression was that she was avoiding her."

"How far is it to Pwll-du Head from Stanley's store—have you ever timed it?"

"Forty-five minutes at least."

"Then from Stanley's store to where we found Christine?"

"About twenty minutes, whichever way you go. From Evelyn's you can get there in ten, if you walk briskly, go through the village, and take the footpath behind the dunes. Or fifteen, if the tide is high and you have to walk over the dunes and down instead of along the beach."

"So if they only walked ten minutes toward Pwll-du, or not at all (it's only their word), they could easily have gone down to Three Cliffs."

"But what would have been their motive?"

"Motives are the hardest part," said Kenneth. "But it looks like they both had the opportunity, and we have no way of verifying that they went as far toward Pwll-du as they said. But if they're telling the truth, the time fits. They walked toward it for twenty, twenty-five minutes. He goes back about 7:30. She goes on for twenty minutes. She spends five at Pwll-du at eight. It takes her forty, forty-five minutes to get back to Stanley's and five to Evelyn's?"

"It makes sense. I don't like her much, but she seemed to be genuinely enjoying Gower. I can't see her trying to find Christine. They knew where she went swimming. But they wanted to see as much of Gower as possible before they left. Still, we should keep an open mind."

He had polished off his curry and was eyeing hers. "You're not already filled up?"

"I am. Would you like some curried beef?"

"I would. I wanted to buy us dessert, too."

"I'll pass on dessert. It was delicious, but I'm stuffed."

"James now. He went out at 7:30, got to Stanley's about 8:20?"

"Right."

"We don't know yet where he went."

"No. He may not remember. He was out long enough and would seem motivated to walk to meet Christine. He had time. He came back for breakfast and left again about nine. James seemed genuinely worried, and at breakfast he acted normal."

"What is normal for James?"

128

"Fatuous. Placating. Greedy. Guilty."

"You've nailed his character. What about my character?"

She lifted her wine glass and looked at him thoughtfully. He was so much fun, so easy, so clear to her. "You?"

"Me."

"It's hard to express."

"Try."

"Not fatuous."

"Oh, good."

"You knew that."

"I was hoping."

"You're clear. I see you like I see something in a glass container. You have a certain steadiness. You attend to people but keep your own counsel."

"I like this. Continue."

She sipped her wine. "There's no emotional garbage clinging to your words or in your tone. You talk straight. The words go in clean, like arrows to their mark. Ah, 'winged words,' like in Homer. Maybe that was what Homer meant: straight talking. No nonsense!"

"Not placating?"

"Definitely not."

"What about the greed?"

"You do have a healthy appetite."

"Definitely. I could have eaten all your curry as well as mine."

"Really?"

"I admit to my greed. There's that. A point in my favor?"

"I haven't said you're greedy. You can control your appetite. You shared your eggplant curry. You pay attention to other people, in, say, a restaurant. You did, however, look interested in my beef curry when it was clear I wasn't likely to finish it."

"You noticed."

"I said you had a healthy appetite. I rather like your appetites."

His hand reached for hers, and his other leg pressed against hers under the table.

"But," she went on, smiling, "you do know how to delay gratification."

"True."

"A mark of an adult."

"I'm glad you think I'm an adult."

"You've treated me as an equal, not like your mum, not like your child."

"Very good. What a relief."

"I think I have room for dessert," she said.

He looked astonished. "Your appetite is healthy, too, then?"

"It is," she said.

"But I am guilty."

"Guilty?".

"I think I love you."

FIFTEEN

The last thing Penny expected to be doing on Sunday morning, after another very satisfying sensual conclusion to an evening with Kenneth, was taking a walk with Ernie. Things had been strained at breakfast. Penny was so happy that she was distracted, but she had noticed Eloise ate hardly anything and couldn't seem to stomach James, who packing away an enormous breakfast in his usual blithe manner. He was definitely recovering.

Ellie excused herself after having scarcely touched her wonderful platter of bacon, eggs, and sausage, to say she was off to Pwll-du for the day. She needed to get away. Ernie acted like he wanted to argue, but he didn't. "You'll be careful?"

"Since we're stuck here, I might as well take the walks I wanted to take."

"We might drive to—"

"I need to be alone, Ernie. I'll be fine. I'll meet you back here at six."

"Go on then. Tonight let's try that Indian restaurant in Swansea we noticed."

She smiled. "Good idea."

Penny didn't mention the excellent curries she and Kenneth had had there. Evelyn and Lucy were aware of what was going on with Kenneth, but she was wary of the other guests knowing anything. Harold's suspicions she'd leave to Kenneth.

She was startled when Ernie turned to her, and asked her if she'd walk with him this morning. He'd like to see the old castle again and Three Cliffs Bay.

Penny had hoped to write. Kenneth had plenty to do that morning. True, she and Kenneth wanted to know more about Ernie. Here was her chance. What if he got amorous? What if he was the killer? Was this wise? "I had planned to spend the morning writing."

"Oh, I see. I wouldn't want to interfere."

"I could walk that way with you and then take off on my own."

"Great. I'd like that." He rose from his chair. "Give me five minutes, and we'll go whenever and wherever you say. A treat, to walk with someone who knows Gower. I'm likely to get lost."

"I've been lost many times, but you're never far from a farm house, a store, or a pub."

"I believe you, but—"

"Okay. Give me ten minutes."

Once she and Ernie were striding along the footpath through the golf links, she wondered why she had worried. He was delightful company, saying he was honored to explore with one of Gower's leading poets and other flattering things. Flattery was a weakness of hers, but she relaxed and talked easily about other Norman castles nearby.

"We saw several in other parts of Wales," Ernie said, "but it was your poetry about this one and that legend about besanding that added the human dimension. They didn't feel populated to me before." He looked at her as though he felt grateful for more than being able to imagine people in castles. What was going on? She'd get him located, explain his direction back, and then take off. She needed time to think. Every time she got her life sorted out, more happened.

They had almost reached the castle when he said, "Actually, more than the castle, I wanted to see where Christine died. It's morbid of me. She was a troubled woman, and I felt that she'd be almost impossible to help, but in my profession you never like to admit that it's too late to do anything. I feel guilty. Maybe I could have said something before it was too late." He put his hand on her arm: "I'm very glad you asked me to talk to James. I didn't want to run out on you, but I was worried about my patients back home."

Running out on me? Where is this leading? They entered the castle ruins. They had a lovely view of the plain that spread itself between the Three Cliffs and Big Tor, the next headland over, with a little river running between the two headlands.

"Beautiful," said Ernie. "A pity that a death should occur in this serene place." He sounded stiff and formal.

She motioned to him to go into one of the remaining room structures. They had an even better view of the plain below where Gower's wild ponies were grazing. "You can see that maze from here, too." Penny pointed to it.

When Penny looked down onto this valley, her eyes following the sensual curve of the quiet river as it wound its way toward the sea, she felt like humankind was being given a second chance. Whatever had happened here, century after century, cave people, the ice age, the stone age, Romans, Vikings, and the Normans, human beings had failed, killed, and gone away, but this beauty stayed. The ponies were here; that maze was here.

"The maze been there since way before the castle."

"Yes. So the fairies were dancing down there? Where exactly was Christine found?"

"On the other side of the river. On the beach. The tide was going out, like it is now. You know high tide is a little later each day."

"How does one get down to the beach"

"There's a footpath—it's deep in sand, but I've done it many times. You can wade across the river. I'll show you how to walk along the cliffs home and then take off myself."

He looked crestfallen. "Won't you walk down to the beach with me?"

Why? Was he was fixing to kill her now? Suddenly she was sure he hadn't killed Christine. He seemed even frightened, as though, in his way, he wanted his mum—some steady, confident, female presence while he dealt with this death. Was that it?

"If you could take me down to where she died. It sounds strange. I'm feeling bad about it, and this will help me. Do you mind?"

"Okay. Then you'll take it from there?"

"I'll take it from there."

The stakes and ropes were gone, and though it was a sunny Sunday morning, not many people were out yet. A few children and their dogs, the adults settling themselves near the rocks, spreading their blankets and towels, putting up canvas screens to block the wind. Penny stopped about where Christine had been lying and stared out to sea. Then she caught sight of a bright blue and orange cloth being pushed back and forth by the waves breaking on the sand. Christine's towel? She walked over to it, Ernie following, and picked it up. It was a large towel, sodden, torn on one end. Definitely Christine's. She wrung it out.

"Someone lost a towel?" asked Ernie, puzzled.

"Christine's. She had one like this, and we didn't find it."

"Doesn't it bother you to pick it up?"

"No. It bothered me to identify her body." She looked hard at Ernie. "Wringing out a towel doesn't bother me."

"It would me," said Ernie. "Where was she then?"

"There," said Penny, pointing back to where they had been standing when she had noticed the towel. "They've removed the stakes and ropes."

He was quiet. He walked back and stood there quietly. For an educated, sophisticated man, he seemed superstitious. Why so involved with where she died?

She was on the point of leaving, when she glanced behind her and saw Kenneth striding toward them.

He'd said he'd be very busy until two, when he was coming to talk to James. He saw them from the caravan camp?

"Good morning, Miss Weaver," he said, "and Mr. Rosewood." He was being awfully formal for someone who had been nuzzling her less than twelve hours before.

"Fancy meeting you here." She could be formal, too.

"Oh, hello, Inspector," said Ernie. "Penny thinks we've found that unfortunate woman's towel. I asked her to show me where she died. So terrible."

"I thought that might be the towel we were missing," said Kenneth. "I saw you down here fetching it. I was up there talking to people in the caravan camp. Does it look like the one you remember, Penny?"

"Yes." She handed it to him. "Should I have waited to wring it out?"

"That's all right. I'll take it. Where are you two headed?"

"I was going off to write." Why did Kenneth look so worried? "Ernie's walking back along the cliffs. I thought you were busy interviewing all those people?"

"I was. But now I'd better go back to Evelyn's. I'll need to get this towel to the lab, and some other things. I need your help actually."

"You want me to help you this morning?"

"If you would."

Something was up. What could she say? "Sure."

Ernie did not seem happy at the thought of Kenneth and her accompanying him even though it guaranteed he wouldn't get lost.

"That's very considerate of you, Inspector, to see us back."

Penny picked up his anger. Because Kenneth didn't trust him? What was the real reason Kenneth had charged down the hill and was walking them back?

If he was going to get jealous that easily, she wanted to know. Her ex-husband had been ridiculously jealous; hadn't wanted her to have any social life by herself or talk to other people when they went to parties. Kenneth was bagging her heart pretty fast, but she'd have to have a little talk with him. True, it had been a relief when Kenneth turned up. Ernie had been so morbid.

They didn't talk much as they clambered over the rocks to Pobbles Beach. Penny and Ernie were both breathless when they reached the top. Kenneth seemed pleased about that, too, like his ability to climb rocks well proved he was superior.

At first Ernie had commented on the views they were passing, but when neither Penny nor Kenneth said much, he walked on ahead of them, as if aware they wanted to walk with each other.

Once Ernie turned to Penny and kicked at some of the stones scattered under the grassy slopes of the cliff they were crossing. "These are the stones that make you think of that besanded village?"

"Yes, exactly."

"It does look like centuries old rubble."

Penny stared out to sea, watching the wind whip at the waves and rush them in to cover the dark feet of these mountains all along the coast. For her these mountains had feet, the wind had passion—desire and rage—that helped her live with her own passions.

As they walked up the road that led to the store, Ernie said, "I'll pop in and get a paper and a coffee. I know my way now. Thanks for bringing me back, Inspector." He sounded annoyed.

Kenneth nodded to Ernie, and took Penny's elbow, steering her toward Evelyn's. Penny said, "Are you upset with me?"

"Yes."

"Why?"

"I don't trust Mr. Rosewood. It wasn't a good idea to go there with him alone. Too many things we don't know."

"You were afraid he'd kill me?"

"I didn't know he wouldn't."

"I'm sorry. I've worried you. But, Kenneth, even though he acted weird about wanting to go there, I don't think he's the murderer."

"You don't think—"

"I trust my intuition."

"Are your intuitions ever wrong?"

"Sometimes. But—"

"Penny, I got a strange feeling in the pit of my stomach when I looked down there and saw you with him. My intuition said something was fishy and to get the hell down there fast."

"You did that."

"You bet I did."

"I felt like a bad child being marched home. Ernie did, too."

"You're also the woman I love—maybe that was some of it. Why would he want to go walking with you? Why wasn't he walking with his wife?"

"She took off." They were almost to Heatherslade Lane. "She didn't encourage him to come. Said she wanted to be alone. He was lonely, I guess."

"Probably so. A pretty woman helps him forget that his wife doesn't want him around."

"I don't like Ernie that much, Kenneth. He's okay, but—" She stopped in front of him. "I like you."

"Good," he said sarcastically. "Mr. Rosewood was upset with me for interrupting his little party with you."

"It wasn't a party, Kenneth. We were taking a walk."

"To see where the body had been?"

"That's what he said—after we got to the castle. It did seem weird, morbid."

"Umm." Kenneth continued walking. "I'd rather you were a bit more circumspect with your person." He put his arm around her waist. It felt very comfortable there. She could tell he'd relaxed again. "I'm rather fond of it."

"I know," said Penny.

SIXTEEN

They walked in silence for a few minutes, more comfortably, but things weren't that harmonious. Penny stopped to look in the craft shop window.

Kenneth could certainly be infuriating. Maybe this wasn't going to work. He was Welsh, not American. Most American men's behavior had been changed by the women's movement. He had been so good about treating her like an equal. What had happened?

"Why are you stopping?"

"I wanted to look in this craft shop."

"Why, for God's sake?"

"Look, there's the mug I love. I'm saving up to buy it at the end of the summer." She pointed to a tall stoneware mug with a beautiful red Welsh dragon on it, and the word *Cymru*, Wales.

"Look, love. I have a lot to do. I want to talk to Stanley, and I have an appointment with James at two."

"Go ahead. I'm perfectly capable of getting back to Evelyn's. I want to admire my mug a minute." She knew she was making him angry. She didn't care. What did he think? That Ernie would come along and do her in while she looked at mugs?

"I'd be happier if you were tucked away at Evelyn's before I went back to Stanley's." He took her arm as if to start them walking again. She didn't move. Might as well have it out. She looked up and into his eyes.

"Kenneth, your protectiveness bothers me. Ernie wasn't going to hurt me. I think you were jealous. I'm in a village street, a block from Evelyn's—broad daylight, people all around. I'll be fine. Are you worried Ernie will come by and talk to me?"

Now he was staring at the mug. He walked around her and into the shop. She followed him in. By the time her eyes had adjusted to the dim interior, she saw him standing at the counter with the dragon mug in his hands, fishing in his pocket for change.

"Kenneth, I didn't mean for you to buy it for me."

He ignored her, handed over several pound coins, and then waited, not looking at her, while the old gentleman wrapped the mug. Then, with the mug tucked under one arm, walked over and very politely offered his other arm. She took it; she wasn't sure why. He had an air, half-defiant, half-authoritative.

"Kenneth?"

"Who said it was for you?"

He stopped outside the door of the shop. "I owe you an apology," he said. "I don't know if Ernie's our murderer or not, but I admit my protectiveness did get out of hand. Of course, you can walk back to Evelyn's by yourself. I forgot you American women are the most independent in the world. Brought up on freedom, aren't you? Don't easily chuck it in?"

He was grinning. She nodded and said, "Plus, I have a bad case of independent-mindedness. I liked you so much because you seemed okay with that. Most men aren't, even Americans."

"I do like it. Why did you say 'liked,' past tense?"

"I did? I used the past tense? I didn't mean that I didn't still like you."

"You do still like me?" He gave her his intense look.

What that did to her. Oh, help. Yes, she was very independent-minded, but why did he have to go and stir up Sappho's "subtle flame that runs under the skin"? She'd turn green soon and have drumming in her ears if he didn't stop. "Yes," she said. "I do still like you."

"I'm glad, and, yes, I'll stop looking at you like that. But promise me something, if you can, if you do honestly feel this way, that you'll give me a few days to solve this case before you make up your mind about me, and also that you will use your common sense about who you go on outings with. I may be jealous, but I think Rosewood's the most likely murderer."

She looked her surprise as he went on, "I may not be able to spend that much time alone with you until I get this case either solved or turned over to our South Wales Major Crimes Department, but I'd a hell of a lot rather solve it myself. I'm independent-minded, too."

He handed her the package. "This is a gift for you, from me, to remind me and you that something has started between us. I treasure that something. It can break like this mug. It can comfort, too, which I want this mug to do when I'm not there, and it—like our feelings for each other—contains a dragon as well, which we'll have to learn to tame if we're going to continue. Not kill," he said, as she took the mug, "but tame. You know, like the Little Prince and his fox?"

"You know that, too?"

"Yes. 'What is essential is invisible to the eye.'" He smiled steadily at her; his eyes looked happy again.

"'You are responsible for what you have tamed,'" she said. "Thank you, Kenneth. You know I love the mug. I already did. More now. I'll use my mind on this case, too. I'll try to do my part with—."

She didn't get to say "the dragon."

Right in the middle of the sidewalk at the curb, as they were moving to cross the street, he suddenly pulled her around to face him, gathered her into his arms, and kissed her.

She wanted to say, "Kenneth! Not here. The whole village will be talking." But he knew villages. He knew what he was doing, hopefully. Her cells quickly forgot her scruples. He certainly knew how to kiss. She was breathless, and her knees were weak. She wouldn't be surprised if she had turned completely green.

As Penny walked slowly down Heatherslade Lane, she thought about how she had met Kenneth only forty-eight hours before, and already he had given her a gift, a symbol of their relationship. Their first significant discomfort with each other had moved them toward a serious commitment. To accept the Welsh dragon cup was to agree to suspend her judgment until he could give her his full attention as clearly he wanted to.

In one way it was a relief not to be so aroused all the time, even though her sensuality still leapt, cavorted, and bathed itself like a happy sea creature in this oceanic bath which Kenneth provided of tender, sensual love. Love had never before been so mutual, so exactly right.

Deep, deep below the surface something was working, like an underground spring. All her life she had let herself be loved, and love. Since adolescence she had embraced those experiences. All the pleasures had brought pain with them, and yet she had never been sorry.

But this promised the most love, the most pleasure, and probably would entail the most pain of any experience so far. Even now, with the slow quieting of her senses following his impulsive kiss, sure to be village gossip by nightfall, she felt the first ache. Had she never met him, this same cup, which she'd have bought at the end of the summer, would have been "enough" comfort. Now it wasn't. She wanted him, not a cup.

What was she going to do with all her stirred feelings? She'd have to learn how to live with them. Wasn't that the essence of emotional pain? To want and not to have? She had read in Proust that suffering is our way of adapting to a better way of life. She had entered a new stage in her life that she wouldn't trade. She'd have to adapt.

Evelyn's front door was locked. Kenneth had insisted she lock both doors when she went out. James' car was gone, too. She let herself in, locked the door, and went into her little room. She drew the curtains and left the top part of the window open for the air. It was cloudy today but not cold.

She had her tea and biscuits with her, so she settled on her bed, plumped up the pillows behind her back, and got out her diary and her lunch. Maybe it would help to write everything down. She'd list the people they were suspicious of and sort out what they knew and didn't know. Curiously, doing this relieved the new ache for Kenneth. She initiated the new cup, pouring tea from her thermos. Dragon, I need your help.

She'd write out her deepest, most honest feelings about each of these people. James. An idiot, blithe and innocent. Totally idolatrous of Christine. He ignored a lot of evidence, so happy that he has what he wants, that he hasn't realized yet that it isn't what he thinks it is.

If he'd killed her, it would have been when he was walking before breakfast. Then he had happily gorged himself. Totally unconcerned while he ate breakfast and had then genuinely worried when she hadn't come back.

When James was in shock, he couldn't hide that. He was devious, but only playing tricks on his "mum" figure, to get to eat more, or when he wanted Christine into bed with him oftener than what she was rationing him. He had every reason not to kill her. He was entirely happy, even if he shouldn't have been. She could feel nothing murderous in James, even toward Christine's killer.

Kenneth thought Ernie had done it. If he and Ellie had lied and been able to bring off the same lie, maybe. They were certainly capable of lying, and, if pushed, of murder. We all are. The dragon lives in us all. She could imagine Ernie killing in self-defense, or in Ellie's defense. But she didn't feel active hatred in Ernie. He was good at working with angry people, even his own angry feelings. He had silly problems, like not eating fast and being obsessed about where Christine had died. How did that fit in?

He might have made that up. He had wanted to walk with her and keep her with him. He was in love with his wife but willing to use other women as a stop-gap when she took off? His sympathetic, interested behavior might be a mask. Did he play those games with his wife to keep her interested, to hide his dependency on her? Was that what was under the surface? He was afraid of losing her? She taunted him a lot, then did what she pleased. She was a very strong woman who knew her own mind. Did she enjoy keeping Ernie powerless as much as possible, though she would never leave him? If so, their game was sick.

As for Eloise, she liked her better now. She genuinely liked Gower and exploring it alone. She was selfish and did what she wanted to do, but that didn't make her a murderer. Christine had made her angry; her temper had flared, but she had left the room, avoided Christine. Anger wasn't murder. Her wanting to leave town could be selfishness. She didn't take in other people's problems. If either one of them had murdered Christine, why would they come back for their clothes? They could have been out of the country before Kenneth could stop them.

It seemed unlikely they had gone toward Three Cliffs instead of toward Pwll-du, either one of them, in order to "do in" Christine, no matter how annoying she was.

Yet she and Kenneth had thought the murderer most likely one of Evelyn's guests. She'd have to ask Kenneth to explain his suspicions of Ernie. She wanted to tell Kenneth that there had been some attraction between her and Ernie, so how could he be a murderer? She wouldn't, however, do that any time soon.

They had all theoretically had the opportunity, but opportunity alone didn't make a murderer. The only thing that nagged was that early morning conversation Friday, that had waked her and Evelyn, about six. It was between two of the guests, but which two? All four were probably awake by then.

Then the little sapphire. She had seen it on someone. Christine? She wore that shade of blue a lot. She wished she noticed what people wore. She could ask James if it belonged to Christine. She'd forgotten to tell Kenneth, too. She'd do that first.

Harold? He knew the Prussian had upset Evelyn, and he was very loyal, though it wouldn't have pleased Evelyn for him to kill off her B and B people, no matter how infuriating they were. She'd make up some excuse for having a chat with him. He might confide in her.

He was an honest, honorable type. Probably there was some easy explanation. He'd been very open about having met Christine that Friday morning. Why didn't he lie about that? He'd admitted to what would arouse suspicion. He didn't like Germans. He was narrow-minded and set in his ways, but his hostilities were open and shared by most of the British who had lived through the London blitz period. He wasn't likely to be Christine's murderer.

Penny had begun to tackle John and Stanley when she heard a car engine stop, car doors shutting, and Evelyn's voice, then her quick, unmistakable, slightly uneven walk up the sidewalk. She had arthritis in her feet.

Penny finished her tea, cold now. Evelyn knocked. "Penny?"

"Come in."

"You're back early? No poems today?"

"No. I wasn't out long. I took Ernie over to the castle and down to the beach. We met up with Kenneth and walked back."

"What a beautiful mug!"

"You like it? Kenneth bought it for me. I've been admiring it in the craft shop window. He bought it for me on the spur of the moment."

"Presents, eh?" said Evelyn, beaming. "Looks like this beau is serious. That's super, Penny. You've deserved a good man. He's taking you out again then tonight? You won't be here for dinner?"

"No, actually, I'll be here, but I can easily go to a pub. I realize the extra feeding of James might be using up all your groceries."

"Penny, no, it's fine. I can make us a ham salad. I had James run me up to the top, and I bought a few things. He insisted on paying for them. Such a sweet man. I didn't even try to do a proper Sunday dinner. Next week."

"I forgot all about that. I was here at noon, but you were gone."

Evelyn heard the front door opening, and her head disappeared. Penny heard, "Right in here, James," and figured James was hauling groceries. She did have a facility for organizing men.

Evelyn was back. "I thought it would do James good to get out. We had a little walk up at the top, then we drove around a bit and then stopped and got a few things. I needed bread, cheese, ham. My stars, Stanley's prices. I'm glad I usually shop in Swansea. I'll get a bite for James and me before Kenneth comes. I see you've eaten, but how about a coffee?"

"That would be lovely," said Penny, and Evelyn pulled her door to and bustled off.

Penny liked Stanley. He was shy, pretty preoccupied with his store. Christine's knocking over the display and driving off John had worried him. He'd had her on his mind before that. Stanley had worried about her not understanding the tides. That suggested concern, not murder.

A knock. Evelyn. "Come in."

"Here's your coffee, Penny. James and I are having a bite. Come visit if you like. Kenneth's due soon, and James is worrying he won't do this interview right. Maybe you can help me relieve his mind?"

The last thing Penny wanted to do was relieve James's mind, but she might help Kenneth. She went dutifully out to join Evelyn and James in the dining room. As she got to the big front window in the lounge, she saw Kenneth coming up Evelyn's walk. James excused himself precipitately and ran for his room, like a child trying to escape punishment.

"He is nervous," Evelyn said. "He probably wanted to freshen up. You get the door. I'll make Kenneth a coffee." She hurried out to the kitchen.

So Penny walked to the door and let him in herself. He didn't have to kiss her. His eyes did all the work of setting her off. The human body certainly had a more efficient communication system than she had ever realized.

Fortunately, he began talking of Stanley. "Great minds run in the same channel," she said lightly. "Come on in. Evelyn is making you a coffee."

"And a sandwich," said Evelyn from the kitchen.

"Thank you, Evelyn. Perfect. I forgot to eat lunch." He looked at Penny as if she were the reason.

"I figured an independent-minded man like you would remember to see about his lunch," she said, sitting in the armchair nearest his when he took the couch.

"Touche! Did you eat?"

"Yes. True, I didn't realize I was hungry until I got back here. But I had the biscuits and tea I'd been carrying."

"Good. I can't make Stanley out," he said, launching into what was apparently uppermost in his mind. She knew that she was on his mind, too, but he had succeeded in getting his mind fully on the case.

"Stanley?"

"Yes, I asked him a few simple questions, and it flustered him. I've known him for years, and I've never seen him act so agitated."

"What did you ask him?"

"If he'd noticed the Rosewoods going by—toward Pwll-du, and when Mr. Rosewood came into the store exactly. If he could tell me anything about the mood Rosewood was in—anything really."

"He couldn't remember anything?"

"Nothing! He kept saying he didn't know, he didn't know. He'd been busy. When I asked his daughter, he tried to send her off on an errand. She didn't know what to do. I said, 'Stanley, I only want to ask her what I asked you. Can't that errand wait?' He shrugged, but he acted funny. Hung around and interrupted, made her totally nervous. Finally, she said she didn't notice anything, and he sent her off. What's his problem? I don't even suspect him."

"Maybe he's afraid you do? I was thinking about him, too, how worried he'd been about Christine not understanding the tides—."

"Tell me about that."

He sat back and listened intently but didn't have time to comment before Evelyn came in carrying a beautifully arranged ploughman's lunch and a coffee.

"You are a dear, Evelyn. Hal was a lucky sod all those years." He said it with feeling and genuine gratitude, and Penny saw tears start into Evelyn's eyes.

"I still miss him," she said.

"I bet you do. This looks super. Sit down. We were talking over the case. Any fresh thoughts on who killed the Prussian?"

"It was John," said Evelyn emphatically. Kenneth looked surprised, as though she'd gotten hold of some information he had missed. Penny knew he didn't suspect John seriously, though John was certainly acting his role as a fugitive from justice lately.

"Oh?" Kenneth put down a piece of bread and cheese he had been about to bite into. "Why do you say that?"

"Who else?" asked Evelyn. "I saw him up at the top a little while ago. He was in Stanley's getting milk. He lives on milk. He ran off, left the milk, when I said 'hello.' He must be guilty. Why else would he do that? Penny told me how you'd hoped to talk to him—was it yesterday?—and he ran off then. If he's innocent, let him come and talk to you. Besides, the Prussian pestered him to death. I'd have killed her, too, if she'd treated me like she did him, poor old sod."

Kenneth resumed eating. "I don't think so, Evelyn. This case makes everyone nervous. That's probably why John ran off. Where's James, by the way?"

"He'll be out. He went to freshen up when he saw you coming."

"He's nervous, too," said Penny.

"See?" said Kenneth. He smiled at Evelyn. "I've got them all terrified, except you and Penny." He smiled at Penny, and she thought, there are so many other emotions charging around inside me, I couldn't feel any fear properly if I had any.

"Right," said Penny. "That's one thing. I'm not scared of you."

"Stanley's out of orbit, too," said Kenneth.

"Stanley? Why?" asked Evelyn.

"I have no idea—same thing, I guess. Finds it hard to talk to me about the case. I wanted to know, if he'd noticed anything that morning in his store, before Christine died, when Ernie and James were in there about eight a.m.?"

"He probably wasn't in his store," said Evelyn. "He never is until 8:30. He goes down for a swim and leaves his daughter in charge."

SEVENTEEN

Sunday afternoon, once Kenneth had closeted himself in Evelyn's lounge with James, about 2:30, turned out to be a free one for Penny. She had decided to forget everything for awhile. This case and her emotions were far too complex. She'd go back to her Grimes, give herself a break. She didn't notice that the wind had picked up until Evelyn knocked on her door about 4:30.

"Like a cup of tea, Penny? It's about to rain. Big black clouds headed in from the sea. My garden needs it. I finally got some weeding done. It looked terrible."

"Sure, I'll have a cup. I've been reading my mystery. I felt like hiding out for awhile."

"Suit yourself, Penny. I'll be right back. I expect the Rosewoods will get back early, too, with this storm coming."

She said it like she thought that might tempt Penny into the lounge. "Didn't Ernie come back yet?"

"No. Wasn't he with her?"

"No, he and I walked down to Three Cliffs. Kenneth and I left him down at Stanley's store about 11:30."

"Maybe he stayed down there. There are some nice benches and good views, too. It's very pleasant."

"Not right now."

"Lord, no. He'll probably be here soon. I'll give him and that wandering wife of his a cup, too. I hope they don't get soaked."

"Why do you say 'that wandering wife of his'?"

"She's always off by herself."

"So am I usually."

"But you're not married."

"You think married women should always be with their husbands?"

"They usually are."

"Not always, Evelyn."

"Hal and I—."

"I know. You and Hal enjoyed walking together. Ellie said at breakfast that she wanted to be alone. Then he proposed going with me."

"Mad at her, I expect."

"That's what I thought, but she does have a right to walk by herself. You can have the Rosewoods and James this afternoon. I'm taking a serious break from everybody."

"Kenneth went next door to talk to Harold, and then he was going to check with Stanley. Why didn't Stanley tell him he'd been swimming? If Kenneth comes back here, are you taking a break from him, too?" asked Evelyn mischievously.

"Him, too," said Penny. "I'm giving my mind a rest all around."

"I'll tell him that if he turns up."

"You'd better not!"

Evelyn laughed. "Be back," she said and closed the door. Penny heard her clattering in the kitchen, the sound of the tea kettle coming to a hard boil and then silence. She reimmersed herself in *I Am the Only Running Footman*.

Detective fiction helped her rest her mind. When she tried to sort out Christine's murder, she only confused herself. Kenneth might be right. Staying closer to home until the murderer was identified might be wise. Being docile and obedient, however, was not her usual mode.

She was fed up with all of them. Kenneth and Evelyn excepted, they all acted like murderers. What a great detective she was. She had used her intuition, and she felt lost in a maze. She liked the Ariadne myth and was usually good at solving labyrinths with a piece of string. But not this one. Let Kenneth do his job. She helped him when he needed her and then made out with him in his spare time.

Was that what was bothering her? Was he only interested in sex? She wasn't reading. She went to the window and opened the curtains. It was bucketing down, and here came Ernie and Ellie running through it. Evelyn knocked.

"Come in. Here come your missing Rosewoods."

Evelyn came over to the window carrying the tea cup on its saucer.

She set it down carefully on the dresser. "My stars, they'll be soaked. I can put their wet clothes in the dryer. Then in the airing closet. Why didn't they wait up at Stanley's until it let up? Sometimes Americans have no sense at all."

"We don't. Not a lick. They knew you were going to make them tea and cosset them."

"Cosset them?"

"Isn't that what you're going to do?"

"I expect so. Penny, drink your tea and read your book. At least you had sense enough to stay out of the rain."

"This time."

"Right. This time. My stars!" Then she hurried out as the Rosewoods came through the little gate. Penny dropped the curtain, picked up her steaming tea, and climbed back in bed.

By staying in her room until 6:30, when Evelyn called her for supper, she managed to avoid the Rosewoods, their wet clothes, and Evelyn's clucking, as well as James's insipid comments. She could hear him advising them about what raincoats to buy.

Kenneth didn't turn up. She had read twenty pages in her book. She had had a vision about her role. In one fell swoop, she'd had two major insights about her life. She'd feel better if she had written a poem about Kenneth.

She couldn't figure everything out about the murder, but she could share her thoughts with Kenneth. They needn't spend all their time kissing. He had strengths, things he could do, but she had gifts to offer: her intuition, her own observations. She'd give him the sapphire. That might be important.

She'd be ready in case she saw him before Tuesday.

When Evelyn called her at 6:30, she leapt up, smoothed her duvet, adjusted her bobby pins, and tucked in a few strands of hair.

Evelyn was setting out their plates of ham and lettuce when she sat down. James was already seated. Through the front window she saw that the Rosewoods' car and Kenneth's were gone. The sun had shone through a hole in the clouds.

Evelyn brought in the tea pot with its accompanying pot of hot water and seated herself next to Penny, with James opposite. "I hope it's all right."

"Marvelous, umm," said James.

"One of my favorite meals," said Penny. They fell to. Evelyn had set out pickled beets and various other salads. She poured them each a cup of tea with milk. Maybe Evelyn had told James that Penny wanted some time off. Both were very respectful of her apparent need for silence, and neither started a conversation. The silence, if unusual to these two and a little conspiratorial, was companionable.

When Penny, over her second cup of tea, commented on the sunshine, the other two began to chat. Yes, that had been quite a storm and those poor Rosewoods. No proper raincoats, caught right in it, and thoroughly soaked.

But before James could tell her the raincoat she ought to buy in London before she returned to America, the front bell rang, and Evelyn hurried to answer it. Kenneth. Penny heard him telling her he'd had a bite up at Stanley's, but could he talk her out of a cup of tea?

"Of course. Sit right here." She indicated the chair next to James and opposite Penny. "I'll put the kettle on." James leapt up and began carrying dishes into the kitchen. Evelyn would have him well-trained by the time he went home.

Kenneth smiled at her and took a seat. His leg moved to touch hers under the table. "Have you had a good afternoon, love?"

His look was only moderately provocative, and it was reassuring to have the pressure of his leg against hers.

"I have," she said. "I read some, and I did some thinking. I feel much better."

"You were feeling bad?" He was concerned. That was pleasant.

"Confused. A lot has happened fast." James reappeared to gather up the salt, pepper, and condiments.

"True." Kenneth smiled. "This has been an eventful few days. I've had a productive afternoon. I'd like a chance to bend your ear. Maybe we could take our tea into the garden, if that's all right, Evelyn?" She had appeared, carrying in a fresh pot, James following with a cup and saucer for Kenneth and the refilled cream pitcher.

"Certainly. Please do. James is going to help me with the washing-up. Then we'll have our tea in front of the telly." James looked surprised but acquiescent. Good for Evelyn. Let the man earn all this extra food he was getting. She was sure James would pay for the additional meals, but Evelyn's labor and help to him in this crisis went beyond anything he could pay for. He obviously was enjoying himself immensely, so soon after his tragedy.

She wondered what exactly Christine had meant to him. He seemed more truly happy with Evelyn bossing and cosseting him. A lot of men wanted that. She had done that, but it had never felt right. Cosseting each other suited her better.

Penny followed Kenneth out the kitchen door into the garden. Evelyn ran out behind them with rags to wipe the rain off the garden chairs and the table. Then she returned to the kitchen. Penny set down her cup and sat down in one of the chairs. What did she want from a relationship?

She wanted it to feel necessary. Was this ordinary-looking Welsh man seating himself and leaning toward her, his eyes full of kindness and amusement, necessary to her?

So far, no one had been. She had loved and lost, but none of it had felt necessary. At the time she had wanted it. Later she hadn't.

"I can tell you've been thinking about us. Want to tell me?"

A big sycamore tree rose high into the air beyond the garden fence. She stared at the tree. "I do want to tell you. I did think about us. It's very big in me, very powerful. Confusing. Scary. I haven't even written a poem about it yet."

"You will," he said softly. She looked over at him. His eyes were shining with love that made her feel loved for all of her, for all that she was and would ever be. Had she ever had that from a man? She looked at the tree again.

"I don't want it just to be sex—."

"Nor I."

"Or even just love. I want to be able to go on being me—writing, and even helping you with this case."

"What I want, too, my love."

"Really?" She looked at him, unable to believe, yet seeing in his eyes that he meant it.

150

"It's why I love you," he said. "You're yourself. You exist without me. You have your work, your ideas, things you like to do alone. You're independent-minded—." He laughed.

Her eyes held his. "You're sure that's not bothering you?"

"I wouldn't trade it. But it does take getting used to. This is all new for me, too. I'm scared and confused, too."

He handed her her tea.

"Thanks. That helps, Kenneth. I wanted to tell you my thoughts. Before I forget, I found this yesterday." She reached in her jeans pocket and got out the little sapphire, still wrapped in her lunch napkin, and gave it to him.

"Where did you find it?" He had unwrapped it with as much care as if her very self were contained in it. In a way it was. She had thought before how the core self was a jewel. Perhaps her self was a sapphire, lost, rolled around by the tide, found, claimed, and protected by her, now given into his hands. Then he lifted the jewel and kissed it. She felt as if he'd kissed her. She couldn't look at him.

He waited, quiet. She heard him sipping his tea.

"I forgot to give it to you earlier." She didn't look at him. "I found it near where Christine's body was, near one of the stakes. It may be important, Kenneth." She looked up.

"I'm sure it is, love," he said. The look in his eyes made her feel deeply and completely loved. That was the necessity then; what she had never had had before. She couldn't see yet where it led, or what it meant, but her life lay with this man. They now had the understanding between them that meant they would be able to work out the details. He again kissed the jewel. Mysterious. Too intense. She was relieved when he rewrapped the sapphire, put it into his pocket and picked up his tea again.

"Tell me your thoughts on the case. Do you think the stone has significance?"

"I've seen it in a ring on someone's hand since I got here. Perhaps there's a tie-in. I wrote down everything in my diary, my intuitive sense of all these people. It may help."

Kenneth settled back, sipped his tea. He was a good listener and didn't interrupt. When she had described her thoughts on James, Ernie, and Ellie, she asked him if he'd learned any more about why Stanley and

Harold had both been lying about Friday morning. Had he been able to talk to John?

"Not John." He set his cup down. "But the other two. It has given me another way to think about Christine that morning.

"I couldn't get James to tell me where he'd walked. 'Along the cliffs,' he said, but he claimed not to remember which direction or how far. Something's funny there. He couldn't have walked more than twenty minutes along the cliffs, between 7:40 and eight. Maybe you and Evelyn can get it out of him. He was back in Stanley's store about eight, and he didn't see Stanley. He only chatted with the daughter.

"He says Ernie came in about five minutes before they headed back here together. So that confirms that Ernie got to the store about 8:20, which he claims. James said Stanley wasn't back when they left. So I used that to confront Stanley. First, though, I went over to see Harold. You were in your room, Evelyn said, having a 'lay down.'"

Penny nodded. You could call it that.

"I've known Harold since he moved here, but it was hard to say, 'Why are you lying to me, Harold?'

"I figured that he was embarrassed about something and covering up. So we chatted awhile. He made me a coffee and was doing his chores. I waited. When he was washing his milk bottles, I said I'd heard that he loved to chat up the milkman. What had he learned about him? I'm rarely up when he comes to my flat in Llangennith. So he got off on the milkman's life—a hard life it is, too, I can tell you.

"Then I quietly asked him to explain why he hadn't gotten his milk in until after seven that Friday morning, and he said, 'Oh, I didn't get home from my walk until about ten after,' then he realized he'd walked into my trap. I assured him I understood there were times when a lie seemed the best solution, but I needed him to be honest about that morning in order to understand all that had happened. He then admitted—this was the embarrassing part—that he found Mrs. Hampton an attractive woman, despite her being so very Prussian. When they met that Friday morning, he walked back toward the beach with her a ways, but she seemed angry and offended.

"He said she was a Prussian bitch all right. She had called him a bastard and a string of other names. He had stayed with her as long as he had to reassure her he meant no harm, but she had said he could help

152

most by getting the hell off the beach where she planned to swim. So he had. He was afraid I'd think he'd killed her. I asked if he'd seen anyone else out, and he said no. He did say that Stanley often swam down there, and John often slept in the hedges in that general vicinity, that I should talk to them."

"Do you think Harold's telling the truth now?" she asked.

" I do. It's a gut reaction."

"It fits. He could be attracted and then embarrassed. It sounds like Christine. It would help if we could narrow down the time of the murder."

"True. Listen to what Stanley told me. When he saw me enter the shop, he turned white. Half the village knows he has his morning swim right after he opens the store. This time he was very compliant. Took me into his little back room, and we had our chat. He went swimming a little after 7:30. He was out from Pobbles. He saw Christine swimming. He was also attracted to her, which he also didn't want to admit. His wife is an invalid, and he has raised his daughter alone the last few years. He didn't need to worry, I said. His feelings were understandable, his being like a widower and all.

"So he swam over and to talk with Mrs. H. He was on about the tides and the danger. She told him very nastily to leave her alone, she'd had enough out of 'these men around here that were only interested in her body.' The tides she could manage, but the men were a damned nuisance. Then she swam farther out. She's a good swimmer, he says, and he went on back to Pobbles and in. Says he got back to his store at 8:30, and his daughter confirms this. She confirmed his lies, too, so I can't rely on her. I need another witness to his return time."

"A customer?"

"I'll ask him who else was in the store when he got back. It would help, to know exactly when Christine died. Stanley's story suggests that when the murderer met up with her—another man who tried to start something?—she was already so agitated, she may have infuriated that person."

"You still think it's Ernie?"

"If I believe Stanley, she was alive at 8:20, and at 8:20 Ernie was in Stanley's store."

"I think we're closer somehow."

"The sapphire clue may help us most. You have no memory of who was wearing a sapphire ring?"

"No. Someone was. Christine wore that color a lot. Perhaps I noticed something, but, if so, I can't bring it up."

"Sleep on it," said Kenneth. He stood. "I want to have another word with James, and then I'll be off. No, stay there. I like leaving you in the garden." He bent over her, kissed the lips she turned up to him and her eyelids, and then he was gone.

EIGHTEEN

Penny sat in Evelyn's garden as it grew dark, staring at the roses and the tall sycamore, watching the antics of Evelyn's robin, who had hopped quite close to her.

What is it about a garden, she wondered. She'd never been very good at making and tending gardens herself. She thought of Joyce Cary in *The Horse's Mouth*: "a garden is a spiritual being." He had used gardens to talk about loving, said people had the choice of creating a hell full of devils or a garden where there was love, but you had to work at it. You had to get the thorns in your hands on purpose instead of in your tender parts by accident.

Could she make a life with Kenneth, and take care of it, like Evelyn did, create a place of real beauty? This garden was real, not like the imaginary ones she'd dreamt up with probably twenty different men who had seemed promising, but none of them had wanted her as this man did.

The lines of a poem began to come to her. She didn't have her notebook. No, wait, she did. She'd brought out her diary to tell Kenneth all her thoughts. There it was, on the ground near her chair. She didn't want to stir. She began to write down the words forming slowly in her mind.

I hadn't planned to be writing
this poem in a garden. I hadn't
planned to be bound to you for
a lifetime.
Here in this garden
are roses: white, yellow, pink,
apricot, and red. Evelyn fusses that
her garden isn't looking very well,
and yet there is beauty on every hand

to greet my eye.
You could ask
anything of me, and I would give it.
A garden like the one I'm sitting in
now is vulnerable to weather and
to time; its blooms depend on
the care it receives; its roots require
thought for their sustenance. The
snapdragon must be set out in the spring;
the bulb that will throw into the summer air
a pink star has to be planted months
beforehand.
I haven't been very good
with gardens, though I understand their
principle. Everything you do counts
in a garden, and what you don't do
is noticed, too. If you want to keep
the roses happy, you have to plan
on engaging with their thorns.
You have to understand and ward
off their diseases and protect them
from insect annoyance. I think
I could do these things.
Every day
in every life there are opportunities.
We can chafe at the hedge life has
thrown up in our faces, or we can
begin where we are to create
a place of serenity and joy, color
and ease and laughter. With a tall
tree beyond the hedge to give
us its look at eternity and to help
us see clearly into each other's
hearts.
You have seen too well
into mine. A door has been opened
by you I could never close again.

It leads me toward a real garden.
It says everything I do will help
the roses and the begonias, the
snapdragons, marigolds, and pinks.
The garden which is our life
will give us its signs to help us.
I know now: this garden, our garden,
is destined and right. My heart says so.
My heart says yes, forever, to you.

It was dark when she finished. She'd scrawled the words down and would read them later. She sat quietly enjoying that feeling of perfect repose and rightness. She never knew when the words would begin to run in her mind. It was mysterious. So was this new love for Kenneth. It had surprised her, yet it felt good and right like a poem did when it welled up from within.

Evelyn got her out of her chair. "Penny? Are you still out there?"

She hadn't wanted to move or to speak. "Yes, I'm here."

"Why are you sitting in the dark?"

"I'm fine. I was thinking."

"You'd better come in. I'm making a milky drink for James and me. Would you like one?"

"Sure."

She walked slowly toward the back door light Evelyn had turned on, hugging her notebook with its new poem.

When Penny entered the lounge, blinking as her eyes adjusted to the lights, James was holding his cup of Ovaltine and sniffing it. Her favorite chair and her drink were waiting.

"Just what I needed, Evelyn. Thanks."

"It's one way to get you back into the house and out of the dark. How can you sit out there by yourself like that, Penny?"

"You should know, Evelyn. I like to be alone sometimes. I was thinking. Now I'm ready for company."

Evelyn flicked off the television. James was quiet, but clearly not unhappy. His grief was abating rapidly under Evelyn's ministrations. He looked composed. Penny had a hunch he remembered what he had done during the crucial twenty minutes when he could have run down to Three Cliffs and killed his wife.

Stanley probably was telling the truth, and he'd seen Christine alive at 8:20.

Could she get James to tell her and Evelyn which way he had walked that morning?

Sometimes people trusted her. What tack could she take with James? Maybe he was embarrassed, too, and it would slip out if she got the right conversation going. He was certainly in a placid mood. Too bad Christine hadn't realized how easy he was to manage if you let him eat.

"Have you had a good day, then, James?"

To Evelyn, she said, "Thanks, this hits the spot. It's delicious."

"Pretty fair," said James. "Yes, Mrs. Trueblood, your milky drink is what I needed to send me off to a good night's rest. I get a little hungry this time of night."

"Your talk with the inspector wasn't so bad then?" Penny continued.

James hesitated, then said blandly, "Not too bad. I'm glad it's over, that I didn't wait until Monday."

Evelyn smiled. "James is feeling much better. Now he's anxious to get all this investigating over with, like the rest of us are, and get on with his life."

"Yes, Penny, it has been a terrible shock, but life goes on. I hope we can settle this dreadful business soon."

"Dreadful business? That maybe Christine was killed?" She'd be straight with him. They'd all been pussy-footing too much with him.

"Exactly," said James. "Whoever did it must be found and locked up. I want to help." He paused and looked to Evelyn. "As much as I can. I've told Inspector Morgan I'll offer 5000 pounds for information leading to the arrest of the killer."

Yet, thought Penny, he won't try to remember what he did from 7:30 until eight. "That's great, James," she said. We all need praise, herself included. "I think we'll find out who did it. In a case like this, it isn't so much one single piece of information as it is lots of little pieces that help sort out the puzzle. That's what Inspector Morgan is doing. He's sorting out the small things to understand what actually happened that morning. We can all help do that. Each of us may have a piece that we don't think matters. It can be embarrassing to admit what we were doing even though it was harmless." She thought of Harold and Stanley. But James?

James interrupted her. Had he been listening? "Mrs. Trueblood, might I have another cup of Ovaltine?"

Evelyn started to get up. "James, I've used all the milk. There won't be any more until the milkman comes in the morning. I have more biscuits."

"Could I?"

"Certainly," said Evelyn. "I could make you a cup of tea?" She rose. "But tea might keep you awake."

James was pushing even Evelyn's indulging tendencies. "A couple of biscuits then. You're right. Tea would keep me awake."

When Evelyn left the room, he suddenly blurted out, "Penny, I guess I wasn't as forthcoming as I might have been with the inspector. He wanted very much to know which way I walked the morning Christine died, and I said—." He hesitated. "I said I didn't remember. I was embarrassed, like you said. I didn't mean to keep the murder from being solved, but I didn't see what difference it made."

So he had been listening. Why did he make himself look more foolish and less competent than he was?

"It can," said Penny, "make a big difference. I'd tell him, even if you're embarrassed."

"Do you think you could tell him for me?" He glanced toward the kitchen, trying to finish his confession before Evelyn returned? He had Penny on the spot, and she could tell that he knew it. She wanted to know what he had to tell. She would tell Kenneth. But she didn't like his pushing her into it. Don't be too fussy, she decided.

"In this case, I think I could," she said evenly. She heard Evelyn putting away dishes in the kitchen. "What is it, James?"

"I didn't walk at all while I was at Stanley's store. I sat on a bench and looked out to sea. I didn't want anyone to know. I was supposed to be walking. Christine would kill me—."

Then tears filled his eyes. His words had the ring of truth. That meant he definitely hadn't killed her. So he had not wanted anyone to know how lazy he was. It fit. He was waiting for her to say something, and here came Evelyn with his biscuits. A whole package. Good grief.

"Thank you, James, I'm glad you've said what you did." Did that leave him his cover? She hoped so.

He took out his pocket handkerchief and blew his nose. Evelyn set the package of biscuits on the little table beside him. He was smiling when he looked up, gratefully, at Evelyn. His confession was a thing of the past. Now he had a package of digestive biscuits to dispose of.

A few minutes later the outer door opened. The Rosewoods. It was nearly eleven. They were pushing their time limit, but Evelyn didn't look perturbed.

Ellie was saying, "No, I won't. I'm not in the mood." They heard her walking back to their room.

A light knock. "Come in," said Evelyn. Ernie pushed the door open, saw Penny, and came in. "You're all still up? Sorry, we were late. Getting ready to turn in?"

"Pretty soon," said Evelyn, "but come in for a minute. Your wife gone to bed?"

"Yes." Ernie looked discouraged. His wife giving him fits again? "You're sure?"

Penny decided, since he was looking at her, that he wanted to be sure that was okay with her. The aftereffects of Kenneth's walking them home and acting like she belonged in Kenneth's territory? She didn't want to encourage him, but she might learn something to help Kenneth. She looked straight into Ernie's eyes, and said, "Come on in. We're going to help James eat all these digestive biscuits he is hoarding." She laughed, affectionately, at James's foolishness, Evelyn's (why had she given him the package?), Ernie's, and her own. She had a weakness for digestive biscuits, too.

When Penny settled in her room for the night, tucked herself under her duvet, she decided to write in her diary to clear her mind so she could sleep. She was suspicious of Ernie now. He had lied in the lounge and was acting very funny.

It had come out who it was who'd been talking in the hall that Friday morning about six. When she had asked the two men if they could tell her who it was, Ernie had shaken his head, as though puzzled, but James had said easily, "It was Christine and Eloise. Don't you remember, Ernie? We talked about it when we walked back later. Christine was in the main loo, and I had planned to go in next when she finished showering, and then your wife knocked. Christine told her I was next, and Eloise thought that was unfair. She said you were taking a shower in your private bathroom, and anyway, it didn't have a tub, and she wanted a real bath. Christine said she was sorry, but we had only the one bath between the four of us, Mrs. Trueblood and Penny, too. But 'you Americans have one for yourselves.'"

James looked smug. "I popped my head out right after that, and Christine motioned me over. It was our bath, and my turn. Your wife isn't used to queuing up?"

Evelyn smiled approvingly at James.

"I guess not," said Ernie lamely. He looked miserable. He said, "Now I remember. She had wanted a bath, and she ended up skipping it then. She had one when she got back from her walk."

Was he embarrassed by his wife's behavior? Or was it this new boundary which Kenneth had set up for them? Something was worrying him.

Penny had, even as they were talking, looked at all their hands to see if she'd remember anything. Ernie had a faint indentation on his left ring finger but no ring. A favorite ring of hers had gotten too tight, so she recognized that mark. It stayed for days after you stopped wearing the ring.

A missing ring. She struggled to remember if she'd seen any ring on Ernie, but she didn't think so. The sapphire was an unusual shape—a rectangle, maybe one-fourth of an inch wide and one-third of an inch tall. In a ring it would look large.

She had often had good luck asking her mind questions and then waking up with answers. She'd still have to interpret the answer, not be fooled like those who had consulted the Delphic Oracle had often been. She'd ask her mind where she'd seen the blue stone.

She put her notebook on the floor, turned out her light, and tossed her robe to the foot of the bed. She'd think of Kenneth kissing the blue stone.

Penny woke up suddenly. What had waked her? She heard footsteps going down the walk, the front door opening. Evelyn getting in her milk. It was seven? She squinted at her alarm clock. Yes. It was Monday.

Then an image came floating up. She could see the ring with its blue stone. Very beautiful—a wide gold band with gold filigree work. The stone was set sideways, not upright. It looked familiar and like a man's ring. Ernie's? No. On James? James had a regular wedding band, no other ring.

No, she still didn't have the whole answer, but she was wide awake. Suddenly, she had the impulse to take the walk down to the beach which Christine had taken and try to imagine what might have happened to Christine. It would give her exercise, help her think, and she'd be back by eight.

She reached for her jeans and her warm shirt. Her sweater, too. Chilly this early. She looked out the curtain. The fog was rolling off, but it would be cold by the water. She laced up her hiking boots, dashed into the bathroom, splashed water on her face, ran back to her room, dried off, brushed and braided her hair, grabbed her stick and backpack, and was off. She stopped first to tell Evelyn where she was going.

"My stars, Penny. You gave me a turn. You're ready for breakfast this early?"

"Sorry, I startled you. I'd like to eat about 8:15. I need to think something through."

"Trying to decide whether to marry Kenneth?"

Evelyn was right onto her again. "Evelyn!"

"You two were pretty happy in the garden last night. He was walking on clouds when he came in."

"You could tell?"

"I peeked out the window. You look super together. Is he bagged yet?"

"*Bagged*, Evelyn?"

"Have you got his heart yet, that he's been wearing on his sleeve?"

"Evelyn, I don't know. I love him, but he's awfully possessive."

"He'd better be if he wants to keep you. Did it bother him that you went off yesterday with Mr. Rosewood?"

"Yes, he was jealous. Why are men so territorial?"

"It's natural, Penny. Like my robin. He thinks it's his garden as much as mine. He doesn't mind my visitors, but if another male robin dares come over the fence, he's after them in a flash."

"But people are different?"

"Not really."

"I'm different. I want to talk with other men sometimes without being treated like I'm out of bounds."

"Kenneth is trying to make sure he has you first, Penny. If he knows he has your heart, he won't be so jealous, even if you go out with Mr. Rosewood. It's the not knowing. So does he have it?"

"He must know he does," said Penny, "and I'm going walking."

"Are you sure he knows?" persisted Evelyn.

"No, I'm not sure, but isn't that his problem, to discover that?"

"I expect you're right, Penny. Have a nice walk. See you in an hour."

As Penny started up Heatherslade Lane, she forgot to imagine herself as Christine and thought about Kenneth, herself, hearts, and territories. She scarcely noticed anything until she came to her favorite yellow and pink roses. She called a halt. Several buds were opening.

"You guys are beautiful, you know that?" she said softly. She liked the buds best—all the colors of Homer's dawn goddess: the rosy fingers had left a blush of color against the saffron mantle they'd been cut from.

They must have a careful gardener. The dead blossoms had been trimmed. In Britain many rose bushes were like little trees. These were. A circle of them, carefully weeded and mulched. Something—a dog?—had been digging in the mulch. Soil was thrown every which way, and a gleam of gold caught her eye. Hmm. An old gold coin buried from some early pirate visit to Gower? There were legends. A bit far from shore though.

Curious. She opened the little white gate and moved toward the dirt that had been dug up recently. She heard loud barking from inside the house, twenty feet away. Better ask, she thought. It's not my gold coin. So, embarrassed—it was early—she walked up to the back door and knocked. The barking became frantic, and she heard a woman's voice answering.

The back door opened. Lucy. "Good morning, Penny. What brings you out so early? Hera is very eager to know, and so am I."

"I didn't know you lived here, Lucy. Are you the rose gardener?"

"I am. Aren't they lovely?"

"They are. I often stop to admire them. I was this morning—I can't believe it's you."

"Who did you think?"

"I didn't know, but I imagined a man."

"Don't you think women can take care of roses?"

"I don't know what I thought. Lucy, where's your car?"

Lucy pointed to a building on the other side of the roses. "In the garage."

"Listen. I came into the yard because I noticed in some loose dirt—."

"Hera, have you been digging where you shouldn't again?" asked Lucy, looking sternly at the dog, who promptly moved under the table, put her head down on her paws, and looked up as if to say, "I honestly didn't mean any harm, and I promise I'll be good from now on."

"Where, Penny? Has she been in the roses?"

"Yes, but I wanted to show you something. Can you come out?"

"Hera, you stay right there," said Lucy firmly, and she followed Penny over to the rose bushes. Penny knelt down and brushed the dirt away from the gold. It wasn't a gold coin. It was a ring, and it had caked dirt in the rectangular place—about one-half by one-third of an inch—where there should have been a stone.

NINETEEN

By the time Penny got back to Evelyn's, through the village and by the footpath behind the dunes down to Pobbles and Three Cliffs, and then back along the cliffs, it was raining hard. The way it was blowing and the dark clouds were swiftly rolling in, it looked like the rain was settling in for the day. She loved the way the ocean looked when it was blowing like this. Like a boiling pot of pewter, dull, metallic gray, being whipped to a froth. Lucky she'd had her backpack and raincoat. She had the ring in her pack, wrapped carefully in a paper Lucy had given her. Lucy had rinsed out the dirt, the dog had been forgiven, had sniffed Penny, and decided she was all right. Penny had refused Lucy's cup of tea. Maybe another time.

The rain was steady all morning, and Penny, after calling Harold's and leaving word also at the Swansea office that she had something for Kenneth, retreated to her room to write. Lucky she'd already had her walk. She didn't expect to see him until teatime. She settled onto her bed with her diary.

At 11:30 Evelyn knocked and asked her if she'd like to make Welsh cakes. "Might as well, Penny. You won't be going anywhere. James is taking his car out to run some errands for him and me, and I've caught up my ironing. Want to?"

So they had worked for hours, both getting covered with flour. Penny wore one of Evelyn's aprons so it didn't matter, and she made notes of the recipe on a clean page of her diary.

By 2:30, they had ten dozen Welsh cakes, and they sat down to have a well-deserved cup of tea. They had already sampled the cakes, but they had some with their tea. Evelyn set out bread, butter, cheese, and some apples. Welsh cakes had never tasted so good to Penny, not even on that first day she'd ever had them, also in Evelyn's kitchen. Maybe it was the blowing rain as backdrop; maybe it was being part of the ritual of baking them, Evelyn telling her stories of how her grandmother had made them on special occasions, like holidays, but also sometimes on a day like this when the wind and rain were working themselves up into a real swivet, and all the children were cooped up inside.

The bell rang, and Evelyn went to get it. Penny drained her cup. She couldn't find room for another crumb. Kenneth came into the kitchen, followed by Evelyn, who was saying: "I'm sure she'll make them beautifully next time by herself. She has written down every single thing I said."

Kenneth beamed at Penny, came over, and squeezed onto the bench beside her. There was barely room. He put his arm around her with Evelyn standing right there watching. Evelyn grinned.

"Penny's pretty nice for an American," he said, knowing this would set off Penny, and, in a different way, Evelyn. Penny decided to let it pass, but Evelyn fell into the trap.

"Now, I've known many lovely Americans," said Evelyn. "Penny's not the first. I'm partial to her though. Do you realize that this is the fifth summer she has stayed with me?"

Kenneth's eyes sparkled, and he squeezed Penny's shoulders. "No!" he said in a shocked voice. "Whatever could be bringing her back to Gower like that, summer after summer?"

"It's the Welsh cakes," said Penny.

"You see?" said Evelyn. "Now will you have some tea, Kenneth?"

He would, and while Evelyn filled the kettle to make a fresh pot, under cover of the tap running, Kenneth said in a low voice, "I've got good news, love."

"So do I," said Penny.

"We'll chat in a bit."

After Evelyn had poured the boiling water into the teapot, she said, "My stars, it's nearly half past three. I haven't straightened James's room yet. Will you two excuse me?"

"Of course." Penny was enjoying the warmth of Kenneth's thigh. She hoped he wouldn't move and sit in the chair opposite. He didn't. When they could hear Evelyn thumping pillows, he kissed her. He was definitely a genius at making a kiss interesting. She might pass out, but she didn't want him to stop. He did, however.

"Darn it!" she said.

"You didn't like that?"

"Oh, I liked it."

He kissed her again briefly.

"I'm losing all my circumspection," she said mournfully.

"So that's why you said, 'darn it'?"

"Exactly."

"Hmm. I have a lot to learn about my American sapphire."

"Kenneth, I found the ring the sapphire fell out of."

"Where, love?"

"In Lucy's garden."

"Lucy?"

"The librarian. I hadn't realized that she lives right around the corner. Her dog had been digging in her rose garden. I saw this gleam of gold. I thought it was an old coin. I knocked and found out Lucy lives there. Kenneth, it's the ring, and it's a man's ring. Also last night I noticed that Ernie has a place on his ring finger where he recently wore a ring."

"Very interesting. Where exactly does Lucy live? Per chance on the road through the village that leads to the footpath? Could one of our suspects have buried it or tossed it there, thinking no one would ever find it?"

"Yes. I was walking the way Christine went, but whoever killed her could have gone that way, too. It's the way Harold walks. He came back that way."

"Harold is clear, love."

"For sure?"

"I found two witnesses: a boy of twelve and his mum, in the caravan camp. The boy was eager to go swim last Friday morning, so he was looking out the window and begging his mum to let him go. She was finishing the washing-up and making him wait. He saw Christine: a tall, blonde woman in a bright blue bikini. She was the only one swimming. He was watching her walk in from swimming. He was admiring her, but his mum made him stop staring and dry the dishes for her. They both saw her alive at 8:25. Ten minutes later—the lad was watching the clock because he'd found a new chum the day before and had promised to meet him at 8:30 to go swim. Then, when he looked out again at 8:35, Christine was in the water again, but her face was down in the water, and she never lifted her head. He hadn't ever seen anyone hold their breath so long.

"His mother was angry at him for looking at her in the first place, so he didn't tell her. She caught him staring out the window again and chased him out the door. She looked again, too, and the woman was definitely lying in the shallow water face down. The mum assumed it was deliberate. Some people like to stay in shallow water. She forgot it, followed her son to the friend's house. The two mums chatted awhile, and the boys played. They ended up driving to Oxwich for the day and swimming there, so they hadn't been around when Christine was found. They hadn't even heard about it."

"So then 8:30 was when she was killed. That means Ernie's out."

"And Stanley, probably. We need to find a customer who can vouch for his being in the store at 8:30. That clears Harold and James. I was pretty sure they didn't do it. It leaves Ellie, unless we can find a witness to verify that she went along to Pwll-du. That's crucial now. I've had people asking at the cottages along the way they took, but so far, no luck. And John," Kenneth said sadly. "I can't believe John did it, though, between us, John has a police record, and his mental stability is not the greatest. I'm going to have to stop protecting him, or protect him better, depending on how you look at it. Now I have to find him and make him talk to me. These Gower folks will pin it on John, guilty or not, if I'm not careful."

"I thought his being a poet was his redeeming feature, that people were happy to have him around."

"Some are. Harold. But you heard Evelyn. She doesn't trust him. A harmless eccentric is one thing. An unresolved murder case with a loose eccentric who has a police record—if they find out—won't fly well. I'm going to have to hunt him up. I'd better get going. Madame, your Welsh cakes were delicious, and I would love for you to show me the ring you found. Possible?"

"Yes, but you'll have to let me out."

As she moved past him, he put his arm around her waist and pulled her back.

"I hope this case is over soon," she said before he kissed her again. She thought she'd end up on the floor. "Kenneth!" He turned her and smiled. "When shall we meet again? When?"

"Soon, love. Get the ring."

She did and, when he let himself out, she followed him out the door and stood there motionless, trying to compose herself. She was aflame. She couldn't stop what was happening to her. Every cell in her body was yearning. So this, after all those years, was love.

Before Kenneth had got to Evelyn's gate, she saw the Rosewoods' car coming. Kenneth stopped. He was taking the ring out and unwrapping it. They had checked. The stone did fit. A jeweler would have to cement the stone in place again.

Kenneth kept it in his hand and put his hand back in his pocket. The Rosewoods' car pulled up. Ellie parked it. The rain had let up. Ellie waited for Ernie to get out, and they approached together.

"Good afternoon," said Kenneth in a normal, cheerful voice. "You folks have a nice day?"

"No," said Ellie. "Too much rain."

"Hello, Inspector Morgan. What about you?" asked Ernie. "Any luck on the case?" Was he using his own urbane civility as cover for his wife's abruptness, which bordered on rudeness—again?

"A few things," said Kenneth vaguely. "Might I ask you something, Mr. Rosewood?"

"Call me Ernie. Shall we go in? Ellie, you go ahead and shower and get ready. Will this take long, Inspector?"

"I'm checking up on one or two things." Kenneth smiled pleasantly and gestured for the Rosewoods to go first. Ellie brushed past Penny, nodding, obviously eager to get on with her shower. She looked fed to the teeth.

Ernie merely nodded as he passed her and went into the lounge.

"You'll be in your room?" Kenneth asked quietly.

"Yes, sure."

"I'll check with you before I leave. A busy evening for me." He winked. A whole paragraph was contained in that wink.

She sat on her bed and tried to calm her reeling senses. What would help? She picked up her diary and reread the poem. The serene stateliness of her own words did help some. She realized, if she hadn't needed so much help from within herself, she probably wouldn't have ended up a poet. What she drew strength from other people did, too. She had never had to live with so much feeling before.

Here the case was, starting to break open. She was playing a key part, even if she didn't understand how. She wrote in her diary: "How will I live with this much explosion of feeling? How will I keep my balance? How will I think? How will I do my work? Do other people go around feeling like a Fourth of July sparkler?

"Can I live with it? Stand being separated from him? Maybe things will quiet down when we're more used to each other, though this physical response may be here to stay. We are separate, distinct, autonomous people, and that has set off a bonding need I've never known before. I don't control it. I could run from it, but he isn't running. He likes our attraction, accepts it, is amused. It fans his jealousy, but—"

There was a knock on her door, different from Evelyn's. Kenneth? Would he come into her room? "Come in," she said. He did.

He closed the door behind him. He grinned at her as she put her feet onto the floor and began hunting her shoes. She knew she'd mussed her hair. When she was thinking hard, she often ran her fingers through her hair or let her hair fall loose around her shoulders, which it was now and probably sticking out in all directions.

"Stay there, love. You look beautiful. Don't tempt me by coming any closer. I need all my rationality, whatever grains I have left. It is Ernie's ring. So that fits, and I have you to thank. He lost it the first night they were here—maybe at the club. It was too tight, and he took it off. He thinks he left it on a table there. He hadn't realized until the next day. So much was happening that he hasn't done any other hunting for it. I want to ask his wife if she remembers anything, so he's fetching her. I doubt she will. She isn't being very helpful. They're very anxious to get home. He has some patients he's worried about. I told him we've about got the case wrapped up. A few loose ends. I'm not telling him the time of death. Let him worry a bit.

"I didn't tell him where the ring had been found, only that the ring had been found separately from the stone, and someone seemed to have been trying to get rid of it. It looked valuable. He said it was a ring that had once belonged to Thomas Jefferson and had come down through his family. One of Jefferson's descendants had come on hard times in the 1930s and had sold it to Ernie's father, who was a jeweler, and Ernie's father gave it to him. The stone is a real sapphire, and it has come loose before. He had gotten it re-glued before he came on this trip. He loves the ring, but you're right. I could see the mark on his finger. He can't be guilty, but he acts nervous. Oops, here they come. I'll be back."

They heard footsteps go by and on into the lounge. Kenneth opened the door, looked out, turned back to grin at her, and popped over to the bathroom. She heard the flush and then him walking down the hall and shutting the lounge door.

Penny had watched Ernie and Ellie drive off and Kenneth get in his little car and follow them. The Rosewoods turned right at the end of Heatherslade, and he turned left. She guessed that Kenneth was going to hunt for John, and the Rosewoods were off to find their dinner. James had returned soon after and proposed taking Evelyn and her out to dinner. Evelyn had come to knock on her door at five, all a-twitter.

James was not her favorite company, but Evelyn looked tired. She deserved a night out, and Penny could put up with James. "Where to?"

Evelyn said they had decided on the Oxwich Hotel, one of her favorites. James had called in a reservation for seven. They all took showers and gussied up a bit, and Penny was driven in the Rolls Royce down to Oxwich. She had always wanted to eat there, but her mind was so full of Kenneth and the case that she wasn't as thrilled as she normally would have been by the lovely view of Oxwich Bay, or the delicious steak and kidney pie in its flaky crust that ordinarily would have gotten her full attention.

While James and Evelyn got down to their usual comfortable chat, Penny stared at Oxwich Bay. It was still very light, and it was a favorite bay for sailboats and wind-surfers. She had often watched them from Oxwich Point, after climbing and walking for hours. Their bright spots of red, yellow, blue, and white, the sails tilted by the wind, the white clouds sailing overhead now in their blue sea, scudding even faster than the boats below.

While she was staring at the sails, it came to her that it had to be Ellie. Who else had had both the motive and the opportunity? She remembered Ellie's hate, from the beginning, as soon as she knew that Christine was German. How Christine had infuriated but fascinated her, too. Could she have dashed back from part-way to Pwll-du and down to Three Cliffs? If she had, she had had the time. If it wasn't Ellie, it had to be John.

If it was John, that would be sad. Her intuition wasn't giving her an absolutely clear reading, but she didn't think it was John. Could a poet be a killer? Poets had all the human failings, as she well knew. They had killed themselves often enough. But other people? She couldn't think of any cases. Ellie seemed more likely.

James had insisted on driving them down to Rhossili to see the view. They missed most of the sunset, but it was beautiful even so, the dark shape of Worm's Head Point jutting out into the sea as the last pinks and purples were fading from the sky to the west and the water below it. The old rock the Vikings had named a "worm" or dragon rose serenely, with majesty and whatever it is that stirs our awe, out of its sea bed. Waves broke against it—the isthmus was long since under water. You couldn't tell it had any connection to the mainland at all. More creature than rock, more living than dead; it caught at one's heart. Maybe the sheer loneliness of it—it had been there at least since the Vikings and how many centuries before that?—rising out of the mist like a benign guardian of this coast—always made her ache. When would she see Kenneth next?

They got back to Pobbles House about ten. It was almost dark. They were in the lounge watching the ten o'clock news when Kenneth knocked. Penny saw the gladness, and exhaustion, in his eyes when he came into the room.

"Have you a minute, Penny? Could you come outside?"

"Of course," she said. "Be right back, Evelyn." Evelyn was smiling, and James was locked into the news.

When they were on the walk outside, he slipped his arm around her waist and then pulled her around to face him and kissed her. Jiminy crickets. She didn't want him to stop whether she collapsed or not. But stop he did.

"Will you walk with me?"

"I will if I can. You make it hard."

He chuckled. "A lot to tell you." When they got well out of range of anyone's hearing them, he began, keeping his arm around her waist. Her cells quieted a little. "I found John. I went door to door in those shacks behind the water tower—the ones that aren't fixed up. He often makes himself a nest there in the winter."

"Yes," said Penny. "Remember, I told you, that day I saw him at the library, that I'd seen him headed that way."

"Oh, right. An old couple lets him stay there when they're not using it. It needs paint, and John had pots set out because the roof leaks. I terrified him. He was sure I thought he had killed her. He said you believed he'd done it. Do you?"

"No," she said. "I don't think it's John. I teased him in the library that morning about Christine's ghost coming back to haunt him. I shouldn't have. As soon as I said it, I could tell he was taking it wrong. He has absolutely no sense of humor."

"You're right about that." Kenneth pulled her to him. "Do I have a sense of humor?"

"Not only that," said Penny. "I can't walk when you do these things to me. Which is it: love or the case? I'm not talented at both at once. Kenneth, I can't think."

"I thought walking was the problem."

"Thinking, too."

"Oh." He was silent, continuing to walk and returning his arm to her waist. "The case first then, the senses later."

"Thank you." She kept pace with him, miraculously. Amazing how calm she sounded. Could she think? She doubted it. She could listen.

He had talked John into going into the police station in Swansea for his own safety. John had spent many nights in jail for vagrancy and talking back to officers. He was not perturbed by that but worried he'd be accused of the murder. Kenneth had patiently explained that, if he had helped Kenneth in the first place, he wouldn't have worked himself into such a state. In the station Kenneth had gotten John's statement. Yes, he had slept behind the dunes that Thursday night, closer to Stanley's store than to Pobbles and Three Cliffs. He hadn't been sure when he had wakened that morning. He had no watch. He had said about eight, judging by how high the sun was. He had gone straight to Stanley's store, to the back door, and Stanley had sold him some milk. They had worked this out because he was terrified of another run-in with Christine. He was afraid his ulcer would start bleeding again."

"If he woke at eight and met Stanley there and Stanley was back, it must have been 8:30 or after."

"Right, love."

"What else did you learn?"

"Mainly that. If we can confirm the time with Stanley, and/or find other witnesses to Stanley's being at the store then, John is safe. I told him that. It relieved him a good bit. He'll try to help. But why didn't Stanley tell me he'd seen John that morning? It would have saved me a lot of trouble."

"You will probably learn that, too. Time and patience seem to be helping. That half-aborigine detective of Arthur Upfield's, Bony, was always saying that that's what it took: time and patience. He thought in time the truth would always come out."

"The truth does come out, all right," said Kenneth and he turned her to face him again. "I love you, dearest Penelope. I must kiss you now and, if you can't walk, I'll carry you."

He held her. They were right there on the sidewalk in front of a house that was dark, true, but still. The man was high risk. It was near the intersection of Heatherslade Lane and the main road. But actually she couldn't care less. That's what it had come to.

They were suddenly aware of a car's headlights and moved apart in time to see a car pass.

"The Rosewoods," said Penny. "My love, I will collapse, if you keep this up. Isn't there somewhere we could go?"

"There is," he said. "Do you trust me?"

"I do," she said.

"Reckless woman."

"You make me reckless."

"All right. What say we go back and collect my car? You have your key?"

"Yes." She felt in her pocket. Thank Athena she had not had a chance to empty her pockets. "Yes, I do."

"Do you love me, Penny?"

He was holding her again, pressing her against him, and how she wanted him to. "I do," she said.

"We need to talk about us."

"Yes," was all she managed.

They had almost reached Pobbles House when they saw the Rosewoods' car lights go on again and heard the sound of the engine starting up, Ernie driving. He stopped when he saw them.

"Inspector, I was looking for you. I've found a witness who saw us going toward Pwll-du that morning."

Ernie looked very happy, had opened his car door, which made the inside light go on. He looked more relaxed than he had for days. He didn't seem perturbed to have found them together, though he must have picked up their intimacy with each other. He was intent on conveying his news to Kenneth, who asked him to explain.

"I knew you didn't have any evidence besides our word, that we'd gone toward Pwll-du, and I figured that was why you were keeping us. I'd expected you to find a witness who saw us, but you hadn't as far as I could tell."

"No," said Kenneth. "I hadn't. Some of the Swansea men have been knocking on doors along your route to Pwll-du, but they hadn't found a witness, and I had other people I had to talk to first."

"I understand," said Ernie, who was all graciousness. "Then you found my ring. You didn't say what you thought that meant. But that worried me, Inspector, I can tell you. I decided to see if I could find anyone in those houses up along the way we walked to Pwll-du, in case—"

Kenneth nodded. "And you did?"

"Yes." He said it, smugly, like a boy who has caught his first fish. "It's an elderly woman, a Mrs. Davies. She lives near the end of that row of houses. She was having an early cup of tea and saw us go by. She was at the window from 7:15 or so until 7:30. She saw us go by right after she sat down, and then some minutes later, about 7:30, she saw me walking back. She could tell we were Americans. She wondered why I wasn't with my wife."

"You got her phone number?" asked Kenneth.

"I did. I'll give it to you. Here. Mrs. Maudie Davies. She's very willing to come to the station to make a statement. She was as sweet about it as she could be."

"Thanks, Mr. Rosewood," said Kenneth. "I'm obliged to you. If you and your wife could come into the Reynoldston station at ten in the morning, I want to talk with you once more, and then if this Mrs. Davies clears you, I'll return your passports and help you reserve your ticket home. I'm sure you'll be relieved to leave. See you then."

He waved Ernie off, after asking him to tell Evelyn he was taking Penny out for a pint and she had her key. Then he turned to Penny. "Hmm. Interesting. What do you make of that, love?"

She didn't know. It was confusing. This witness would seem to clear the Rosewoods, or at least verify their story. "Something's bothering me about it," she said, "though I'm not sure what it is. It's not rational."

"Let's leave the case to itself for a couple of hours and forget rationality." He reclaimed her waist and steered her toward his car, saw her into the passenger side, walked around, and settled in the driver's seat. "Should we have gone back to tell Evelyn ourselves? Will she worry?"

"I don't think so. She's in the plot."

"The plot, eh?" He reached over and put his hand on her thigh. "Which plot is that?"

"The plot to—" Maybe he didn't want to marry her. She was assuming he did. In any case, was it only a marriage plot? Was that all it was? No, it was a quest plot, too, for her at least. What to say?

"I think you'd better talk to her," she finally said. "Evelyn sees plots differently than I do. I'm not sure how you and I see plots yet either."

"We need to talk about that, love," he said, letting out the clutch and pulling away from the curb.

"We do," she said. "Where are you taking me?"

"You said you trusted me."

"Yes, I think I do."

"You think so? What do you feel, Penny?"

"Kenneth, what does all this mean to you? If we sleep together . . . "

"You mean, when I finally get to love you all over and do everything I've imagined?"

TWENTY

On Tuesday morning, so much happened so fast that, when Penny thought back on it later, she couldn't believe there'd been time for that much to occur between seven a.m. and lunch time.

The milkman had awakened her—and after not getting in until 3 a.m. They had gone from Pobbles House to Kenneth's apartment, had had hot chocolate and buns, and talked through as much of their future as they could sort out. Kenneth would keep his inspector job, which he liked, and Penny would move to Wales as soon as she could, but she'd make regular visits to the States to see her friends and her children and keep up her American writing contacts.

He'd go to North Carolina as often as he could get time off, but definitely for Christmas. By the next summer they hoped to marry in the little church of St. Cennydd, where Penny had always wanted to be married since she'd found it several summers earlier. They'd keep on with their different interests and friends. Meantime Penny was going to move into his flat, as soon as she had broken the news to Evelyn, and they'd have eight weeks before she had to go back to the States. She had ongoing responsibilities there: her teaching job, at least for another year.

She should have been tired when she heard the milk bottles clanking into their holder, but she wasn't. Her happiness from the night before rushed back into her mind. She put on her glasses and walked in her underwear to the little mirror on the door of the wardrobe. He keeps saying I'm beautiful. I never ever thought so. I figured I'd have to be loved for myself alone. But she could see, when she smiled, some of what Kenneth saw. She was shining. She looked vital, interesting, happy, lively. How about that? She pulled on her jeans, felt in her pocket (her key was still there), pulled on the same shirt and sweater.

Lucy had been up yesterday at this hour. Maybe she'd invite her for tea today, if she dropped by. She had to see Lucy.

She found Evelyn in the hall, reorganizing her airing closet. "Penny! You scared me. You're getting up early a lot. What's up?"

"I'm out for a little walk before breakfast again. Okay?"

"Certainly. Penny, weren't you a little late getting in?" Evelyn looked like she was dying to know what was up and knew very well that something was.

"I *was* late." .

"I thought you'd sleep till eight. Any new developments on the Kenneth front?"

"Yes. We're getting married."

"Penny!" Evelyn shrieked and then caught herself.

"Not for a year, Evelyn, and it's a secret for now. Evelyn, he's so lovely! I'm so happy." She gave her a bear hug, which knocked Evelyn's glasses askew, but had her beaming.

"Oh, all right, Penny, I won't tell a soul. That's super. I'll hear more later," she whispered conspiratorially. "You go have your walk. My stars, I did shriek. I probably woke everybody up."

Lucy was awake but still in her robe, and Hera, wagging her tail furiously, welcomed Penny into the kitchen where Lucy was making herself wholemeal toast and Earl Grey tea.

"I have news, Lucy," said Penny, settling into the little breakfast nook with its wooden benches on either side of the table, which was laid with a white cloth and a vase of those lovely yellow and pink roses.

"News. Hmm. Find the murderer?" Lucy muttered under her breath for the toast to hurry. She seemed distracted. Penny waited for her to settle opposite her. Lucy offered Penny toast, with homemade bramble jam. Then she poured them each a cup of steaming tea.

"I'm having breakfast at Evelyn's, but, okay, one piece. Mmm, this is great jam. Did you make it?"

"No, I'm all thumbs in the kitchen. I can barely make toast. But a friend takes pity on me and shares her jam. Good, isn't it? It's local. She goes out and collects the berries herself in September."

"Speaking of September, that's my news. I'm staying until mid-September."

"Oh, that's nice. What made you decide to do that?"

178

Penny smiled. "I'm going to live with Kenneth, so I'll save money and can stay longer."

Finally Lucy tuned in to what Penny was saying. She opened her eyes wide. "Live with Kenneth? You mean marry him?"

"Not yet, but next year. What do you think? Can I have both a marriage plot and a quest plot?"

Lucy smiled. "Ah, Penny, I expect you can—you and Kenneth both—if you work at it. I've been asking the goddess to look out for you."

"Which goddess?" asked Penny.

"Hera, of course. She looks after long-term relationships." Hera yipped. She was sitting quietly, waiting for toast crumbs to fall. If any did, they wouldn't go to waste. "Aphrodite, too. I talked to her. Plus, I prayed to Athena that you wouldn't lose your head altogether."

"I have, I'm afraid," said Penny. "I'm head over heels." Hera yipped again.

"Hera approves. So do I. That's smashing, Penny. Will you live here?"

"As much as I can. We each want to keep on with what we're interested in. I'll go back to the States in mid-September. By the time I'm your age, I'll probably be here more than there. This is a little unusual, I realize, as I'm only getting to know you, but would you be my maid of honor or whatever it's called over here?"

Lucy laughed loudly and got up to get the kettle to pour more hot water on the tea leaves. "Of course, Penny. I'd be honored. How's your virtue?"

"All gone."

Lucy roared and almost poured the hot water on Hera. She was laughing so hard, she had to sit down. Hera looked utterly baffled.

When their laughter had subsided, and they'd resumed tea drinking, Lucy asked, "By the way, how's this dreadful case coming along? Has Kenneth got it solved yet?"

"Not only Kenneth," said Penny. "I've been helping the police with their inquiries."

"I bet you have." Lucy laughed again.

"No, listen." She filled her in on the ring's being Ernie's, yes, the American psychiatrist's, and how the Rosewoods had found a witness to back up their story, how John had apparently been at Stanley's that morning, so he was out of danger, if they could find someone who'd seen him, and how that Friday morning two people had seen Christine alive at 8:25 and dead at close to 8:35.

"Penny, what time was it you needed someone who saw John last Friday?"

"John says he went into Stanley's store about 8:30."

"He did. I saw him. I was up there Friday, my morning off. I go to town to shop and run errands. I ran up to Stanley's first to get a paper and a couple of items I like to buy there. John was walking toward the back door of the shop."

"You saw him? You're sure about the time?"

Lucy nodded. "Of course. Let's see. Yes, I like to leave here about then. I try to get my car started and leave it running a few minutes, and then head out at 8:30. So it couldn't have been more than 8:35. It only takes a few minutes to drive up there. I circled around and was parking, and I saw John loping toward Stanley's back door. I wondered why he was going to the back door."

"This is a real help, Lucy. We hadn't yet found someone who could verify that Stanley was in the store at 8:30. You must have seen him, too."

"Oh, yes, he waited on me. His daughter came in from the back and asked if it was all right to sell that poet milk at the back door, and he said, yes, so she collected two pints and carried them back there. Why he was at the back door?"

"Stanley says because he was trying to avoid Christine. This helps, Lucy. Could you come over to Reynoldston or into the Swansea police and let Kenneth take your statement? I know he would want you to. He doesn't think John did it, and he has been worrying John would get scapegoated."

"When do I need to go?"

"Ideally this morning. The sooner the better. If Kenneth can't tie up the case, he'll have to turn it over to his higher ups."

"The library opens at ten. I could ask my substitute to go in. She's usually willing. Let's see. It's eight now."

"Eight? I'd better get back. Lucy, in any case, call the Swansea police station and leave Kenneth a message, okay? See what he wants you to do. I need to go. Evelyn will be fit to be tied if I'm late."

"Certainly, Penny. I'll call. Do you think you could ride in with me?

For company. I've never done this before. It would help to have a friend along. Then we can talk more about you and Kenneth. I'm so glad you two got together. What fun. I've never been a maid of honor, Penny. This will be super. Who will be the best man?"

"I don't know yet. We didn't get very far in our planning."

Lucy roared. "You two have known each other how many days?"

Penny counted on her fingers: "Friday, Saturday, Sunday, Monday, Tuesday. That's five, counting today. I haven't seen him yet today." Lucy pushed her out the door, still laughing.

☞

Every summer she'd been on Gower Penny had been in Reynoldston to walk up to Arthur's Stone on Cefn Bryn, the low mountain that was visible from most points on the peninsula. She'd ride the bus to the Reynoldston green, opposite the King Arthur Hotel, and walk up the road that crossed the mountain and then through bracken over to the ancient stone called Arthur's, with its broken piece lying flat beside it. To Penny it represented the place where Arthur had pulled his sword, Excalibur, out of the stone. She found it a perfect place to renew her vows for her life and to put things in perspective for another year. She wished she could walk up there today to freshen her sight and remake her vow to keep to her own quest plot as well as this new marriage plot, but maybe that walk was best done with Kenneth when he was free of this troubling case.

She'd never noticed the little police station next to the hotel. When Lucy parked her small green car beside the village green, Penny spotted the blue globe in front of the station, between the hotel and a craft shop. It was quarter to ten. Kenneth had asked Lucy to come there to make and sign her statement. James was to be there at 10:30 to change his statement. Evelyn had promised to accompany him.

When Lucy pulled open the heavy outer door, there were two people waiting in the small anteroom, where a desk officer with greying hair, a small goatee, and glasses was presiding. Lucy walked up to him and gave her name, then introduced Penny. They were asked to have a seat. Inspector Morgan was due any time. On one of the benches along the wall toward the craft shop were a woman in her early thirties and a boy of about twelve. Probably Tod and Mrs. Matthews, the witnesses who had seen Christine alive, then dead shortly afterwards. Lucy sat down on the bench along the street wall, and Penny sat next to her. The mood in the room was solemn. The Matthews' evidence had been vital and had cleared a lot of people, but they could be nervous.

Mrs. Matthews smoothed her son's dark hair and straightened the collar of his white sports shirt. Her blonde hair was pulled into a neat bun, and she wore a sleeveless, summery dress. The boy had on long trousers and new white trainers, as the British called tennis shoes. He was as relaxed and eager as she was nervous and twitchy. Penny watched his eyes take in the room, especially every move the man on the desk made. His mother fidgeted, shifted her position on the hard bench, straightened her skirt, and avoided looking at Penny and Lucy, who had both brought books. Lucy had opened hers immediately. Penny was opening her Grimes when the poet John walked in, followed by a small, thin, elderly woman wearing tinted glasses and a hearing aid, and then Kenneth, who nodded first to the desk officer, then glanced around the room, caught Penny's eye, smiled, and then walked over to Mrs. Matthews.

"Good morning, Mrs. Matthews, Tod. Thank you for coming in. I have two people to see first, but I'll be with you very soon."

He turned to Lucy. "Ah, Ms. Straley. Sorry to take you from the library this morning, but I appreciate your coming. I have a few people to see before I can get your statement, but I'll be with you soon. Then you can get back to your book lovers."

He smiled at Penny, all his gladness in his eyes. The man spoke volumes with his eyes. She hoped he might yet tie up this case so his life and hers could return to normal—not exactly normal—as everything had changed for them both—but to a new normal—a normal they hadn't had time to invent yet.

When he'd disappeared with John and Mrs. Davies, Lucy whispered, "What a lucky woman you are, Penny. Few men love with such ardor and the respect he obviously has for who you are."

"I know," she whispered back. "Sometimes I still can't believe it."

Next Ernie and Ellie Rosewood entered. Ernie noticed her and Lucy immediately. He stopped in the middle of the room as if he wanted to come over, but Ellie walked straight up to the desk. "We're here to see Inspector Morgan about getting our passports back. Did a Mrs. Davies make her statement yet?"

The officer looked unruffled and replied politely. "And you would be?"

"Ernest and Eloise Rosewood, Americans," she said, like that nationality deserved special consideration. Ernie had gone to stand beside her.

"I'll tell Inspector Morgan you're here. Please be seated." He gestured to the benches.

"Could you tell him it's urgent? We were told we could leave today and fly home."

"Please be seated. Inspector Morgan will be with you as soon as he is able to."

Ellie looked like she wanted to argue, but Ernie took her arm and turned toward the benches. "Let's sit down, Ellie." He walked over and sat down by Lucy. Ellie broke away, saying, "I'll be right outside. It's crowded and stuffy in here. Come get me, Ernie, when he can see us."

It hit Penny that finally she could introduce Ernie to Lucy. She caught Ernie's eye and said, "Ernie, here's someone who has been dying to meet you—our Gower librarian, Lucy Straley. She heard you were an American psychoanalyst and wanted to ask you some questions, if you don't mind?"

Lucy closed her book and beamed at Ernie. "I'm delighted to meet you, Dr.—."

"Rosewood. Call me Ernie. I'm happy to answer questions, but I hope we won't have to wait long. Penny, do you know what's up? Is Inspector Morgan here?"

Penny nodded. "He brought your witness in, Mrs. Davies. These other people are also here to make statements. I'm sure he'll see to everyone as quickly as possible. You talk to Lucy. I'll go out and get some fresh air. Be back shortly."

As Penny crossed the street to the green, Ellie looked up from her pacing. "He's ready for us?"

"No, not yet. I came out to get some fresh air, too. It shouldn't be too long. He's talking to Mrs. Davies now."

"It was a complete waste of time for us to stay," said Ellie. "I never met anybody as inconsiderate as that inspector."

Penny couldn't believe her ears. "What inspector?"

"This Morgan—or whatever. We've been hanging around because of his whim since Friday, and he never found a witness. We had to find one ourselves. I can't believe these British. No wonder the Americans rebelled and started their own country."

Penny could think of nothing to say. She determined not to let this woman upset her. Then a Rolls Royce slowed to a smooth stop at the edge of the green behind Lucy's car. James and Evelyn. Good. "I'm going to see how Evelyn's doing," she said to Ellie. What bitterness Ellie had. She was determined to see the worst in people. Of course, no one else knew Kenneth as she did. How small-minded and unfair she was, how utterly self-centered. She was as bad as Christine.

Lucy and Ernie were deep in Freud's view of infant sexuality when Penny, followed by Evelyn and James, walked back into the waiting room. Evelyn led James over to the desk, and then they took the last two places on the benches. Evelyn immediately began chatting with James. Good, she'd keep him steady and focused.

They'd all been caught up in the puzzle of who had killed Christine, but there it was: death. Some people in this world got angry enough to take the lives of other people. She was again present in that moment when she had had to identify Christine. She'd never forget James's white, shocked face when he came into the post office that morning. He looked sad now. He must be reliving it, too. Bless Evelyn for sticking by him. She was telling him that Arthur's Stone was less than a mile away. They could easily drive up to see it after he'd given his statement.

The outer door opened again, and Stanley and Harold came in. Hadn't they already made their statements? Harold walked over to them while Stanley checked in at the desk. "We have to correct our statements, Evelyn. Hello, Mr. Hampton. Is it a long wait?"

Evelyn turned to James. "Mr. Hampton is correcting his, too, and these other people. She nodded toward Mrs. Matthews and Tod. Then she smiled. "Join the queue." There being no seats left, the two men, once they'd checked in, stood waiting by the desk.

It was 10:20 by the wall clock when Kenneth returned to the waiting room, leading John up to the desk, and then leading Mrs. Davies over to Penny and Lucy. "I wonder, Ms. Straley, if you might take Mrs. Davies home when you've given your statement. She doesn't live far from you. I'll get yours as soon as I get the Mathews ones. Would you be willing?" He glanced at Penny, his eyes happy. Was he able to attend to all these people as he needed to? He looked like he might float away.

Ernie jumped up so that Mrs. Davies could sit by Lucy, and said, "Thank you, Inspector, for seeing Mrs. Davies. Everything's okay then? We can leave?"

Kenneth looked sober suddenly as he focused on Ernie. "I'll be able to see you and your wife in about thirty minutes. I have three people ahead of you."

"But we're cleared?"

"I'll want to talk to you first. Please wait here." He glanced around at the full waiting room, nodded to Stanley and Harold. "Or right outside. I'm taking these folks next, so that will free some seats. Sorry, it's a small station but more convenient than driving into Swansea." Then he led the Mathews mother and son back into his office.

John had turned from the desk, evidently cleared to leave, then hurried to the outer door and disappeared. One poet who could return to normal. Ernie, looking unhappy, walked out the door, no doubt in quest of his wife.

By 11:30 they were all back home. Evelyn bustled into her kitchen to make herself and James a bite to eat. Penny had said she'd head out for the cliffs. Kenneth was delayed; he had no choice but to call in the Major Crimes Department. All their possible suspects were apparently innocent. Ellie and Ernie were free to fly home and had their new reservation. They were in their room packing up.

Something was nagging at Penny, but she couldn't get ahold of it. Perhaps getting out on the cliffs would help. There no longer was any reason for worrying about going out on her own. She went in her room to gather lunch makings: digestive biscuits, peanut butter. She changed into shorts and put on her hiking boots. It was already up to 80. The sun was bright. Not a single cloud.

Ernie passed her door, carrying suitcases out. They'd be gone. She was glad. She wasn't eager to see the Rosewoods again. She hadn't enjoyed Ernie much lately, though Lucy had. Let her fill her thermos with water, and she'd be off.

She crossed the hall, saw that the bathroom door was ajar, and walked in. But it wasn't empty. Ellie turned around quickly to face her. She looked furious. "I'm sorry," said Penny. "I didn't think anyone was in here."

"You never do think, do you?" snapped Ellie. Why was she so angry?

Those eyes. Such rage. For so little cause. This was definitely an un-happy woman. Penny began to back up. "I was going to fill my thermos, but I can get water in the kitchen. Sorry," she said again, quickly, em-phatically, but unemotionally, the way the British say it.

Ellie continued to look very angry. Then Penny remembered that morning when Ellie had been so angry at Christine and had wanted to leave the breakfast table but had seemed frozen, held there listening to what she didn't want to hear, almost against her will. Suddenly it came back to Penny: Ellie had been wearing the ring with the blue stone that morning. She had seen it on Ellie's finger, not on Ernie's. Had Ernie lost it or given it to Ellie to wear?

She stepped back. Ellie apparently picked up something in her face as she took hold of the door as if she planned to close it and lock it as soon as Penny moved out of the way. But Penny didn't move.

"You were wearing Ernie's ring. So it must have been you who lost the stone."

"Ring?" Ellie grabbed the door. She wanted Penny out. "I don't know what you're talking about. I need to close this door."

"I want to talk to you about Ernie's ring. You lost the stone down at Three Cliffs and then threw the ring itself into a rose garden. Why?"

"You're crazy," shrieked Ellie. "I'm shutting this door. Move or I'll get your foot in it."

Penny left her foot where it was. Her foot—both feet—were in their hiking boots, providentially, so Ellie's pushing on the door, held open only by her foot now, wasn't hurting much.

"You must have been down there the morning Christine was killed," said Penny.

"I was at Pwll-du, I told you. That old biddy told you, too. Get out!" She was screaming.

"I think you killed Christine," said Penny calmly. "Prove you didn't."

Suddenly Ellie lurched at her, a truly mad look in her eyes, and grabbed her throat.

Even though Penny had accused her of murder, she wasn't expect-ing Ellie immediately to try to throttle her. When she felt Ellie's hands on her throat, she instinctively began to poke Ellie in the ribs, tickle her. But then she lost her balance, felt herself falling, and blacked out.

Penny learned later that Evelyn had come running in with her teakettle when she heard Ellie scream, and seeing Ellie going for Penny's throat again, where she lay on the floor, she had thrown the teakettle at Ellie. This effectively stopped Ellie cold. She, too, fell to the floor, and an enormous lump began to form on her forehead where the teakettle had hit. Evelyn thought she'd killed her, leaned back against the wall, fainted, and slumped to the floor, too.

When Ernie came in, followed by Kenneth, who'd also arrived, and James, who was coming out of the lounge to see what the commotion was, the three women were lying in the hall in a heap, all of them out cold.

Penny learned later that Ernie had guessed immediately that his wife had had a post traumatic stress episode. He rushed to her, partly pulled her, partly carried her into their bedroom. Kenneth, after checking Evelyn's pulse, went right for Penny, listened to her heart, gently touched the bruise marks on her face and neck. She opened her eyes. "My love, let me help you up. Are you all right?"

Penny remembered. "Ellie, Kenneth. I accused her of killing Christine, and she tried to choke me. Where is she? She didn't get away?"

"No, she's here. Can you stand?"

"Yes."

"I want you to go in your room and lie down."

Penny saw Evelyn and panicked. "Did she kill Evelyn?"

"No, no, Evelyn almost killed her. Evelyn fainted, but she must have thrown this teakettle first. Ellie has a big knot on her head."

Penny wasn't quite up to a laugh, but she smiled and turned to look at Evelyn. James was fanning her with his handkerchief.

"I checked her pulse," Kenneth said, as Penny walked into her room. "She's fine. James, why don't you go wet that handkerchief, and we'll see if we can bring her around." They did, and Penny heard them leading Evelyn into her bedroom.

About this time Ernie reappeared and said to Kenneth, "I'm afraid my wife has had a bad episode. It hasn't happened for years, and I wanted to believe she was cured. Inspector, given how she behaved just now—she tried to strangle Penny, right?"

Kenneth nodded.

"I'm afraid she may have killed Christine. I've given her a sedative. I'd like to get her to a hospital. Can you call an ambulance? Tell them to be sure they have restraining straps. She's not going to like waking up."

Kenneth said later that he had seldom seen such sad eyes as Ernie Rosewood's as he spoke about his wife. Then Ernie had gone back into the bedroom to stay with Ellie while Kenneth called the ambulance.

Evelyn was soon on her feet again, and Penny rested for only ten minutes, then joined the others in the kitchen. Evelyn filled the teakettle. It was only a little dented. James set out plates and cups, and all of them sat down to drink tea and wait for the ambulance.

"I never liked her," said James.

As Penny sipped her tea, Kenneth beside her with his left hand on her leg under the table, she thought how sad it was. James had lost his wife, and so had Ernie, though neither had truly had them. Neither marriage had been happy, and both were over now. Yet here she was beginning her own.

Ernie appeared again. He stood drinking the tea they offered him. "I feel responsible, Inspector. I did lie about one thing. I didn't lose the ring. I took it off in the pub that first night, and I said Ellie could wear it. When you found it, I was afraid, but I couldn't face it. I found that old woman who had seen us go by. I wanted to believe that saved us. I couldn't bear the truth staring me in the face." He looked miserable.

"Are you certain she did it?" asked Kenneth.

"Yes. I think she'll admit it now. She'll have to be hospitalized for the rest of her life. The doctor she has worked with told me that she might relapse, that I should be alert. She had medicine, and I tried to make sure she was taking it. I thought I was on top of it—I have tried to be—God knows—for years, but I wasn't alert enough. I'm so sorry."

The ambulance arrived then, and Ernie went with them to the hospital in Swansea.

When the ambulance was gone, Evelyn lay down, saying it was too much excitement in one day. James walked up to the top for a newspaper. Kenneth and Penny urged him to walk along the cliffs. He looked like he might.

They settled in the lounge on Evelyn's couch.

Penny said, "I have a surprise for you."

"You won't throw a teakettle at me?"

They collapsed giggling. "No, no," said Penny. "I want to read you a poem." And she did.

EPILOGUE

July 10. Thursday morning.

Dear Cathy,

Finally I have a chance to write you a real letter. A lot has happened. Don't you think there are moments in our lives when a lot of loose strands inside us get gathered up into one bunch and then get knotted together? Ten days ago I had the foreground of my life's painting sketched in, though I still hoped to find someone to be in the foreground with me, and I've found him, Cathy, right here on Gower. Not even a whole week ago. Kenneth and I are planning to get married next year. A week from Monday I'm moving in with him, so write me there.

I think I told you that a German woman who was staying with Evelyn got murdered last Friday, and the detective inspector turned out to be a single man my age, and it developed quickly.

I've thought of your telling me how you tried to give up Rick and how your inability to do so helped you see that you should marry him. Then I think of Amanda Cross's words in *Sweet Death, Kind Death*: "Only those can genuinely marry who are already married. It is as though you know you are married when you come to see that you cannot divorce, that is, when you find that your lives simply will not disentangle. If your love is lucky, this knowledge will be greeted with laughter." I'm laughing. I wish you were here to laugh with me.

It has been a raging sexual attraction, hitting me so below the belt that I wondered if I could be wise. Kenneth and I are determined to continue as we were, adding this new ingredient.

While we were falling in love, we were solving the murder. It turned out to be a fellow countrywoman. Her husband's a shrink. She had a tough childhood. Both women did. Both were victims of World War II.

The Sands of Gower

We think World War II is over. They're still fighting it here. Like it's so hard to do away with racism in the U.S.—I know how discouraged you get—so it's hard for Europeans to get over their hatred of Germans and anti-Semitism.

Ellie's mother was in the French underground. The Germans arrested her in front of Ellie when she was only three. Later they tortured and killed her. Ellie became obsessed with any signs of anti-Semitism, and she hated Germans. Those Gestapo officers left scars that set off rage years later. Her husband finally told us that she was susceptible to rages, a symptom of her post traumatic stress disorder. She'd had ten years without any episodes, was on medication, but he had grown careless, he admits.

She almost got away with it because he was so protective of her. On Tuesday morning, it still wasn't clear. Then a gut reaction caused me to accuse Ellie of killing Christine, and she nearly killed me. Fortunately, Evelyn was a good shot with a tea kettle.

Ellie did confess then, but Kenneth went back to Mrs. Davies, the witness Ernie had found who had seen them both heading for Pwll-du, and it turned out that she had also seen Ellie going back by. She hadn't understood that that was crucial evidence. But she doesn't hear well, and Ernie was mainly determined to have a witness that they had both gone toward Pwll-du. Ellie had cut behind some houses and gone through the village down to Three Cliffs Bay.

I didn't like Christine. You know how some people radiate their positive energy, their pleasure in life, their zest at being alive. She radiated the opposite. She expected and got the worst side of everyone. Nor was she able to stop herself. She went rushing on, creating anger around her as if she fed off of it. In a way, her own hopelessness, her narcissistic rattling around in her own cage, drew her death right to her.

When Ellie woke up in the emergency room of the Swansea hospital late Tuesday afternoon, Ernie and Kenneth were both there. Ernie had drugged her before they called an ambulance, and they had put her in a straightjacket, rather awful. She couldn't move. She was strapped down to a table. They had a hypodermic ready to give her if she got violent.

Ernie had agreed to talk to her while Kenneth was there, so that he could write down and record what she said. First, as she was coming to, she was really sad. She began crying when she realized she was strapped down. Kenneth said Ernie was crying, too, and he felt like it himself even after all he'd been through with this case. But he reminded me: murder is always tragic. No matter what. So here was Ellie, sobbing and trying to reach out to her husband, and he wasn't touching her, too aware of how fast her tears could turn to rage, but he was using his voice to soothe her. Kenneth said he was good—it would have soothed him. It came as close to touching as a voice can.

When he asked her to tell what she had done to Christine, she began to shriek: "She deserved it. She asked for it, the bitch. Bitches like her killed my mother, helped men rape her, put needles in her. She was a goddamned German bitch. She deserved to die."

Then tears again. "She said my mother was a no-good Jew. She said the Jews had had to be stopped. She said the French underground was worse than the Nazis, and they were just as cruel. I couldn't let her say that. I told her to stop. She wouldn't listen. She was splashing water on herself and acting as if I weren't even there. She thought she looked so great in that little blue bikini of hers.

"She didn't care about anything but making men want to lay her. How could she say those things? My mother was good. She died because of those horrid Germans, and I couldn't let that German bitch keep talking like that. I couldn't. She wouldn't shut up. I had to shut her up. Then she lost her balance and fell, and I grabbed her by the hair and shook her. She yelled, 'Get away. Don't you touch me, filthy Jew!' I had to make her stop. The ocean was polluted with her. She was the filthy one. I was glad when she stopped talking. I didn't want her ugly body in the ocean rotting and polluting it, but I didn't know what else to do. The tide was taking her out. So I left. She deserved it.

"Why didn't the ocean keep her? Even the ocean hated her. It brought her back. Ernie, let me out of this thing. Ernie!" When he shook his head slowly, she began to shriek again. "I hate you. You're no husband. You always take the other side. You're as bad as the filthy Germans. I'm glad I threw your ring away. Stupid old ring. Why should a Jew have a ring that belonged to Jefferson? What did he do to help Jews? What did you ever do? You hate me." Then a nurse moved in to give her the sedative, while Ernie turned away, his eyes pouring tears, looking unable even to stand up.

Kenneth said he stayed with Ernie awhile. Cathy, I liked Ernie. I don't blame him, even though his carelessness almost cost me my own life. Kenneth is real good with people. Ernie's the shrink, but Kenneth is wiser, wiser than science has learned to be wise. He understood Ernie's dilemma, and Christine's and Ellie's. Ellie lost her mother too young, Ernie said; and had too many substitutes, and all of them hated the Germans.

Christine, Ernie thinks, must have had an equally hard time growing up during the period when Germany was being occupied and the German people were going through that terrible defeat. They'd brought it on themselves, but it was still humiliating and difficult. The Allies were so determined they should never be able to make war on other nations again. Christine was in Germany until her late teens. Then her mother died, and she came to England. James was her second husband. She'd had an earlier and very miserable marriage to a lorry driver. He was cruel to her for years, James told us, which kept her from marrying anyone else for awhile. But she always had men fluttering around her, like moths to a sputtering candle, and she always dressed fit to kill. Her tragedy was that she made everyone want to kill her. We suspected everyone, because everybody wanted her gone.

It's over now. We're trying to get back to normal. Kenneth had to see to a lot of paperwork yesterday, and today he and Ernie are working out how Ellie will be flown home. Very sedated, I gather, and with a plainclothes guard, and then handed over to police at JFK. She'll have to be in a prison hospital for awhile, and she'll never be able to live outside a hospital again.

By Friday afternoon Kenneth thinks he'll be free, and we're going to Oxwich for a picnic and a swim, if the weather's okay. It's pouring rain today, but maybe the sun will return when we want it to. You never know in Wales.

Christine's husband had offered five thousand pounds for information leading to the arrest of the murderer. Guess who is five thousand pounds richer? Yes, your very own friend. It will help launch me on this new double-career, which I've watched you handle with such grace, of a marriage plus a quest plot. Write me, and think of me a week from Monday. Marriage number two, but the first one that Old Necessity chose for me.

Love, Penny

Judy Hogan is a postmenopausal woman who loves to write, farm, think, and laugh. She has one foot in Erik Erikson's Generativity vs Stagnation phase, and the other foot in his Ego Integrity vs Despair stage. She's determined to share whatever she has learned over nearly eight decades and also keep her sense of self strong. We live in a century where our two most urgent issues are: accepting all other people as equally human and taking care of our earth. If we can't learn fast enough, we will lose our planet village. I myself have been in all the basic situations in which my sleuth Penny Weaver finds herself, but of course no murder occurred.

Judy's first two published mysteries, *Killer Frost* (2012) and *Farm Fresh and Fatal* (2013) were the sixth and seventh written in her Penny Weaver series, and she now begins a new project of publishing the other thirteen mysteries through Hoganvillaea Books, beginning with the first one, *The Sands of Gower*, which was written in 1991.

Judy has a flock of White Rock hens and grows half her food. When her community is threatened by injustice and/or pollution, she's an activist, like Penny Weaver. Her Odysseus has been elusive, but Kenneth Morgan found Penny in her mid-fifties and hangs onto her. Penny is better behaved than her author, but bolder when she's solving crimes. Hogan is also a published poet and non-fiction writer and would like to live to a hundred, if she can, and put many more books into print. She lives and farms in Moncure, N.C., near the Haw and Deep Rivers. Enjoy these books. May they comfort and sustain you in your amazing gift of humanity.

judyhogan.home.mindspring.com
postmenopausalzest.blogspot.com

Made in the USA
Charleston, SC
07 February 2016